"What are you doing?"

"Giving you a lesson on sound engineering principles. You badly need one. Now, raise your arm."

"Why?" She eyed him warily.

He kept his hands on her shoulders. "You paid for instruction. I'm offering to show you what's wrong with your design."

"You thrive on pointing out my shortcomings, don't you?"

"I should have expected that. Look, your design is good. It just needs a few adjustments."

He closed his fingers around her hand, lifting her arm to the level of her shoulder. She stood as rigid as a brick wall, mindful that he still held her hand.

"Relax," he said, giving her shoulder a slight squeeze. The intimate gesture sent a thousand tiny shivers loping across her flesh.

"Miss Delaney, I promise I'm not going to pounce on you."

**Harlequin Historicals is proud to introduce
Paula Hampton
with her charming debut title
THE RELUCTANT TUTOR**

**THE RELUCTANT TUTOR
Harlequin Historical #534—October 2000**

THE RELUCTANT TUTOR

PAULA HAMPTON

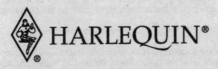

HARLEQUIN®

TORONTO • NEW YORK • LONDON
AMSTERDAM • PARIS • SYDNEY • HAMBURG
STOCKHOLM • ATHENS • TOKYO • MILAN • MADRID
PRAGUE • WARSAW • BUDAPEST • AUCKLAND

ISBN 0-373-29134-5

THE RELUCTANT TUTOR

Visit us at www.eHarlequin.com

Printed in U.S.A.

Available from Harlequin Historicals and
PAULA HAMPTON

The Reluctant Tutor #534

To Dad, who taught me about heroes,
Mom, who showed me the power of love
and my husband, Chet, who makes writing possible.

Chapter One

Winter, 1899

Kate Delaney squeezed her eyes shut and exhaled a whispered prayer for luck. Only the scarred oak door stood between her and the rest of her life. She gave the door a sharp rap with the handle of her large black umbrella.

"Hello," she called, her voice deceptively calm. Beneath the skirt of her tailored gray travel suit, she tapped her foot to the anxious hammering of her heart. Every minute she waited tightened the knot in her stomach.

Relax. Kate scolded herself. *Being this nervous makes as much sense as relying on luck.* At twenty-two she knew better than to trust her dream to chance.

Of course, a woman on her own in New York City couldn't overlook any possibilities. Life hadn't made her cynical, foolish or cocky enough to completely discount the power of a good-luck charm.

She wore hers, a dainty gold shamrock that had belonged to her mother, pinned to the lapel of her fitted jacket.

Today she wouldn't need its help. Kate had prepared for this all her life and she knew everything would be fine. If only she could calm down. Hard as she tried, she couldn't quiet the fluttering in her stomach. In just a few minutes she would meet the man who had agreed to apprentice her. Her moment had arrived and with it a severe case of the jitters.

Taking a deep breath to steady herself, she concentrated on remaining calm and making a good impression. She couldn't arrive looking like she'd climbed from one of the overflowing trash bins that spilled onto the sidewalk.

Kate nervously fussed with the rebellious coil of copper-red hair that lay at the nape of her neck and adjusted the tilt of her ostrich-plumed hat.

"Hello," she called again, this time raising her voice above the snarl of carriages and push carts.

"The door's unlocked," a man shouted back. "Come on in."

Kate's pulse quickened. *This is it.* Hefting her leather valise and matching portfolio, she pushed the door open and marched ahead with a purposeful stride. Dead center she stopped.

The studio was no more than a large airless room overlooking a narrow alley between oppressive brick walls. Slowly her eyes adjusted to the dreary light that filtered through the grimy panes of a single north-facing window. She set her portfolio down, rested it against the wall, then looked around.

There was no well-appointed reception room for entertaining clients. No flowers or tea tables. Instead of the amenities she expected to find, piles of blueprints and technical journals were stacked on every horizontal surface, including the chairs.

Kate picked her way across the room, stepping around architectural models that littered the floor like the ruins of a miniature Pompeii. A thin coating of plaster dust settled on everything and stuck to her Parisian walking boots, still damp from the snow. *This is it?*

Disappointment dropped like a stone to the pit of her stomach. "Good Lord," she murmured to herself. "How can anyone work in this mess?"

"Can I help you?"

The male voice came from behind her. Kate spun around, surprised and embarrassed at being heard. If her remark insulted him, it didn't show. He leaned comfortably against a large oak drafting table, bracing the toe of one boot against its base.

The sleeves of his shirt were rolled to his elbows and his open collar enhanced his relaxed posture. He had a casual, Bohemian air. A man she might expect to find sitting in a Paris café or strolling along the Left Bank.

He placed his pen down to look her over. Kate realized she was staring, but it never occurred to her that the man she'd written to might be just a few years her senior. She hid her surprise behind a pleasant smile and took a step closer.

"I'm Kate Delaney." She offered her hand.

He wiped the ink from his hands with a soiled

cloth hooked on the side of his table. ''Gabe Murray,'' he said, accepting the handshake. ''What can I do for you?''

Kate paused when he didn't react to her name. ''Don't you know why I'm here?''

''Should I?'' He seemed to be waiting for her reaction as intently as she'd awaited his a moment before.

''We corresponded,'' she said. ''You reviewed my work.''

''I did?'' Confusion knitted his brow. He really didn't know.

Her composure slipped a notch as she admitted to herself something was wrong. ''I don't understand. I have your letter.''

Her hands trembled slightly as she reached into her purse for the dog-eared envelope embossed with his name and address. She held it up between her thumb and forefinger.

''Oh, I get it,'' he said, rolling his shirtsleeves down. ''You're looking for my father. We have the same name.''

Kate exhaled, feeling the tension ease from her shoulders. ''Well, that explains it.''

Gabe returned a sober nod. ''This sort of thing happened all the time when he was alive.''

Her eyes flashed to his as the valise slid from her hand smacking the floor with a loud thud.

Baffled, Gabe stared back at her. ''Are you all right?''

She couldn't have been further from all right. Her

mouth went dry and it was all she could do to nod. She felt the blood drain from her face.

Gabe pushed a stack of papers from the straight-backed chair, brushing the dust from the seat. "Maybe you'd better sit down."

Dazed, she slumped onto the chair. She turned the buff-colored envelope over and over in her hands, trying to absorb what had happened. She felt her whole body sag as reality sank in. The one architect she'd found who was willing to apprentice her was dead. And for the moment, so was her future.

"Miss, are you okay?" His voice drew her back.

Kate raised her eyes slowly. She had been so immersed in her own trouble she forgot he was standing there. Now, as she saw his questioning look, she realized how callous she'd been. She might have lost her instructor, but he'd lost his father.

She pushed herself up out of the chair, flattening her palm on his table to steady herself. "Mr. Murray, I'm so sorry for your loss."

"Thank you," he said, searching her face. "What business did you have with my father?"

Still numb, Kate explained, "He agreed to apprentice me."

"Not as an architect?"

His tone jarred her from her stupor. Kate's head came up sharply. This wasn't the first time she'd seen that doubting look. She hadn't taken him for such a mossback and any other time she would have told him so, but even as a dozen responses came to mind, the seriousness of her situation left her mute.

Kate pressed her hand against her churning stomach and fought a surging wave of panic. She knew she had little hope of finding another instructor and no doubt her grandfather would make good his threat to disinherit her after the harsh words they'd had. Suddenly it seemed all her hard work had been for nothing. If she didn't complete her training and prove her independence by this time next year, she'd be doomed to spend her life married to a stodgy man of her grandfather's choosing.

"This can't be happening," she groaned, staring blankly at the vision of that bleak future. Unwanted tears pooled in her eyes.

"Oh, don't do that," Gabe said as he cringed visibly.

Kate quickly turned away, unwilling to let him see her cry. She stood with her back to him, facing his drafting table.

"Is there anything I can do?" he added in a hushed tone.

Kate shook her head, struggling to swallow the huge lump that lodged in her throat. Absently she brushed her fingers across the small gold shamrock pinned to her lapel. She had never been a quitter and she couldn't give up now. She had to think.

Pressing her fingers to the bridge of her nose to ease the throbbing in her head, she forced herself to concentrate. For the first time she noticed his crisp clean-lined rendering lying on the table in front of her. The simple design was as masterfully executed as anything she had ever seen. It suddenly struck her that he and his father shared more than a name.

Kate turned to look at Gabe. There certainly was

something he could do. Her dream was within reach and at this moment he appeared to be the shortest distance to it.

"You could apprentice me."

"Oh, no." He flatly refused. "That's out of the question."

"Why?"

"Because I've already paid the last of my father's debts," he answered quickly.

"No, you haven't."

Kate snatched up the envelope she'd left lying on the chair and held it out to him. "Your father had an obligation to me."

Gabe stared at her, his dark brows drawn more firmly together. "What does that have to do with me? I can't be expected to keep his promises." He pushed her hand away.

A piece of paper slid from the envelope and fell at her feet. As Gabe picked it up, she noticed it was her processed tuition check drawn on her grandfather's account at the Bank of Elmira. That check had been cashed. It seemed he had some explaining to do.

"Mr. Murray, when did your father pass on?"

He eyed her skeptically. "Last month. Why?"

"If your father died last month, who endorsed my check two weeks ago?"

Gabe looked at the check, then back at her. "Well, I guess I did." He shrugged. "I thought it was payment for some odd job he'd done."

"I see." She nodded. "Technically, that makes me one of his creditors, doesn't it?"

Gabe paled, but his expression didn't change. "It was a mistake. I'll pay you back. But, right now I'm a little short of cash."

"You don't understand," she said. "This is about more than getting my money back. I have to complete my apprenticeship."

"Well, you'll have to find someone else. I'm not putting my projects on hold again. I've already wasted enough time on other people's problems."

The desperation in his eyes momentarily silenced her. Kate understood that look. How often had she wrestled the cold dread that life would leave her with unrealized dreams? In that instant she felt oddly connected with him. "Mr. Murray—" she began, but he cut her off breaking the spell.

"No," he said. "I've paid his debts. That's the end of it."

She gave him a look she hoped would singe his eyebrows. "Maybe we should let the courts decide."

"What?" He pushed a tumble of sable hair from his forehead. "Are you threatening me with legal action?"

Taking the offensive seemed her only chance. "You stole my money," she said.

"Now wait just a minute."

"No, you wait. You already admitted that you cashed my check and when you endorsed it, you signed a binding contract to apprentice me."

Gabe made a face. "You're crazy."

"Am I?" she said, her chin inching higher. "Are you claiming you didn't cash the check?"

"No. But I didn't agree to anything."

"Well, then you forged your father's signature and stole my money."

"I don't believe this." He gestured helplessly. "All I'm guilty of is paying my father's creditors. You can take this to court, but I swear any judge worth his salt will throw you out on your well-tailored little rump."

He had a point. That angered her even more than his crass remark. She knew she'd never win a court battle, but she wasn't about to admit that to him. Especially since the possibility seemed to worry him.

"I'll take my chances," she bluffed.

"Oh, for pity's sake, lady. You can't prosecute a man for making a mistake."

Kate bristled. Her future was at risk and he called it a mistake? "It's a simple solution, Mr. Murray."

A small vein pulsed at his temple. "I said I can't."

"Why not?"

"Because you're a woman, all right?"

That did it. She took a step toward him, her lips compressed in an angry line. "You're not my ideal instructor, either. But I won't let you cheat me. Getting an education wasn't easy for me and I've defied the opinions of better men than you to get this far."

He shot her a look that would have backed a burly teamster into a corner. "I only meant I can't accommodate your special needs."

"Oh?" She paused, sensing he might be swayed.

"I don't expect to be treated any differently from a male apprentice."

Gabe looked doubtful.

Kate went on. "When you accepted my money, you accepted me as a student and you can't quit unless I do."

"Do you mean that?" Something flickered in his eyes and the sudden thawing in his voice put her on the defensive.

"Do I mean what?"

"What you just said. If you quit, the deal is off."

Kate frowned, realizing her mistake too late.

"I think we have an agreement, Miss Delaney."

"Do we?"

"One year or until you quit." He paused for effect. "Whichever comes first."

"I never quit." She met his triumphant stare.

"We'll see about that," he said. "Now, why don't I show you around so you can settle in?"

"You mean here?" She gave the studio a second look.

In all the confusion she hadn't seen beyond the clutter. Her stomach pitched as she noticed the adjoining rooms. A cast iron woodstove and filthy porcelain sink crowded the dreary little kitchen. Through the greenish shadows cast by a single gas lamp, she saw the outline of an old-fashioned mahogany bedstead. It sat beside a chest of drawers, cramped into the alcove, beneath a high-perched loft library.

Kate swallowed hard as her eyes met his. "You live here?"

Gabe flashed a warm smile she wasn't naive enough to trust. "We live here," he corrected her. "The bath is just down the hall."

"How convenient. And where's my room?"

"I don't have an extra room," he said in a mocking tone. "But you're welcome to share my bed. Just as a male apprentice would."

It took all her control not to broadside him with her umbrella. "That's very generous, Mr. Murray, but room and board means I'm to have a room. Where is it?"

Gabe rubbed his jaw and thought deeply for a moment. "Well, I guess there is my supply closet."

He directed her toward the door beside the fireplace. Kate braced herself as she peered inside. The closet couldn't have been more than ten feet square, filled with wooden packing crates and drafting supplies. She jiggled the doorknob, making a mental note of the missing lock.

"What do you think?" he asked.

She didn't have to look at him to know he was gloating. He probably expected her to take one look at the filthy little hole in the wall and race back to Grand Central Terminal. Well, she wasn't going to make it easy for him. Sharing a cramped closet with whatever might be crawling about in the dark appealed to her more than the future her grandfather had planned.

She wiped the dust from her hands and slapped a smile back on her face. "This will suit me just fine."

"You mean you're staying?" His sour expression

made the prospect of sleeping on the cold floor tolerable.

"Of course, Mr. Murray, we have an understanding, remember? One year."

"Or until you quit." He was quick to add. "Don't make yourself too comfortable, Miss Delaney." He left her standing there and snatched his coat from the tarnished brass coatrack.

"Where are you going?" She followed him.

"Not that it's any of your business, but I'm going out for a walk." He jerked open the door.

A swirl of snow caught her skirt. Kate shivered, but it was from more than the cold. She watched him walk off, wondering how much she would learn from such a reluctant tutor. She had to do something.

"Mr. Murray, please." She called out to him above the street noise. "We have to discuss my apprenticeship. Come back. We're not finished yet."

"Oh, yes we are." He never broke his stride.

Chapter Two

Kate slammed the door behind him. "Perfect," she said. "Just perfect."

She had herself an instructor, all right. Now all she had to do was convince him to teach her. Arms folded, she paced the studio. Her immediate future was bound with that of an angry man who appeared incapable of finding joy in anything, except making her miserable. And what had she done to deserve that treatment? It made no sense. If anything, she was the one with the grievance.

She picked up her pace and with each agitated step the hem of her skirt sent dust motes dancing ahead of her. She had hoped that by now the constant quarreling with men would have been a memory. She was quickly realizing the warfare had just begun.

Time and again her grandfather had told her that resistance and reproach were the price of being different. Kate understood that, especially how it felt to be different. She'd always been considered too tall, too thin and too outspoken.

Even as a child, when other girls were content to play with dolls and learn to sew, Kate preferred sketching whimsical fairy-tale castles. Her grandfather criticized her. Daydreams were a waste of time. He constantly reminded her if she were a boy she might have put her talent to use and become an architect like her truant father. But women had no business in business.

That her life would have been easier had she been a man was the one thing she and her grandfather could agree on. Kate bit her bottom lip and wrestled down the stinging memory of the arguments and faultfinding. That was all behind her now. She had proved her grandfather wrong. An architect was exactly what she had become. Almost.

Now she had to prove herself all over again. *Men,* she thought angrily. She would never live long enough to understand them. Of one thing she was certain, she would be the best apprentice Gabe Murray ever knew. Like it or not, he was her instructor and he was going to start behaving like one. She'd paid her tuition and she wasn't going to be dismissed.

At the supply closet door she stopped pacing and stared into the cramped, dark space. Her resolve crumbled as she imagined living in that filthy little room for a year. A hot sting of tears made her bring her head up to counter the negative thought.

Kate brushed the tears from her cheek and reminded herself that in order to survive she had to adapt. And she would adapt to this. She'd already insisted she didn't need special treatment. She had no choice but to move into his little grubby closet. Or did she? Her gaze drifted up to the large airy loft.

Kate saw no reason why she couldn't move up there. No reason at all. And he thought he was so clever. Anticipating his surprise brought a smile to her face and buoyed her spirits. Hiking up her skirt, she carefully climbed the ladderlike stairs attached to an oak balustrade. The wobbly rungs, covered with dust, creaked mournfully with each footfall.

She reached the top only to be halted by an enormous bookcase. It blocked her path like a hulking dark sentinel. Gripping the railing, she squeezed by and looked around. The loft, like the ground floor, was cluttered with crates and boxes, notebooks and journals of every kind. But, unlike the closet, it had windows, air and more importantly, its location put some distance between her and whatever vermin might be scurrying about in the dark. Including Gabe Murray.

Removing her hat and jacket, she rolled up her sleeves and went to work hauling wooden packing crates across the floor. She stacked them along the railing, one on top of the other, constructing a makeshift wall surrounding a large open space. By the time she finished, her hands were filled with splinters but she had some privacy.

Straightening, Kate took a deep breath and mopped her brow before turning her attention to the immense bookcase. She studied it more closely, taken by the fine craftsmanship. Carved oval doors with insets of beveled glass, etched in a floral motif, graced the cabinet. Drawing her fingers across the lustrous black walnut finish, she wondered how such a striking piece had found its way to this rat's nest. Surely a coarse cretin like Mr. Murray didn't have the refinement to appreciate furniture like this. She considered him for a minute then shook herself and focused her attention on her work. She had no time to waste if she was going to build her fortress before he returned.

Stepping back, she sized up the bookcase once more. Its massive bulk matched its elegance pound for pound. She decided it would make a perfect wardrobe. If she could move it. Mustering all her strength, she flattened her palms against its side, locked her elbows and pushed. It didn't budge. She tried again, harder. Her face flushed as she strained against the cumbersome piece.

"Criminy." She exhaled, frustration swelling inside her. The cabinet seemed as unyielding as its implacable owner.

Kate tried once more, but the bookcase might just as well have been anchored to the floor. Irritated yet unwilling to give up, she attacked it with a vengeance. Pressing her back against the side, she braced her knees and pushed with all her might.

"Move," she commanded, gritting her teeth.

The bookcase lurched backward, her feet slid from under her and she hit the floor with an unladylike grunt. Her lace petticoats bunched up around what he'd so indelicately referred to as her well-tailored rump.

"Lord, give me strength." Kate closed her eyes as, exhausted, she sat on the floor, resting her head against the cabinet.

If today was any indication of what the rest of her apprenticeship would be, she would need all the help she could find.

No matter how far or how fast he walked, Kate's words still grated on him. Gabe turned up his collar, bent his head against the wind and tried to lose himself in the early darkness of late December. Large wet flakes dimmed the incandescent lamps along the avenue and the cracks in the sidewalk were filling with snow.

Jamming his hands deep into the pockets of his gray chesterfield, he continued at a brisk pace, determined to put some distance between himself and that uppity female. "*Nouvelle femme,*" he grumped sourly.

The last few weeks had been hell. As if the parade of collection agents wasn't enough, now he had to contend with *her.* What could his father have been thinking? Struggling to keep his footing on the slick cobbles, he dodged streetcars and carriages, eager for the warmth of the Green Harp Tavern.

The neighborhood rapidly went from shabbiness to squalor. As he neared the Harp, the welcome sound of laughter spilled onto the street. He pushed through the door into the seedy, smoke-filled bar, shaking the snow from his hair. The room had the familiar smell of malt and wet woolen sweaters. Sawdust clung to the soles of his shoes as he made his way between dirty tables where men sat hunched over cards and poker chips. Halfway to the bar the sound of Finn Hurley's laughter rose above the drone of voices and hacking coughs.

Finn didn't make Gabe wait. The tall, strapping old Irishman with bright-blue eyes and a generous smile lifted a glass from the mirrored shelf and poured a shot of his best Scotch. Regulars were treated well at the Harp. Gabe knew he was treated better. He'd known Finn Hurley all his life. The man had been like a favorite uncle.

Gabe couldn't count the number of times he'd listened to the story of how his mother and Finn had met during their Atlantic crossing and how Finn tried, unsuccessfully, to dissuade her from her forthcoming marriage to Gabe's father. Honoring commitments is a curse on your family, Finn would joke.

Gabe was beginning to believe in that curse. Distracted, he slapped a few coins on the bar and rested his weight on the brass foot rail.

"'Tis on the house," said Finn, his voice thick with a Dublin cadence. He brushed a wisp of flyaway white hair from his brow as he swept a damp rag across the long mahogany.

"Thanks." Gabe downed his drink, still seething over his predicament. How the hell was he going to get rid of her?

"What's eating you?" asked Finn.

Gabe looked at him, feeling trapped. "My studio's getting a little crowded."

"I see." Finn nodded sagely. "So you came here seeking fresh air and open space, did you?"

Gabe ignored Finn's sarcasm, but his silence drew more questions. "For God's sake, lad. What's wrong with you?"

"Nothing," he mumbled.

"You're sure about that?" The older man rested his elbows on the bar and rolled a toothpick across his tongue. Gabe knew he wouldn't get away without an explanation so he told Finn what had happened.

"Now I'm stuck with her." His voice trailed off.

"Oh, that is a misery, isn't it?" Finn said, refilling Gabe's glass. "I can see why you're so upset. After all, who needs a woman moving in?" A puckish grin swept his ruddy face.

"Don't start," Gabe warned. "The last thing I need is you playing Cupid."

Finn laughed it off. "Are you daft, man? There's a woman camped in your studio."

"I know that, damn it."

"Well, what the hell are you doing here? You should be cozying up near the fire with her, for Pete's sake."

"Not with this one," Gabe snorted disdainfully. "You should see her. My old T-square has more curves."

"Aw, saints help us, lad. You didn't leave that poor creature alone in this vile city?"

"That poor creature can take care of herself," Gabe defended, recalling how she'd deftly backed him into a corner.

Finn's mocking laughter irritated him. "What's so funny?"

"You," Finn said. "There are other things in life besides work and coming here for my delightful company, you know."

"You're absolutely right," Gabe exhaled, conceding the point. "But work I understand. Women are another animal altogether. There's not one who knows what they really want."

Finn pulled a five-cent draft for another customer and dropped a solitary coin in the till. "You can't keep blaming all females for the fickleness of one."

"I don't. Hell, I just don't want a woman around. You know what they're like. Give this one a few days and she'll be rearranging my place. Cleaning. Hanging frilly curtains. I won't have that. If a man can't find solace in his own studio, where can he?"

"Oh, bull. I know better. 'Tis the episode with that Hartford woman that's soured you."

"Eve has nothing to do with this." Gabe's voice hardened as the familiar knot tightened in his gut. A year hadn't eased the pain of losing Eve to his former partner.

"I work alone," he said. "That's all there is to it. She has to go."

"And how do you propose to get rid of the lass?"

"I don't know. That's the sticking point," Gabe said, mulling it over. "How hard could it be to take the starch out of her?" He caught Finn eyeing him and decided he needed a plan.

"What do you think she'd do if I went back smelling of whiskey and feeling amorous?"

"Well, now, I don't know. You're the expert on females. What do you think?"

"She'll probably wallop me with her umbrella," Gabe said, slipping deeper into his gloom.

"Just let her stay," said Finn. "Teach her what you can, then send her off."

"No," Gabe adamantly refused. "She has to go. Now."

Finn leaned across the bar and spoke in a soft voice. "In case you haven't noticed there's a new breed of women around. If you got out more, you'd see them parading about Fifth Avenue with their suffrage banners flappin' in the breeze. Get used to it, Gabe. If she's one of those, she knows her mind all right, and she won't be giving up easily."

Gabe's shoulders slumped. "For crying out loud, Finn. You're no help."

"What can you do, lad? Seems to me you've got an obligation. You can't just throw her to the wolves."

Obligation. The word riled Gabe. To hell with obligations. If he hadn't felt bound to pay his father's debts, he wouldn't be in this mess.

"I'll throw her to the wolves," he thought aloud. Then, it hit him. "Or the sisters," he said. A smile curled his lips and he looked at Finn. "Why, you old goat. You're a genius."

Finn scratched his stubbled chin, looking puzzled.

"It's perfect," Gabe explained. "Hattie and Vera Goodhue. The wolves."

"Now, you've lost me."

"Just think about it, Finn. Those two old biddies

have been driving me crazy for months with their endless design changes. I'll put her in charge of drafting the plans for their blasted project. If they can't dampen her enthusiasm, nothing will." He laughed. "She'll think I'm doing her a favor. Trusting her with the entire job and in no time, they'll frustrate that little plague right out of my life." He paused to savor the beauty of his plan.

"I'll bet you that by this time next week, I'll be minus one troublesome apprentice."

Finn looked skeptical. "Would you like to put your money where your mouth is?"

"Why not?" Gabe said, feeling agreeable. He noticed Finn's gaze shift just as he felt someone move behind him.

"Can anyone get in on this, Gabey?"

Recognition was instantaneous. Only one man called him by that name. Lloyd Peyton. Gabe turned and glared at his former partner. "Well, well. If it isn't the ferret from Fifth Avenue."

Peyton grinned, showing off a set of perfect white teeth. He removed his derby and ran his hand through his slicked-back hair. Macassar oil deepened the baby-fine strands to the color of caramel.

"Now, Gabey. Is that any way to greet an old friend?" His pale eyes bit into Gabe as he opened his cashmere coat, flaunting a diamond tie tack.

Gabe studied him with contempt. "I thought I'd seen the last of you when you joined Kendall, McKee and Hartford. What brings you here, Lloyd? Were all the uptown saloons closed?"

Peyton sniggered, resting one arm on the bar. He

gave the Harp a quick once-over. "Just thought I'd pay a visit to the old neighborhood and reminisce a bit. I see you're visiting, too." He clamped his teeth around the end of the cigar and flashed a condescending smile.

Gabe's face reddened. Peyton knew damned well he still lived in this part of town.

"Oh, now I've offended you," Peyton said. "Irish," he commanded. "Pour me and my old friend Gabey a brandy."

Gabe's temper boiled but he held it in. "Keep your drink."

"Suit yourself." Peyton pulled a gold money clip from his breast pocket and dropped a few crisp new greenbacks on the bar.

"What do you say, Gabey? Why don't we up the stakes and make this wager more interesting. You get rid of your little apprentice and I won't bid on the new art museum."

Gabe masked his surprise, wondering how long Peyton had been standing there listening. The conversation had a distinct smell to it and Lloyd Peyton was the last person he'd ever be fool enough to make a bet with.

"Who are you kidding? Every architect in New York knows the bidding on that project is a farce. Kendall, McKee and Hartford has it locked up."

"So you're not interested?" Peyton said, exhaling a stream of blue smoke.

"I'm interested in designing the art museum. Not in dealing with you."

"Come on, Gabey. We were partners, remember?"

"Yeah, we were." Gabe's mouth quirked in distaste. "And I don't recall your being the kind of man to risk a sure thing."

"You have a good memory."

"Too good," said Gabe. "So, what's this really about?"

Peyton studied the end of his cigar reflectively. "I'm bored," he said in a rare moment of honesty. "Hartford's connections at City Hall have eliminated any competition. Winning without an opponent isn't any fun."

Gabe shot him a go-to-hell smile. "I see your new position has enhanced your arrogance as well as your wallet."

"Don't be that way, Gabey. Being here makes me long for the good old days. Working independently has a certain excitement that being part of a large successful firm lacks. I envy you."

Gabe couldn't stop a self-derisive laugh.

"I'm serious," said Peyton. "I've always admired your work. When I overheard your conversation with our friendly barkeep here, I thought the risk of losing to you might inspire me again."

"Go to hell." Gabe turned back to the bar. Once. Just once he wanted to hit the son of a bitch.

"What harm is there in a friendly wager?" Peyton clapped him on the shoulder.

Gabe shrugged off his hand. "I said beat it."

Peyton backed away. "All right, all right. I can see I've upset you."

Tucking his ebony walking stick beneath one arm, he pulled on his fine kid gloves and looked around. ''As much as I enjoy the ambiance of this place, I should be leaving. I'm meeting Eve for dinner at the Yacht Club. I'll be sure to give her your best.'' His smile was sugar-coated steel.

Gabe ground his teeth, wishing he could bury his fist in the middle of the bastard's face. He managed to control himself. Finn couldn't.

''Don't be putting on airs, Lloyd. I remember when you were just a street rat hauling pails of beer over to the flophouses. You'd be doing that still if Gabe's father hadn't taken you in, fed and educated you.''

Peyton shot Finn an angry look and arrogantly blew smoke across the bar. He turned a calculating look on Gabe. ''I was saddened to learn about your father,'' he said. ''I would have done anything to have been his son. I hope someday you realize how lucky you were.'' He turned toward the door.

Remorse tightened Gabe's throat. Suddenly winning the museum project was all that mattered. He could do it. He'd get rid of the girl, defeat Peyton and prove his designs could work all at one time. He owed his father that much. People might finally stop questioning his character and start noticing his work. He knew the high price of dealing with Peyton, but he figured this time it was worth it. Hell, what more did he have to lose?

''Wait,'' he called.

Peyton turned back. ''Change your mind?''

From the corner of his eye Gabe saw Finn shaking

his head in warning. He pretended not to notice. "Let me get this straight," he said. "If the girl quits before proposals for the museum are due, you won't submit your design. And if she doesn't quit, I won't submit mine. Are those your terms?" Gabe looked at him steadily.

"That's the gist of it. We have three months before bids are due. Interested?"

"She'll be gone long before that."

Peyton stared at him, ice in his smile. "Then it's a deal." He shoved the cigar between his teeth and offered his hand.

Gabe refused the handshake in a deliberate slight.

Peyton laughed. Taking the cigar from his mouth, he let his hand drop to his side. With perfect graciousness he said, "Good evening, gentlemen." He walked away without a backward look.

Gabe drew a long breath, then exhaled slowly. Finally he had a chance to beat that weasel. Besting Peyton while ridding himself of the girl was perfect.

"You're a bigger fool than I thought," Finn said. "Letting him rope you in like that was plain stupid. And putting the poor lass in the middle of your fray isn't right."

Finn's reproach released a flood of pent-up anger. Gabe slammed his fist on the bar. "Just let this fool have his due for once, damn it." He didn't need Finn Hurley or anyone else acting as keeper of his conscience. Lately he'd been doing a fine job on his own.

As his temper cooled, Gabe groaned aloud. Finn didn't deserve his anger. "I'm just sick and tired of doing the right thing while men like Peyton prosper. If putting her in the middle of it is unfair, too bad. Life is unfair. Learning that will be her first lesson.''

Gabe added softly, ''It's not as if I asked her to show up at my door.''

''Aye.'' Finn stepped away, resting his weight against the back bar.

The awkward silence stretched out until Gabe couldn't stand it. ''Oh, hell, Finn. I'm sorry.''

''I'm sorry, too. And I'm sure I don't have to tell you why.''

''But you will.''

''You're darn right I will.'' Finn raised his voice. ''What the devil has gotten into you? That man is like a cancer. From the day you met him, he was trouble, doing whatever he could to come between you and your father. Being at odds with you broke your old man's heart.''

Gabe summoned his anger to hide his grief. ''Why do you think I want to win this project?''

''I understand,'' Finn said. ''But not by using the lass. Listen, Gabe, your father wasn't stupid. If he agreed to apprentice her, he must have thought she had talent. What you're doing is wrong.''

Gabe stared him down, unwilling to be swayed. He'd waited too long for a fair chance in an honest competition.

''So be it,'' said Finn, eyeing Gabe with resignation. He took the money Peyton had left on the bar and placed it in an empty cigar box, adding a few bills of his own to the wager.

''You're like a son to me, Gabe, and I don't relish

being on the side of that viper, Peyton. But my money is still on the lass and don't you forget it.''

Gabe knew Finn wouldn't let him forget it. Neither would his own conscience. He pulled the gold pocket watch his father had given him from his vest, the case inscribed with the words *Trust your instincts*.

He snapped the watch shut, the feeling he'd walked into something he'd regret already forming in his stomach. He fought off his doubt. No one, not Finn Hurley nor some wide-eyed little apprentice was going to keep him from beating Lloyd Peyton.

"No sense putting this off," he said.

Gabe left the Harp with a new sense of purpose. The snow was tapering off and the winter moon peeked through broken clouds, washing the sidewalk in a silvery glow. The blustery wind blasting his cheeks suddenly didn't sting so much.

A few hours ago he would have traded places with anyone. Now, he couldn't believe his luck. Drawing a long satisfied breath of icy air, Gabe started for home.

Maybe. Just maybe his father and little Miss High-and-Mighty had done him a favor.

Chapter Three

Kate whipped her head around as the front door swung open. Long damp strands of freshly washed hair swept from the back of her bathrobe and slapped her cheek. She braced herself for another volley of insults as she watched Gabe from the loft.

He didn't seem to notice her. Crossing the room, he hung his coat and paused before the dark supply closet. He looked inside, his self-satisfied grin sending a flush of anger to her cheeks. Kate bit her tongue, holding her temper, biding her time.

She watched from her perch as Gabe flopped onto his chair, jiggled open the top drawer of his desk and removed a cigar. Placing it between his teeth, he struck a match and tilted his head to touch the tip of the Havana to the flame.

Shaking the match, he settled back, stretching his long legs out. He rested his heels on the desk and puffed away. A wisp of smoke curled from the end of the cigar and drifted up to the loft. Kate swiped at it, wrinkling her nose. She hadn't spent the evening cleaning the place just to have him sully it again. Grabbing her perfume atomizer she retaliated by spraying the foul air with lavender scent. It wasn't long before the fragrant mist rained down on him.

"What in tarnation?" He bolted from his seat, sniffing the air. "It smells like a French harlot's boudoir in here."

Kate folded her arms and smiled down at him. "Obviously, a French harlot's boudoir smells a lot better than your studio, Mr. Murray."

He tossed a disapproving glance in her direction. "You're still here."

"Yes, I'm still here and I'm hungry. Don't you keep food in this place?"

He answered, caught off guard. "I take my meals at the local tavern."

"Fine," she said. Turning her back, she descended the steps. "Then, beginning tomorrow, I'll take my meals at the tavern with you." She paused as her feet touched the floor. "Just as a male apprentice would."

Even in the dim firelight she could see his jaw clamp in anger. Kate smiled to herself, thinking years of tolerating her grandfather's surliness had been worth something after all.

"Excuse me." She pushed passed him, yanked a quilt and pillow from his bed and hauled them back to the ladder. Giving him a curt smile she started up to the loft once more. Gabe looked on.

"You're turning my studio into a damned squatter's hovel."

Kate stood poised on the rickety step and replied with a half turn. ''I couldn't take all the credit for that. You gave me such a good start.''

The words barely crossed her lips when the shift in her weight tipped the loose rung up, throwing her off balance. ''Oh,'' she gasped, her eyes round with alarm. The bedding flew from her arms as she pitched backward off the ladder, slamming into Gabe's chest.

The impact knocked the cigar from his mouth. He staggered back, arms locked around her. Kate caught her breath, quickly becoming aware of his broad chest pressed against her back. His hands spanned her waist, holding her fast, testing the curves.

''Guess I was wrong about the T-square,'' he said. His warm breath brushed her cheek as he lowered his face to within inches of hers.

Kate felt her whole body flush. ''T-square?'' She whirled on him. ''What are you implying?''

He returned a long appraising look that made the fine hair on the back of her neck stand on end. She followed the direction of his gaze down the front of her robe and realized it had fallen open to reveal her ivory flannel nightgown.

''You're incorrigible,'' she said, pulling her robe tightly around herself.

''Forget it.'' Gabe dismissed her with a weary wave. He stooped to pick up his cigar and returned to his chair.

Kate would be a long time forgetting the look on his face and the odd quiver that particular look sent rippling through her. She walked across the room, planting herself in front of him, determined not to let this happen again. "Mr. Murray, your familiarity is completely unwelcome."

"Fine. The next time I'll just let you fall on your—"

"There won't be a next time," she cut him off. "If we're going to share this studio, we're going to set down some rules."

Gabe ripped the cigar from his mouth. "Rules? What kind of rules?" His voice rumbled like thunder through the Adirondacks.

Kate squared her shoulders and responded to his outburst. "You know what kind of rules."

"I don't know," he said, eyes boring into her. "Why don't you tell me?"

Slowly he rose from the chair, glaring down at her. God, he was even more imposing than she'd thought. Kate nervously wet her lips. "I think we should have a schedule," she said. "So neither of us gets caught indecent."

"A schedule?" He raised one eyebrow.

"Yes," she said, managing just barely to keep a formal edge to her voice. "For instance, I generally rise early, so I'll use the bath from six until seven each morning."

"Fine. Anything else?"

Kate swallowed hard, recalling the heat of his gaze. "As a matter of fact, there is. For the duration of my stay it's best if we remain on opposite sides of the room. After a decent hour, neither of us crosses this line."

With her toe she drew a ragged line in the dust

covering the floor, separating his bedroom from the base of her ladder. Gabe took a step forward, obliterating the line with the sole of his shoe. "Anything else you'd like, Miss Delaney?"

So much for propriety. She took a deep breath and kept her voice even. "Is a little privacy so much to ask?"

"Miss Delaney," he said, his voice deep, rich and mocking. "I assure you, the last thing you have to worry about is my violating your privacy."

He spoke as if she were the most undesirable woman on the planet. Kate concealed her injured pride and struck back with a blow to his honor. "Why should I trust you?"

Gabe nearly swore an oath as he pulled the cigar from his mouth. "Look," he said. "I'm tired. It's been a long day in a year of long weeks and I'd like to get some sleep, if you don't mind. I have an early meeting with clients tomorrow." He turned to walk away.

Kate tested him. "You mean we have a meeting, don't you?"

He stopped short. His shoulders slumped. "Right," he said without argument.

Kate eyed him warily. She knew better than to believe in miraculous transformations, especially when it came to men. "Who are your clients?" she asked.

He turned to face her and flicked the gray ash from his cigar. It hit the floor just short of her toes. Kate didn't flinch and kept her eyes fixed on his face. He seemed to enjoy her defiance, smiling with genuine pleasure for the first time since she'd arrived.

"The Goodhue sisters are two delightful old ladies who want to build a rambling retreat for artists on Long Island. You'll love them."

"I'm sure I will." She held his gaze, almost afraid to break eye contact. There was something very unsettling about his sudden eagerness to oblige. Still, she supposed as long as he was willing to take her along, she didn't have to like, or trust him. All the better if she didn't, she decided. A smile like his could charm the chill out of winter.

"I'm glad you've changed your mind, Mr. Murray. You won't regret this. By the time we're finished we might even be friends."

Gabe replied, "Friendship comes at a price you can't afford, Miss Delaney. Remember that. It may be the most valuable thing I teach you."

His sudden philosophical tone came as a surprise. Kate didn't know what to say.

"You'd better get some sleep," he added. "We have a schedule, remember?" Without giving her a second look or showing a smidgeon of modesty, he stripped off his vest and started unbuttoning his shirt.

Kate quickly gathered up the pillow and quilt, scurrying back to the relative safety of the loft. She sat for a long time, knees drawn up to her chest, listening to the unfamiliar sounds of her new home. She heard Gabe moving about in the dark, stripping down. The loud thud of his boots hitting the floor made her start and she held her breath until she heard the creaking of springs as he fell into bed.

At last quiet settled into the studio, broken only by the sporadic barking of dogs. Tired as she was, she couldn't sleep. A tangle of emotions knotted her stomach until she didn't know whether she felt more like a child awaiting Christmas morning or a condemned prisoner facing execution. She wondered if Gabe was really giving her a chance or simply giving her the chance to fail? She would find out soon enough. Turning down the lamp, she curled up on her quilt and stared at the sky through the small window.

The stars seemed dimmer than she remembered them from her grandfather's country estate. Their light appeared dull, as if they'd been tarnished by too many wishes. Kate closed her eyes, making a wish of her own. Somehow before she was through she would convince Gabe Murray that she was as talented, as serious and as ambitious as any man. She had to.

Chapter Four

Gabe woke early with a slight hangover and an unwavering determination to get Kate Delaney out of his studio and put his life back in order. As he struggled with the knot of his pearl-gray cravat, he caught sight of her reflection in the hall mirror. Both wearing dark woolen suits, they looked like a pair of bookends. He turned and their eyes met.

"Good morning." She gave him a cautious smile. "Sleep well?"

Her hesitance restored his belief that he had the situation under control. Gabe grunted his response, certain that small talk would only get him into trouble. He finished buttoning his vest and pulled on his suit jacket while taking her in from head to toe.

She looked nice. Too nice, and he wondered how she could be so perky after spending the night on that hard icy floor. She had to be exhausted. He'd heard her scurrying about the cold studio well before dawn. Probably trying to avoid running into him before she was *decent*.

She looked damned decent now, her skin soft and creamy against the starched lace collar of her fitted shirtwaist. "Neat as a package from Tiffany's," he said without thinking.

Kate glanced up from fastening the row of pearl buttons that ran along the seam of her glove. "Thank you. You look very handsome, too."

He could have kicked himself for his unintended compliment. He grabbed his coat, punched his arms through the sleeves and reached for the doorknob.

"Mr. Murray?"

Gabe ignored her, determined not to make any more foolish remarks.

"Mr. Murray?" Her voice was insistent.

"What is it?"

"Why are you so angry?" she asked. "I'd hoped we could get through the day without arguing."

Her innocent appeal shook him all the way to his toes and turned his insides to jelly. *Don't be a sap.* He quickly caught himself and he tore his gaze away from her. "We'd better get a carriage," was all he said.

He tucked the cardboard cylinder containing his blueprints beneath one arm, hurried to the street and hailed a carriage. "Madison and Thirty-Seventh," he instructed the driver.

Absentmindedly, he opened the door for Kate.

"Thank you," she said, lifting her hem. She placed one foot on the carriage.

Gabe couldn't help noticing the neat display of ankle. He shifted his attention to her face. The cold air had blossomed into roses on her cheeks. Her complexion glowed with excitement. He couldn't recall the last time he'd felt the thrill of youthful expectation that sent his pulse racing. All at once he felt very old.

She climbed in. Gabe watched her from behind. The neat tuck of her waist and the feminine sway of her hips brought a smile to his face. She turned to seat herself and caught him staring. He quickly covered his mouth, pretending to hide a yawn.

He sat opposite her, placing the cardboard container on the seat beside him. The driver snapped the reins and the jostling carriage lurched forward. The blueprints rolled from the seat, falling on the floor between them. They both reached for them at once, his forehead colliding with the brim of her hat, knocking it to one side. Once more their eyes met. Hers were smoky-green, touched by the early morning sun.

"Sorry," he said, his voice barely audible.

She smiled self-consciously and handed him the cylinder, then slid back in her seat, adjusting her hat. The jingle of harness bells and the sound of the carriage wheels crunching over crystalline snow punctuated the uneasy silence.

Gabe returned the blueprints to his lap and sat back. His knees brushed hers. She shifted hastily to one side of her seat. There she sat, back rigid as a rod of reinforced steel.

"Sorry," he said again.

He felt like a dolt, unable to remember ever being so clumsy around a woman. Gabe raked his fingers through his hair, struggling to keep his long legs far away from her. The walls of the carriage seemed to be closing in on him. He tugged at his collar, willing the driver to speed up. Traffic was thick and the carriage inched its way along streets narrowed by loaflike snowdrifts.

For what seemed an endless ride, she remained perched primly at the edge of her seat, gazing out the window. Gabe studied her, regretting his mistake. If he'd made his move last night when that rickety old step put her in his arms, he might have been taking her to the train station instead of to meet the Goodhue sisters.

She turned to him, her eyes suspiciously bright. ''I can't tell you how much this means to me, Mr. Murray. All my life I've dreamed of apprenticing in New York City.''

Guilt slammed his chest. *Don't think about it,* he told himself. *All that matters is beating Peyton.* He tried not to listen.

''I came to New York before,'' she said looking out the window again. He sensed she'd turned away to hide her tears.

''My grandfather brought me to see the Wild West show,'' she said in a low voice, leaning back in her seat. ''He was furious because I was more interested in seeing the buildings.'' A pained expression settled on her face.

Gabe's heart sank. This was going to be more difficult than he'd thought. Maybe if he pretended to be asleep he could just close his eyes and shut everything out.

God, he was tired. He lay awake for most of last

night after his run-in with Lloyd Peyton. Even now he couldn't relax. Kate's silence unnerved him. He wondered what she was thinking and opened one eye a slit, peeking at her through a haze of thick dark lashes. He'd never met a woman like her and didn't know quite how to behave. Of course, that didn't really matter because she wasn't sticking around.

"Mr. Murray?"

Startled from his reverie, his eyes flipped open.

She smiled at him. "Could we stop at the station on the way back to pick up my trunk?"

"Sure." Gabe felt like a jerk. There seemed no point in hauling a trunk up the flight of stairs to his studio just to lug it back down in a day or so.

"May I see the plans?" she asked, extending her gloved hand toward the blueprints resting on his lap.

He handed them to her, seeing no harm in letting her study them. Wasting her time with blueprints that were likely already changed by the Goodhues would frustrate the hell out of her.

He studied her while she reviewed the blueprints, recalling how she looked last night when he returned from the Harp. Bathed in firelight with her wet, russet hair tumbling across her shoulders, she had an unexpected sensual appeal.

Not one strand of that lustrous hair was out of place this morning. Controlled, he thought to himself. The poor creature has probably never danced or drunk or been made love to in her life. While the overall severity of her schoolmarm demeanor disappointed him, it also ensured his success. He would not be tempted by Saint Kate.

He almost chuckled aloud at her absurd notion that he'd be enticed to cross that silly line and enter the holy of holies. No, sir. He'd crossed that imaginary threshold with Eve Hartford and he wasn't about to be made a fool of by a woman again. Ever.

Kate glanced up, once more capturing him with her moss-green eyes. "They're really quite wonderful," she said, returning the blueprints.

Gabe nodded, absently, thinking her eyes were really wonderful. Long lashed and expressive, they were her best feature. Mentally, he kicked himself. *Don't be a fool for a little dewy-eyed flattery.*

Yet, her praise sparked another twinge of guilt. He seized the blueprints, fighting his conscience. Recalling the bet, he focused on his mission.

All he had to do was be nice, win her trust and let the Goodhue sisters do the rest. Ridding himself of her was a simple task really. Trusting Peyton had been his undoing. Trusting him would be hers. Never put your faith in anyone. That would be the second lesson she'd learn from him.

As the carriage snailed its way up Madison Avenue, Gabe settled back, feeling confident once more. All he had to do was relax and let nature take its course.

Chapter Five

"Everyone called old Goodhue 'the Admiral' because he was a giant in the shipping industry. When he died, his daughter Vera took over running the business." Gabe stepped from the carriage and offered Kate his hand.

Sunlight reflecting off the snow blinded her. Shading her eyes, she caught her first glimpse of Fairweather, the Goodhue mansion. Its ornate Indiana limestone facade overwhelmed the long row of flat-topped brownstones nearby.

She cast her head back and studied the unusual nautical motif. Four street-level bay windows resembled those at the stern of a ship and actual portholes were used as windows on the second floor. Kate smiled, noting the whimsical carved sea serpents and mermaids that capped the curved hood molding over the front entry.

The mansion fascinated her so, she spoke without thinking. "Didn't Mr. Goodhue have any sons to take over the business?'' One look at Gabe and she quickly regretted opening her mouth.

''Why, Miss Delaney, don't you think a woman is capable of running a steamship company?'' He flashed a wry smile and walked ahead of her up to the front door.

Kate wanted to throttle him, but she'd matched wits with men all her life and she knew how to handle Gabe Murray. She couldn't let him know he irritated her and responded with a slight chuckle. ''If only all men were as open-minded as you.''

She caught him grinning as he tapped the brass knocker against the heavy strike plate. He obviously enjoyed her quick comeback. Strange, she thought. Kate felt him watching her, but resisted looking at him. It seemed an eternity before the butler came to the door. When he did, she took a step back, put off by his imposing girth.

''Fräulein Vera is expecting you, sir.'' He spoke with a German accent and as he stepped aside to let them pass, the sun gleamed on his shaved head.

Kate hesitated, but Gabe said, ''Morning, Josef,'' and walked in as if he owned the place.

She followed Gabe through the vestibule, impressed by the elegant surroundings. The entry rose nearly twenty feet to a Louis Tiffany stained-glass skylight. Polished walls of dark wood paneling were fastened with brass ship's lanterns and, mounted low on a thin slab of sandstone, off to one side of the entry, was a large carving of a woman. She looked like she might have been a ship's figurehead. Her arms rested at her sides as an unfelt ocean breeze swept back her long golden hair and carved folds of her deep-blue gown. Her painted indigo eyes seemed to gaze out toward an imaginary horizon while her toes skimmed the crystal water of a crescent-shaped reflecting pool of alabaster marble.

Kate looked to Gabe, hoping for an explanation, but Josef urged them on before she could ask. ''Fräulein Vera is waiting.''

He took their coats and led them down a corridor lit by soft gaslight. Kate slowed her pace, craning her neck, taking in the formal dining room, feeling as if she'd been deposited in the hull of a sailing ship. Her curious gaze followed the gently vaulted ceiling to massive curved oak timbers, resting on thick columns which rose from a floor of sea-green marble. She could almost feel the waters of the Atlantic lapping at her toes.

Farther down the hall, through a pair of open pocket doors she glimpsed the brightly colored music room. Hand-painted murals filled the niches between mock Doric columns with lyrical vignettes and pastoral scenes. An antique harpsichord sat at one side of the great hall and in the center of the room, beneath a glistening chandelier, were two high-backed chairs resembling thrones.

''For der Fräuleins Goodhue.'' Kate dropped her voice, mimicking the butler, then stifled a laugh, afraid he might have heard.

Glancing around she found Gabe and Josef were far ahead and she hurried to catch up. Her heels echoed on the marble floor. Gabe reproached her with a glance, which she ignored. Nothing was going to ruin this glorious moment.

"Please, make yourselves comfortable," Josef said. "Fräulein Vera will meet you here." He threw open a pair of etched oval glass doors that led to the winter garden, where he left them.

Kate caught her breath as she crossed the threshold into the conservatory. The pungent aroma of lush ferns and palm trees teased her senses as the sultry air caressed her cheeks still fresh from the cold. She walked around with complete abandon, taken by the humbling space.

"It's a tropical paradise," she said. She turned and caught Gabe watching her.

He smiled self-consciously, answering in a low tone, "The Crystal Palace was a great influence on my father."

"Your father designed this? Why didn't you say so?"

There was something vague and unreadable in his face as he replied. "It was a long time ago."

Kate glanced around, awed by the incredible elegance of the room. "But the engineering looks so advanced."

"It was for its time," he said. To her delight he soon began pointing out details she might have missed. "That cast-iron floor grating conceals a subterranean heat system. And hidden water towers on the roof provide the fine mist that regulates the amount of moisture."

Kate didn't interrupt. For the first time she recognized sincerity in his voice. She found herself studying Gabe and the palm house with equal interest, noticing the tiny creases that framed the corners of his mouth and the length of his dark lashes. When he caught her staring she quickly tilted her head, squinting her eyes against the sunlight pouring in through the glass dome.

It sat on an arcade carried by richly decorated cast-iron columns. Ornate swags and sculptured figures adorned the support structures, and filigree ironwork encased the pivoting windows.

"Fascinating," she said, puzzling over Gabe's reluctance to talk about his father.

The sound of the opening door and tap of a cane on the Italian tiles cut short her speculation. Kate turned as Vera Goodhue crossed the room with regal bearing. She smoothed the pale gray strands of hair pulled tightly over her veined temples. A gossamer wisp of lace turned over the high starched collar of her black silk dress and a delicate shell-pink brooch hinted at her femininity. Yet frail as she appeared, her presence filled the room with dignity and poise.

"Mr. Murray. It's good to see you." She extended her hand to Gabe.

He smiled. "You look well, Vera. Did you have a good Christmas?"

"Oh, yes," she said while studying Kate. "But I was saddened to think of you spending the day alone." Her gaze sharpened. "Who is this?"

Gabe introduced them. "Vera Goodhue, Kate Delaney. My apprentice."

His quick acknowledgment seemed as much of a

surprise to Vera as it did to Kate. "I didn't know you had an apprentice."

Though she addressed Gabe she looked squarely at Kate leaving no doubt the comment was directed at her.

"I've just started my apprenticeship," Kate replied.

Vera's eyes gleamed with interest as she turned attention to Gabe. "How nice. I'd like to hear more about this enterprise. Let's have some refreshment, shall we?"

She directed them to a cluster of white wicker chairs at the center of the room. Shimmering silver service and bone china cups were neatly arranged on an elaborate wooden tea cart. Gabe made himself at home in the high-back chair beside Vera. Kate sat opposite, unable to escape the old woman's scrutiny.

"The name Delaney is familiar," Vera said. "Though I can't place it."

Kate cleared her throat and explained. "My grandfather owns apple orchards upstate and waterfront warehouses here in the city. Perhaps you saw our name on one of his buildings."

"Of course." Vera smiled.

She lifted the silver dome from a cut crystal serving dish that held petite triangular sandwiches, each with its crust scrupulously trimmed. She offered them to Kate, observing her, making her uncomfortable.

"Thank you." Careful to take just one sandwich between her thumb and forefinger, Kate placed it on the gilt-edged plate.

"Oh, come now," Vera scolded with a light chuckle. "Do have more than that."

Kate declined, her stomach so tight she didn't know if she could keep anything down. Gabe didn't suffer from nerves. He piled his plate high. Napkin folded over one leg, he balanced the dish on his knee.

Vera placed the silver tray aside, smiling at Kate. "What does your husband think of your ambitions?"

"I'm not married," Kate replied.

"I see," Vera said, settling back in her chair.

Kate sipped some tea to calm her nerves, trying to escape the older woman's contemplative gaze. The creaking hinges of the glass doors drew Vera's attention away from her as the second Miss Goodhue entered.

"Good morning," Hattie said.

Kate shifted in her chair to look at her. Hattie Goodhue wore pale lavender and the placid expression of a woman who had turned her back on the cares of the world years ago. She seated herself in the chair beside Kate, carefully arranging her skirt around her legs.

Vera smiled at her. "What took you so long?"

"Wrong?" Hattie twittered, pressing a lace handkerchief to her throat. "Heaven knows, Vera. We haven't done anything wrong in years."

She lifted the delicate cozy from the teapot and filled her cup. She turned to Gabe. "How are you, Mr. Murray?"

He smiled amiably. "Just fine, Hattie. How are you?"

Hattie appeared not to be listening. By now her rheumy blue eyes were fixed on Kate. Vera tapped her on the shoulder to get her attention. "Why don't you use your hearing device, dear?"

"Oh, yes." Hattie clicked her tongue. "The ice is dreadful, isn't it, Mr. Murray? Was traveling difficult, dear?"

Kate pressed her napkin to her lips to cover a smile as Gabe rebuked her with a warning glance.

"Hattie, my dear," he said. "No storm could deprive me of your pleasant company." His unabashed display of charm surprised Kate.

Hattie patted his knee with her liver-spotted hand and smiled. "I'm glad you're here. I'm eager to get this project going. At our age we can't afford to dally, can we?" she said with a soft laugh, turning to Vera.

Vera held the brass ear trumpet out to her. "Please use this. I don't want to be repeating everything." Her voice was soft but not lacking command.

Hattie snatched the contrivance from Vera, discreetly tucking it between the seat cushion and the folds of her skirt, showing no intention of using it. She looked at Kate. "Isn't anyone going to introduce me to our charming guest?"

"This is Miss Delaney," Vera said. "She's Mr. Murray's apprentice."

Hattie's eyes brightened as Vera added, "Imagine

being young, unattached and on your own in New York City.''

Smiling, Hattie assessed Kate. ''How do you know Mr. Murray? Did you study in Paris together?''

''No. No, I didn't,'' Kate replied, eyeing Gabe. ''You studied in Paris?''

''Yes, he did,'' Hattie answered for him. ''Mr. Murray is one of the first American architects to graduate from the Beaux Arts Academy. Isn't that right?'' They both looked at him.

Gabe nodded while swallowing a mouthful of food.

Kate couldn't resist saying, ''So, that explains why Mr. Murray is such an authority on French perfume.''

His eyes met hers and a wisp of a smile curled his lips as he toasted her with his teacup. Kate returned a smile, enjoying their exchange. She noticed the sisters looking on with interest and quickly changed the subject.

''You have an exquisite home.''

''Mr. Murray's father designed it for the Admiral,'' Vera told her. ''He was a dear, dear friend. Wasn't he, Hattie?''

''Oh, yes. It was quite a feat convincing the Admiral to allow a young, untried architect to design this house. He had his heart set on the Vanderbilts' man. But we were such good friends, we wanted to give Mr. Murray's father a chance to prove himself.''

''And we did just that,'' Vera added, her eyes

fixed on Gabe. "Now we've commissioned Mr. Murray to design our project. You see, collaboration between the Goodhues and Murrays is a family tradition."

Gabe set his cup aside, clearing his throat. "Why don't we look over these plans?" As he rolled out the blueprints on the side table, Hattie inclined her head to study them. Vera didn't.

"We've already reviewed the design you sent over last week," she said.

"Oh, I'm sure you have," Gabe replied with a smile, his tone of voice hinting that he'd been through this routine several times already. He arranged the blueprint on the table, glancing up to explain. "I had some additional ideas that weren't included in those plans. I think you'll like them."

He'd barely finished talking when Vera pulled a piece of paper from the deep pocket of her dress. "As long as we're discussing changes, I have some of my own."

Gabe's face dropped. "What kind of changes?"

Vera remained straight-backed in her chair, a pleasant smile on her face. "We were hoping for something with a little more aesthetic spirit."

Her affable expression didn't soften the sting of her criticism. The air between them crackled as Gabe replied with a slight edge. "The building is aesthetic in itself."

"I like it." Hattie chimed in, breaking the tension. "This in particular."

Kate looked on, once more admiring the subtle mastery of his design as Hattie traced the same area that had caught her attention earlier. The ceiling spanned at least a hundred feet yet she saw no columns or support structures. The entire space had a light ethereal quality that seemed to soar like the music it would house. She sat forward in her chair about to question Gabe when Vera abruptly ended the discussion.

"We've looked at your idea, now I want you to consider mine." She handed him the folded piece of paper.

Gabe looked hot enough to explode as he gave the notes a cursory glance then passed the paper to Kate. "I'm sure Miss Delaney can come up with something more to your liking."

"Me?" Her eyes flashed to his.

She felt a tightness that started in her chest and settled in the pit of her stomach. She wondered what he was thinking. It occurred to her that he was giving her the chance of a lifetime. If she fell short of this challenge, she'd never win his trust or respect. Suddenly that mattered very much. She pulled herself together, took the paper from him and read Vera's notes aloud.

"Ornamentation along the frieze or bracing. That's easily done, isn't it?" She looked to Gabe for affirmation.

He didn't utter a word, but Vera's eyes turned dark and stormy. Kate felt her palms grow moist as her uncomfortable position crystallized and she realized no matter what she said, someone would be angry. Taking a deep breath she did the only thing she could under the circumstances. She read on.

"Oh, and decorative buttresses," she said over a trace of nervous laughter. "That would be lovely, wouldn't it?"

"It's your project," Gabe said. His voice tightened a bit.

Kate felt her heart thump as Vera's gray eyes narrowed upon her. "You're turning our project over to your apprentice?"

"I'll oversee the work," he assured her.

Kate searched his face, wrestling with an odd mix of emotions. Part of her wanted to throw her arms around him and thank him. Another part cautioned her, reminding her that only yesterday he'd vowed to make her quit. She couldn't shake the nagging suspicion that he might be setting her up. Gabe Murray had the uncanny ability to conjure up in her the most contradictory feelings. Yet he was her only hope and the Goodhue project an opportunity. The whole situation confused and disturbed her.

"Then it's settled," Hattie said. "You can bring your design with you when you come to dinner on New Year's Eve."

"Thank you," Gabe declined. "But I can't make it."

"I know, dear. You never accept. I was addressing Miss Delaney."

Kate snapped to attention. Vera smiled at her. "We'll send a carriage to pick you up at nine. Where are you staying, dear?"

A flush of embarrassment colored her cheeks at the idea of explaining her living arrangements. She looked at Gabe as she answered, willing him to be quiet.

"Actually I'll be working late at Mr. Murray's studio that night. Why don't you send the carriage there?"

Gabe looked amused. Kate turned away more annoyed with herself for lying than with him for enjoying her dilemma.

"Then our business for today is finished?" Vera said.

They all rose as one. Hattie took Kate by the arm, leading her toward the door. "I'm sure you'll enjoy yourself, dear. Mr. and Mrs. Peyton will be there. He's an architect, too. Isn't he, Mr. Murray?"

Kate glanced over her shoulder back at Gabe.

"Oh, yes," he said with a heavy dose of sarcasm. "You'll enjoy Mr. Peyton. He adores decorative buttresses."

He moved toward the door, leaving the cylinder with his blueprints lying on the table. Kate retrieved it before leaving the palm house.

As Gabe walked a few steps ahead of them to the vestibule, Kate puzzled over his sudden hostility. She couldn't understand his reluctance to do what Vera wanted.

"We'll see you at the party?" Hattie said as they reached the entry.

Kate hadn't been listening and returned a blank stare.

"New Year's Eve," Hattie reminded her, smiling with well-bred indulgence.

Kate felt like a fool for letting herself be so distracted by Gabe. She clasped Hattie's hands and smiled apologetically. "I'm looking forward to it."

The butler handed them their coats. Vera stopped Gabe at the entry. "Mr. Murray," she said in a voice so soft Kate strained to hear. "Don't you think you should escort Miss Delaney to the ball?"

Gabe glanced at Kate while slipping his arms through his coat sleeves. Caught listening, she quickly looked away.

"Miss Delaney will be fine, Vera. I really can't make it."

"*C'est dommage.*" She expressed her regrets in French. "Perhaps another time?"

"*Oui, c'est dommage,*" Gabe replied. His flawless French momentarily stunned Kate.

He said goodbye and was out of the house before she had a chance to recover and put on her gloves.

The cold air hit Gabe hard. Tension burst into a headache at the base of his skull as he tried to figure out what went wrong. Damn it, they weren't supposed to like her. How could he have been so shortsighted? He'd let his anger over what Vera had done to his design cloud his judgment. He should have accepted the invitation to make sure Lloyd Peyton didn't have a chance to influence Kate. Of course, going to the party would have meant seeing Eve.

Gabe walked down the stairs, heedless of the ice. Why couldn't he just put the past behind him and get on with his life?

"Mr. Murray, wait."

He watched Kate struggle to keep her footing on

the slippery steps. God, she was like a splinter he couldn't extricate.

"What on earth is wrong?" she asked.

By now he wanted to lash out at something and her innocent question was all it took. "Don't you ever suggest corrupting my designs with bric-a-brac. Do you understand?" He turned to walk away.

She caught him by the arm. "No, I don't understand. You said this was my project and I think we should give Vera what she wants."

Gabe flexed his fingers, fighting his frustration. He didn't know who he was angrier with; himself, Vera or his father for getting him into this mess. "Just don't tamper with my design, all right?"

He grabbed the end of the cardboard tube containing his blueprints. "Here, give me those."

"Oh, no, you don't," she said as she pulled back on it and held fast. "You gave me this project. Besides, I don't think this has anything to do with changing your precious designs."

"Really?" He gave the cylinder another yank.

"Really." She replied with a sharp tug. "You're upset because they invited me to the party."

"Oh, that's rich, Miss Delaney. If you want to waste your time sipping champagne with Lloyd Peyton on New Year's Eve, you go right ahead."

"And I'll remind you, Mr. Murray, that you have nothing to say about it if I do. You're my tutor. Not my guardian. I might even learn something about architecture from Mr. Peyton." She jerked hard on the cylinder once more.

That was more than he could stand. Gabe let go

of his end, sending her hurtling backward. "Oh," she gasped, windmilling her arms. With the plumes on her hat fluttering, she looked like a large flightless bird as she fought to regain her balance.

Gabe tried to catch her but missed by inches. She fell in a deep mound of snow, her hat sailing off her head as she landed.

"You barbarian," she screamed, cheeks flushed and eyes burning like hot coals.

He quickly offered her his hand. She slapped him away. "Just leave me alone. You might speak French like a gentleman, but you're a brute and a philistine." Her tirade escaped as frosty vapor.

"Philistine?" he said, laughing.

He stepped back, beginning to enjoy her struggle.

Each time she managed to push herself up, her feet slipped from under her. Once more he offered to help. Kate shot him a fiery look, but clasped both his hands. As he started to pull her up, she let go.

Gabe lost his balance, slipping on the icy concrete. His legs flew out from under him, his back slammed the trunk of a small tree and he slid to the base, where he sat, shaking his head.

Through the ringing in his ears, he heard a soughing sound, like wind through the pines. He glanced up as a small avalanche sifted down through the snow-laden branches.

Thundering tarnation. He rolled to one side. Too late. The snow hit with a muffled thud, burying him in a cold, wet blanket. The sound of her laughter echoed through his head as he blinked his eyes and shook the snow from his hair. He must look a fool.

So did she, plopped down in a drift, hair skewed to one side.

Her contagious laughter brought a smile to his face that erupted into an explosive belly laugh. The release of tension felt so good, he flopped on his back in the snow, laughing.

A few curious passersby gathered at the iron fence surrounding the property, among them a policeman. "Is there a problem here?" He eyeballed Gabe as he tapped a menacing billy club against his open palm.

"No. No problem, officer. Just had a little slip." Gabe pushed himself up.

Brushing the snow from his pants and coat, he reached over to help Kate regain her feet. Still chuckling, she shook the snow from her skirt.

"I guess that cooled you off," she said, glancing at Gabe.

It had. Bowing deeply, he swept up her hat from the ground with a flourish, dusted snow from its brim and presented it to her. His chivalrous performance brought laughter and a round of applause from the crowd at the fence. As he straightened, he noticed Vera and Hattie watching them from the upstairs window.

"Oh, terrific," he groaned, wondering what they must be thinking. He alerted Kate. "Behave yourself, they're watching."

She glanced up at the window, smiled and waved. The old sisters gave her a pleasant smile and let the curtain fall. Gabe watched Kate, struck by how she'd won them over. "Truce?" he said, offering his hand.

"Truce," she replied, shaking his hand.

The onlookers cheered Gabe as he retrieved his blueprints and offered Kate his arm. Linking her arm through his, she smiled amiably as they marched through the front gate away from the crowd.

Once around the corner, she burst out laughing. "How embarrassing," she said. "I'm soaking wet. I can't imagine what Vera must be thinking."

She smoothed her coat collar still trying to pull herself together. "Maybe you should give up architecture and go into Vaudeville."

Gabe replied in a playful mood. "I tried that, but they hauled me off stage with a cane."

As her eyes met his, a full smile lit her face. "That was fun," she said. "What do you do for an encore?"

It was fun, he silently admitted to himself, afraid to let her know how much he enjoyed her company.

"Is the truce still on?" she asked.

"For now." Gabe searched for a carriage. Kate walked beside him.

"Then, can I ask you a question?"

He braced himself, not knowing what to expect. "All right."

"Why didn't you tell me your father designed Fairweather?"

"That's it?" he said. "What difference does it make?"

"I've never seen anything like it," she said. "If my father had designed it, I'd be proud."

Her remark hit a nerve, changing his mood. Avoiding a direct answer, he stepped from the curb to hail a carriage. "Fairweather is all sentimental fluff. Ornamentation, like the feathers on your hat. They're pretty, but serve no purpose."

"Serve no purpose?" Kate blinked her eyes, staring at him in disbelief. "You are an enigma, Mr. Murray. The palm house is beautifully ornamented. You didn't mind explaining that. You are supposed to be teaching me, aren't you?" Her voice held an unmistakable challenge.

"The palm house has structural significance that might serve you in the future," he said. "Like the warmth provided by your hat. Do you understand the difference, Miss Delaney?" He instantly regretted his patronizing tone, but he was her instructor after all.

Kate returned one of her regally condemning glances. "Yes, Mr. Murray, I do understand. Fashion would be very dull had you been a haberdasher."

If they'd had a truce, it ended then. She smacked her hat against her thigh, squared her shoulders and marched away from him toward the waiting carriage. A feather fluttered from her hat, landing in the snow.

Gabe picked it up, absently rolling it between his thumb and forefinger. He watched her walk away, grinning in spite of himself. He'd never met a woman who could insult him so completely yet leave him smiling. Here was a female whose company he genuinely enjoyed, even if it wasn't in his best interest. He found himself wishing they'd met under different circumstances, but the fact remained she had to go.

Gabe shifted his thinking to what needed to be done. He had to be careful. He had to remember his plan. Nothing could interfere with that. Nothing. Letting the feather fall, he strode to the carriage, determined not to be sidetracked by her sweet face or quick wit again. He had an idea.

"Maybe we should continue our debate over dinner," he said, climbing into the carriage behind her.

Kate looked at him, the angry flush fading from her face. "I'd like that."

"Good." Gabe settled back, his self-assurance restored. She'd taken the bait. Dinner at the Harp might be just the thing that would push her over the edge and out of his studio.

Chapter Six

"I'll only be a minute," Kate assured him. She pulled a clean blouse and skirt from her oversize steamer trunk and hurried up to the loft, eager to change out of her wet clothes.

The day had been filled with excitement and laughter and she looked forward to an evening out, continuing their conversation and furthering their friendship. She secured the crook-necked hanger on a nail and shook the folds from her green velvet skirt. Finally it seemed she was making progress. Their tumble in the snow had broken the tension. She even discovered that Gabe had a sense of humor, astonishing in one normally so aloof and serious.

Slipping out of her suit jacket, she considered their unfortunate start and understood how he might have found her as intolerable as she had found him. After all, she had invaded his life and been demanding. But all that would change now. She felt they had made a start today. She'd scratched the surface of his granitelike facade and glimpsed another side of Gabe. A side she liked.

As she lifted her blouse up and over her head, a hook at the collar snagged her hair, sending a cascade of unruly ringlets tumbling down her back. "Oh, drat."

She didn't have time to fuss with her hair. The last thing she needed was for him to think her a dawdling woman just when he was beginning to accept her. Peeking over the balustrade she saw Gabe impatiently pacing the studio.

"I'll be right there, Mr. Murray." She lifted her silver hairbrush and stepped before the large oval mirror, wearing only her chemise and camisole.

The sound of her voice stopped his pacing. Gabe glanced up to realize that from where he stood he could see her reflection in the mirror. His gaze remained fixed on the arresting image. The flimsy garments skimmed the fullness of her hips putting a formidable knot in his stomach.

His breath caught as she leaned over, tossing her hair to brush out the knots, her full breasts nearly spilling from her camisole. The heat of desire shot to his groin. Gabe tried to sever his gaze, but her movements were magnetic and he watched, enthralled as she straightened to catch her hair at her temples with two tortoiseshell combs. She shifted her weight from one leg to the other, the sensual thrust of her hips mimicking the moves of an exotic dancer.

He squeezed his eyes tight, but the image came back. He couldn't desire her. He wouldn't. He'd just gone too long without a woman. A few lively hours with one of the vaudeville girls from the Fourth Street Theater would cure what ailed him. He turned away, reasoning with himself, shoring up his resolve. Deep down he knew he had to remove the temptation before he weakened.

Kate cinched her belt, smoothing the fabric of her shirt, taking one last look at herself. Satisfied with her appearance, she started down the steps to meet Gabe. "All set," she said.

He turned, looking at her as if he just realized she was a woman. Kate thought she'd left one of her buttons undone. A quick glance at the front of her pleated blouse assured her everything was in place. Her eyes returned to his.

"Is something wrong?"

He shook his head, looking her over, his dumbstruck expression adding to her confusion. "Your hair is different."

"Don't you like it?" she asked, drawing her fingers across the wavy strands falling over her shoulder.

Gabe swallowed hard, his eyes following the movement of her hand, dallying at the curve of her breasts for a moment longer than proper before shifting his gaze.

"It's fine," he said, and reached for his coat. "I thought we'd walk."

"All right," she agreed. Taking her coat, she followed him from the studio.

As they crossed the street she noticed he'd become quiet and remote once more. Eager to make the most of the evening, she double-stepped to keep up with his long stride, a pace that made conversation difficult. Kate tried, a little winded. "What do you think of the new Stanley Steamer, Mr. Murray?"

"I haven't thought about it. Why do you ask?"

She hustled to keep up, anxious to share her thoughts. "I think people are going to flock to them and when everyone in America owns a machine like that, they'll want a place to keep it. Roads will have to be widened, streets paved, the boundaries of the city will expand and we'll be able to build houses in places we haven't dreamed of."

Gabe slowed his pace causing her to nearly bump into him. He gave her a furtive glance, then looked away. "Interesting," he said, turning the corner.

Shaking her head, Kate tried to make sense of his odd mood. She followed close behind until he stopped abruptly in front of a dingy-looking tavern. "We're here," he said.

Surely he was joking. She glanced up at the sorry-looking placard that hung above the chipped and splintered door. A tipsy man stumbled out onto the street. Kate backed away.

She felt like a fool for being so gullible. She'd actually thought Gabe was beginning to accept her. Her heart sank as she realized she was mistaken.

"What's wrong, Miss Delaney? Lost your appetite?"

Kate swallowed her disappointment and looked him straight in the eye. "I'm famished, Mr. Murray. Simply famished."

She turned her back on him, pushed open the door and marched ahead into the Green Harp Tavern.

The room fell silent. Heads turned and hands remained poised above poker chips as men stopped playing cards to gape at her. She stopped short, staring into the face of the snowy-haired bartender. His cobalt-blue eyes remained fixed on her face, his hand clamped around the tap handle until beer sloshed over the rim of the glass.

"What the devil?" He wiped his hands on the front of his apron.

Kate ventured a quick look around, noting the shocked expression on each patron's face. Her first impulse was to turn tail and quietly leave, then she realized that was the exact reaction Gabe expected. She would sooner die than give him the satisfaction of knowing he'd upset her.

The stream of amber light spilling from the narrow galley kitchen at the rear of the room fell like a beacon across a small square table. Kate straightened her spine, held her head high and assumed a brisk pace as she made her way toward the table.

Sawdust clotted on the soles of her high-buttoned shoes and clung to the hem of her brushed velvet skirt. Every eye was on her, watching her as if she had two heads. She avoided eye contact, keeping her gaze focused on a tattered lithograph of *Custer's Last Stand*. It hung on the wall squarely ahead of her.

Her stride faltered when she noticed some of the figures were moving. Kate strained to see in the dim light. Her mouth dropped open and her stomach turned as she stared at the roaches scurrying up the stark plaster wall.

"Are you still hungry, Miss Delaney?" Gabe asked, leaning close.

His taunting tone of voice made her fume. She shot him a murderous glare. Nothing would have pleased her more than to wipe the smug look from his face with the flat of her hand.

He seized another opportunity to jab at her. "You did say you wanted to be treated just as a male apprentice, didn't you?"

God, she detested him. Turning on her heel, she continued on to the table with the old bartender close behind. He maneuvered around her, pulling a chair out from the table with the flare of a Waldorf concierge. He dusted the seat. "To what do I owe the pleasure of such delightful company?"

He looked from Gabe to Kate, then back at Gabe. "You should have told me you were bringing a lady to dinner, Gabe. I would have made the proper arrangements."

Kate eyed Gabe with mounting distaste as she seated herself with her back to the ogling clientele. Obviously the proper arrangements were the furthest thing from his mind where she was concerned.

He took the chair opposite her, meeting her angry stare from across the small round table. The cold air seeping beneath the back door felt tepid compared to the chill passing between them. The old man spoke up at last, breaking the tension.

"If you don't mind my saying so, lass, the Harp isn't often graced by such a fine lady. I hope you're not uncomfortable here.'' His concern diffused her anger.

Kate gave him a sweet smile as she primly placed the napkin on her lap. ''I'm quite comfortable. Thank you, Mr.....?''

''Hurley,'' he said, bowing deeply. ''Finn Hurley, proprietor of the Harp at your service, lass.''

''Thank you, Mr. Hurley. It's refreshing to be in the company of a gentleman.'' She shot Gabe a scathing look. He ignored her. Their animosity was palpable.

Finn cleared his throat. ''Are you hungry, lass?''

''Starving,'' she replied, keeping her fiery gaze leveled on Gabe. ''What's on the menu, Mr. Hurley?''

''Please, call me Finn. How does a bowl of hearty beef stew laced with tiny peas, diced carrots and new potatoes sound?''

''Sounds wonderful,'' she said, sitting back. Even if he offered her a plate of sawdust she was going to enjoy every bite.

''Splendid,'' said Finn. ''I have a nice crusty loaf of black bread fresh from Rosen's Bakery. 'Tis still warm from the brick oven.''

Gabe snapped open his napkin. ''Why don't you bring us a bottle of wine, too.''

''Aye,'' Finn nodded, chafing his hands. He headed in the direction of the kitchen.

Gabe called out, stopping him. ''Don't serve any roaches with it, all right?'' He leveled his gaze on Kate.

Her stomach roiled but she managed not to react.

Left alone, the oppressive quiet slammed around them like the door of a tomb. Kate recalled all the tense silent meals she'd shared with her grandfather. She shifted uncomfortably in her seat, wishing things could be different between her and Gabe. At last Finn returned, cradling two glasses and a bottle of red wine.

"Here we are," he said, placing a glass in front of her. He gave it a quick inspection, lifted the grimy glass and wiped it clean with his apron.

"That's better." He gave her a smile.

It seemed the more Finn went out of his way to please her, the more Gabe scowled. They were behaving like schoolboys in a game of one-upmanship and she was beginning to feel like the rope in a tug-of-war.

Finn poured a glass of wine as he glanced at Gabe. "Would you be a good lad and catch the newsboy for me?"

Gabe narrowed his eyes on the crafty old man. "You want me to get you a paper now?"

"Sure," Finn replied. "I hear there's a shake-up at City Hall and I want to read about it. Come on," he cajoled. "For the sake of me old bones, lad, don't make me go out in the cold."

Kate smiled inwardly, sensing he was up to something. The old leprechaun appeared as sound as an ox. He obviously wanted some time alone with her. He probably thought she had a romantic interest in Gabe and intended to give her some fatherly advice on how to win him. She'd set him straight.

Gabe didn't budge. He eyed them both.

"Go on." Finn elbowed him. "Don't worry, I'll protect the lady with me life."

"Oh, all right." Gabe relented, slapping his napkin on the table. He pushed back his chair and dug a coin from his pocket. "I won't be long," he told Kate.

"Don't hurry back on my account," she replied, toying with her spoon.

Gabe grumbled something under his breath as he walked away. Finn spun the chair around, straddling the seat. He draped his forearms casually over the high back, then half turned to make sure Gabe was out of earshot.

"So, lass," he said with a wink. "How are the two of you getting on?"

"Getting on?"

"You know," Finn said, cocking his head in Gabe's direction. "Him teaching you. How's it going?"

She hadn't expected that. "You mean you know who I am?"

"Sure. You're the student. Gabe never let on you were so fair a pupil." Finn assessed her with an approving glance, then shook his head in disbelief. "The lad is even dumber than I figured him to be."

Kate chuckled, yet found it odd that Gabe had mentioned her to Finn. She sat forward, resting her elbows on the table, thinking Finn Hurley seemed to have more than a passing friendship with Gabe, a friendship that might help her find a way around the stubborn oaf.

"How long have you known Mr. Murray, Finn?"

Pride brightened his eyes, he puffed up his chest and sat straight in the chair. "Why I was there the night the lad was born."

"Really?" she said, thoughtfully pressing one finger to her lips. "Then maybe you could explain why he's being so...so..." She didn't have a chance to find the word before he spoke.

"Giving you a hard time, is he?"

Kate drew a deep breath, exhaled slowly and nodded.

"I thought as much," Finn said, frowning. "You just got to remember lass, people can only get your goat if you let them know where you keep it."

Her perfectly arched brows drew together. "What do you mean?"

"Simple. You can't let people see what riles you. Don't let him get you down. Protect your vulnerable side." He pulled up his fists like a sparring boxer feinting blows. "Old Gabe may be stubborn as they come but he has a good heart and he's a fine teacher."

"I wouldn't know," Kate said, lowering her eyes to hide her despondence. "I haven't seen evidence of either quality in him."

Finn smothered her hand with his own and spoke in a soft compassionate voice. "There's more to that man than meets the eye."

Kate shot back. "He's bullheaded and arrogant."

"No denying that." Finn laughed richly. "But mostly he just doesn't know how to talk to people, if you know what I mean."

"I do know what you mean," she said. "Especially women. He's like Dr. Jekyll and Mr. Hyde. Just when I think he's beginning to accept me, he turns around and goes out of his way to be rude." She caught herself before saying too much. Finn was his friend, after all.

He gave her a knowing smile. "Well, that's understandable."

"Is it?" She searched his face.

"Of course. If he talks to you, he might get to know you. Maybe even like you."

"I hadn't thought of that."

Finn squeezed her hand once, then let go. "Cut him some slack, lass. He'll come around. Truth is, the lad's afraid."

"Afraid?" she asked. "Afraid of what?" Before Finn could answer her, Gabe returned.

"Isn't this cozy," he said, eyeing Finn.

He relinquished the chair to Gabe. "I'll fetch your dinner." He turned to leave.

"What about your paper?" Gabe asked.

"I'll be back."

Gabe placed the newspaper on the table as he took his seat. "The two of you seemed pretty chummy when I walked in. What were you talking about?"

His defensiveness lent credence to Finn's remark. "Nothing," she said, meeting his gaze straight on. "He promised there wouldn't be any roaches in my food."

"Right," Gabe said. His doubtfulness sparked her curiosity and made her wonder if cynicism was just his way of keeping people from getting too close. She had often used sarcasm as a shield when she felt threatened. But why would a man as attractive and talented as Gabe Murray see her as a threat?

Kate sipped her wine and settled back, wondering if she'd misjudged Gabe. He certainly hadn't given her reason to think so. Gabe Murray was so ill-tempered she couldn't imagine anyone wanting to get close enough to him to become a threat.

"Why are you looking at me like that?"

His voice cut through the fog of her thoughts, making her realize she'd been staring. Flustered at being caught, she groped for something to say. "I was just wondering if you always knew you would be an architect."

"There was never any question," he said, snapping open the newspaper.

Kate wasn't going to let him shut her out and hide behind the daily. Finn had a point. She had to find a way to communicate with him. Yet, as she studied Gabe, the small table separating them seemed as vast as the Atlantic Ocean. She reasoned she'd already plunged into his life, so she drew a deep breath and dove into his indifference.

"Mr. Murray, I'm curious. Why didn't you ever go into business with your father?"

He lowered the paper to look at her in a way that made her think she'd struck a chord. "My father and I had very different ideas," he said.

Kate replied, "On more than design, I suspect."

Again, he lifted the paper to shut her out. Determined to get through to him, Kate folded her hands on the table, cleared her throat and began picking away at what she saw as a weakness in his armor.

"You're very lucky to have had a father who encouraged you. And to study in Paris must have been wonderful," she said. "I've always dreamed of seeing Paris."

She paused, hoping for some response. Gabe didn't look up.

"Mr. Murray?"

Nothing. Closing her eyes, she slowly counted to ten.

When she opened them again, she was still faced with the black-and-white printed wall of newspaper he'd erected between them.

"Did anyone ever tell you what a wonderful conversationalist you are?"

Again nothing.

Kate dropped her voice an octave, answering herself. "Why, yes, Miss Delaney. I have been told that."

Gabe turned the page with an exaggerated motion. Kate rolled her eyes. She was wasting her time yet she wouldn't give up. Settling back, she sipped her wine and pressed on. "I'm sorry I never got to meet your father. From his letters, he seemed a different sort of man. Very different from you and my grandfather..." she said, voice trailing off as her thoughts wandered. It seemed she'd been fated to live her life with troublesome men.

"We argued a lot," she said, remembering. "I can't tell you how many times I raced from the house in tears to hide in the stable. I'd lay awake on cold clear nights for hours. The scent of burning leaves filling the autumn air and crystal stars dotting the sky. I played a game, connecting the dots. I passed the time, designing cities, building with windows lit by starlight.''

The rustling of the newspaper brought her head up. Kate found Gabe watching her. For a moment their gazes flowed together. She looked away, embarrassed by the intimate things she revealed. ''I never told anyone that before.''

''Why did you tell me?'' He sounded genuinely curious and the softness in his voice came as a surprise. Still, she felt she couldn't trust him. That realization brought her back to her problem.

''The only reason you gave me the Goodhue project is because you think I'll fail, don't you?''

The compassion left his face and she felt something threatening in his attitude once more. ''I have no reason to believe you won't.''

Kate stared at him, convinced he didn't have a sympathetic bone in his body. Whatever crazy idea she'd had about reaching him and changing his opinion dissolved. She felt her cheeks grow hot with anger.

''How dare you? You don't know what I'm capable of doing.''

Gabe sat back, regarding her over the rim of his wineglass. ''I know you're very capable of backing yourself into a corner, Miss Delaney. The question is, are you clever enough to get out?''

''What are you saying?''

''How are you going to complete a design and full set of blueprints in time for Vera's party? That is what you promised her.''

Gabe smiled and the same smile that she swore could melt the coolest female heart now made her shudder. She had promised Vera and Hattie a new design and until that moment she believed Gabe would help her. The depth of her foolishness brought the hot sting of tears to her eyes as she realized she'd behaved just as she had with her grandfather. The same naive self-assurance that had allowed her grandfather to maneuver her into this awful situation had now given Gabe the upper hand.

He had no idea to what he was sentencing her. A choking feeling of panic pushed her close to telling him about her grandfather's edict. Just as fast, she understood he wouldn't care. Gabe Murray was just like her grandfather and men like them would sooner see a woman hobbled by a loveless marriage than succeed in their man's world.

Kate contemplated a quiet subservient life as cold silence hardened around them. If only she could find a man who loved her enough to allow her the freedom she craved. Yet that kind of love seemed as elusive as a warming breeze in winter. Everything about her appeared to bring out the worst in men. She looked at Gabe, wondering if he saw her as a threat, then pushed the silly notion aside. She wasn't competing with him. All she wanted was the instruction she'd paid for.

Finn returned with their food, jolting her from her thoughts. He placed a bowl of piping hot stew on the table in front of her. "There you go, lass, enjoy your meal."

"Thank you," she lied. "I will."

Gabe dipped his fork into the stew without showing the slightest sign of compunction. She hadn't finished with him yet and she intended to have the last word. She waited until Finn left.

"You forgot one small detail, Mr. Murray."

"And what is that?" he asked, glancing up.

In the depths of his dark eyes she saw determination that matched her own. Kate spoke in the most even tone she could manage. "You promised Vera you would oversee the work."

"And I will," he said. "But I doubt there will be much work to oversee if you don't come up with a design."

Once more he dipped his fork into his plate. He glanced up, smiling with the smug self-assurance she was fast growing to hate. "There's an early train tomorrow, Miss Delaney."

Kate simmered. "Well, don't expect to find me on it, Mr. Murray. I'll have a design for Vera with or without your help."

She ground her teeth and stabbed a gravy-soaked potato, pretending it was his thick skull. They finished their meal in strained silence, which seemed to suit Gabe just fine.

Chapter Seven

For the next several days Kate struggled with her design while Gabe diligently avoided her.

She wouldn't have believed the man could be so brassbound. Stubbornness seemed the one thing they had in common. She wanted to wring his miserable neck for twisting things around and using her own mulish nature against her. Pushing the loose hair back from her forehead she stared in hapless defeat at her drawing.

It seemed the more she worked at it the worse it looked. The entire structure was bogged down and heavy, lacking the light, airiness she'd found so appealing in *his* original plan.

A similar feeling of heaviness settled in her heart as time ran out and she confronted the impossibility of completing her design. Even if she worked day and night for the rest of the week, a simple rendering was the best she could hope to have for Vera. If Vera approved, a full set of blueprints would have to follow. Kate's spirits sank further. She had never drawn up a complete set of blueprints as complex as this. No matter how she hated to admit it, she needed Gabe's help.

She frowned, certain that would never happen. As soon as she asked he'd have a carriage ready to escort her to the train station.

"Irascible man," she mumbled to herself. "It's no wonder he has no clients. Except for Finn Hurley, he probably has no friends."

Resting her chin in her hand she looked around the untidy room, puzzling over the lack of public interest in Gabe's work. Something just didn't add up. He had talent and good ideas. Looking for an excuse to avoid tackling her design, she found herself thinking of ways to improve the appearance of the studio.

The spacious room with its high ceiling had potential. A little elbow grease and some spirits of ammonia applied to the windowpanes would do wonders to enhance the natural lighting and a few carefully chosen paintings and draperies would add color. She envisioned a comfortable reception area accented by fresh flowers and a tea table for entertaining clients. If there were clients.

The nagging question surfaced again and she thought about Gabe. She found it strange that he went out of his way to alienate the very people who could enhance his career. Why? she wondered.

It seemed to Kate that a party hosted by the Goodhue sisters was the kind of social event that could bring future opportunities and business prospects to

a man like him. *And what kind of man is that?* she
asked herself.

Gabe Murray was a riddle and the more she tried
to make sense of him, the more questions arose.
Questions she had no time to dwell on if she was
going to come up with a design and save her skin.
That pressing reality shook her into action. She
didn't have time to stand here thinking about him
when she had so much to do.

She looked at the drawing lying on the table in
front of her, feeling the tightening grip of failure.
Nothing she came up with captured her imagination
as much as the plans Gabe had already presented to,
and had rejected by, Vera. Tapping her pencil on the
table she debated what to do. Finishing her design
far outweighed swallowing her pride and asking for
help. What would she gain by winning a battle of
wills if she went to Vera empty-handed? She could
either find a way around Gabe and get him to help
her, which seemed unlikely under the circumstances.
Or, she could ask Vera and Hattie for more time. As
much as she hated taking her problem to them, it
seemed her only chance. After all, the worst that
could happen is they would refuse and she'd be
forced to ask Gabe for help, anyway. She would do
it.

Before she could change her mind, she left her
work lying on the drafting table, grabbed her cloak
and headed off to Fairweather.

Gabe felt so good he bounded up the steps to the
front door of his studio two at a time. He could

hardly keep from grinning. She was reaching her limit. He'd seen the frustration growing in her eyes for days now and victory was so close he could taste it.

He'd spent enough time with her to sense her moods. He'd even come to know her little habits, like the cute way she chewed her lower lip while puzzling out a problem.

He chuckled, thinking she was certainly puzzling over the problem he'd dumped in her lap. Cradling the package of freshly laundered shirts beneath one arm, he dug through his coat pocket for his keys. He could just imagine Vera's unceremonious rejection of the new design. Poor Kate would be devastated. Of course, he'd be there to console her. But solace wasn't all he was prepared to offer.

He brushed his hand across his breast pocket, making sure the one-way train ticket he'd bought was secure. As soon as Kate quit, he would personally escort her to Grand Central Terminal. Then he could relax, knowing the museum project was his.

Gabe smiled, anticipating the pleasure he'd take at seeing the shock on Peyton's face as he snatched the museum project out from under him. No one deserved losing more than Lloyd Peyton. But no one deserved deception less than Kate. His smile dissolved as he once again found himself wrestling with his guilt over winning at her expense.

If only there were some other way. He didn't want to hurt her. He admired her perseverance. No matter what he confronted her with, she met his torment with determination. Kate Delaney was a far cry from other women he knew. She was no simpering little frilly thing. She had substance. She also had opinions about everything from three-dimensional design to the economic impact of the horseless carriage. And she wasn't afraid to express them. He liked baiting her, challenging her, arguing with her. She stimulated him intellectually as few women could. The memory of the way she looked standing before the mirror wearing only her shimmies stimulated him in other ways. Gabe wrestled with his uncomfortable attraction, caught his thoughts heading down that dangerous road and made a swift mental about-face. He had to resist her and remain focused on his purpose. The sooner he got rid of her, the sooner he could get on with his life and forget her. But could he forget knowing he'd deprived her of her dream? And what was his life, anyway? Certainly not full of spectacular successes.

He stood at his front door for a long time contemplating that as his feelings of triumph diminished. His mistakes already hung like an albatross around his neck. He didn't relish adding guilt over Kate to that weight. But, damn it, winning the art museum meant more than just evening the score with Peyton. It meant salvaging his reputation and restoring his good name. It meant stepping from the shadow of doubt and disgrace that his stupidity had cast over his family. He could make it up to Kate later. Once the museum project belonged to him, he saw no reason why they couldn't be friends. No reason at all. Except that she would never forgive him for using her this way. He wouldn't blame her.

The idea of how hard she'd worked to please Vera further softened his heart. Would it be such a mistake to help her with her design? Gabe had no doubt Vera would reject whatever Kate presented just to punish him for giving the project to his apprentice. He really had nothing to lose by offering Kate his help. Or did he? Still debating, he opened the door and walked in.

He dropped the package of clean laundry on a chair and absently placed his keys on the small wooden table beside the door. He was so deep in concentration, he didn't notice Kate was gone until the silence hit him. He looked around.

Gabe saw her work lying on the drafting table and walked to it. He'd been curious for days, but refrained from showing any interest in her design, afraid she'd misconstrue his curiosity for approval. He stopped short of the table and smiled, certain the little fox stood watching him from the loft right now, waiting to trick him. He raised his eyes only to be disappointed by her absence.

"Miss Delaney?" His voice reverberated through the empty studio, filling him with an odd sense of remorse. He wondered if she'd gone, then pushed the thought aside.

A fresh pot of coffee sat on the stove. He poured himself a cup and sipped it while he walked back to the table. The coffee was surprisingly good. So was her design. He placed the cup aside to study her drawing more closely. She'd followed Vera's suggestions as if they were religious doctrine. Poor thing, he thought. She had no idea how fast dogma changed with Vera in charge.

Still, he couldn't deny her rendering showed promise. And talent. Gabe became more interested when he saw how she'd taken his idea and softened the edges ever so slightly with a touch of decorative scrolling. Curious, he decided it was time he looked at her other work.

He walked to his desk where her portfolio sat, untouched, since her arrival. Untying the black satin ribbons that secured it on three sides, he lay it open and quickly ruffled through sheet after sheet of typical student drawings. He stopped when he came to several unexpected watercolors and design posters. A feeling of respect twitched to life. Her technique was more than adequate. The way she executed her designs showed the kind of confidence that came only with hours of practice and dedicated study. Her delicate watercolors of ethereal female figures exhibited a deep understanding of two-dimensional design and showed a balance between darkness and light, line and curve.

What impressed him most was her design for a large frieze, a panel depicting two female figures clutching rosebuds. Gabe was struck by the lovely tension she'd achieved between decorative curves within the framework of an asymmetrical rectangle.

Reluctant to let her know he'd looked at her work, he arranged the drawings just as he'd found them, tied up the portfolio and returned it to its place beside his desk.

Allowing his gaze to drift up to the loft, he wondered where she'd gone.

He returned to the table, studied her design and smiled at the way she'd completely overlooked sound engineering principle for the sake of her precious ornamentation. He looked forward to pointing that out to her when she returned. Yet, as much as he anticipated teasing her, he couldn't deny that with a few minor adjustments he could include her decoration and keep the structure from collapsing.

Gabe couldn't resist the urge to correct her mistakes. He reached for the pen, then stopped short, realizing if he made even one change he'd have to explain why. Or worse, admit she had talent. He rubbed his jaw, fighting with himself, knowing the slightest alteration would work against him. Then, again, helping her just a little might ease his conscience and help him sleep.

Gabe debated, drumming his fingers on the table. Impulse won at last and he touched the pen to the paper.

Chapter Eight

"I'll wait here," Kate told Josef.

Seated on an elaborate carved bench in the vestibule, she fidgeted with her gloves, rehearsing what she would say. Hattie and Vera Goodhue didn't strike her as women who tolerated excuses. Lord knows, Vera must have dealt with her share of cantankerous men in her life. Kate decided she would approach them with confidence and appeal to Vera's sense of business.

The sound of female voices coming from the hall sent her pulse racing. She forgot her prepared speech, shot to her feet and tugged nervously at the hem of her jacket.

Hattie approached, escorting a statuesque young woman. Kate studied the younger woman, noting she wore a tailored winter suit in the latest Paris style. The lace veil of her black silk hat covered her face to her lips, adding a striking touch of mystery.

Kate smiled, catching Hattie's attention.

"Miss Delaney, what a pleasant surprise." She

took Kate by the hand, drawing her toward them, making an intimate circle.

"I'm so glad you're here. I want you to meet Mrs. Peyton." Hattie turned to the other woman. "Eve, you remember I mentioned Miss Delaney would be attending the New Year's ball."

"Of course." Eve smiled, but there was no warmth in her eyes. "I'm pleased to meet you," she said.

"Likewise," Kate said, ill at ease. "I've interrupted."

"No," Eve assured her. "I was just leaving. I promised my husband I'd be at home when he arrived." She pulled on her gloves and glanced at Kate. "I'll see you at the ball?"

"I look forward to it."

Josef opened the door and Eve left. Kate found herself staring, thinking the woman appeared to be everything she wasn't, everything her grandfather wanted her to be.

"She's a lovely creature, isn't she?" Hattie's voice drew her back.

"Yes, very beautiful."

"I doubt you would be studying with Mr. Murray if she hadn't broken their engagement."

"What?" Kate looked at her askance. "Mr. Murray was engaged to be married to her?"

"Oh, yes," Hattie said matter-of-factly. "But, with that dreadful scandal…" Shaking her head, she clicked her tongue.

"What scandal?" Kate asked.

"Why the scandal that sent him off to Cuba with

the Rough Riders, of course.'' Hattie spoke as if everyone who was anyone knew the details.

''Of course,'' Kate said softly, wondering what kind of man she was sharing a studio with. As Gabe's dark brooding features took shape in her mind, she recalled what Finn had told her and realized she'd been so absorbed in her own problem, she'd missed the obvious reason for his surliness. Eve Peyton had broken his heart and now she was paying the price. Just as she'd paid the price for her mother's rebelliousness.

Kate couldn't believe it. It seemed she'd spent her whole life trying to convince her grandfather that she wasn't anything like her mother and now, fate had doomed her to spend her apprenticeship fighting with Gabe Murray because of another woman's actions. Kate felt an instant dislike for Eve Peyton.

''Was there something you came to talk about, dear?''

She looked at Hattie, thinking there was a lot she wanted to talk about. Unfortunately, she couldn't think of a graceful way to approach the subject of Gabe Murray's past. She pushed the thought aside and went straight to the point.

''I came to discuss the new design.''

Hattie looked nonplussed. ''You mean you're finished already?''

Kate blushed, unable to hide her embarrassment. ''I'm afraid not. I have an idea I think you'll like, but it will take some additional planning.''

''Well, let's discuss it with Vera, shall we?'' Hattie directed her to the study, furnished with forest-green upholstery and walls of polished oak. Vera stood at the window, sipping sherry. As she turned, sunlight streaming through the lacy curtains fell in a delicate pattern across her wrinkled cheek.

"Sit down, dear," Hattie said. She took her place on the awning-striped settee, patted the plump cushion beside her and looked at Vera.

"Miss Delaney has some design ideas to go over with us."

"More ideas?" Vera said with a slight chuckle. "Will I live long enough to see a finished project?"

Kate smiled, feeling a little less awkward. "Of course you will."

Vera topped off her glass with sherry. "Would you like some?"

"No, thank you," Kate said.

"Then, let's hear your idea." Vera sat opposite her.

Kate began slowly, recalling her reaction to Gabe's revisions. "What I had in mind was an area that could be used for out-of-doors concerts."

"Out of doors?" Vera looked interested, yet skeptical.

"In summer," Kate went on to explain. "The concert hall will be covered, but open on all sides to take advantage of the ocean breeze."

"Interesting," Vera said, studying her. She pressed her steepled fingers to her lips. "How do you propose to support a covered roof without sides?"

Kate had no idea, but she knew Gabe Murray did. "That's what I'm working on," she said, crossing her fingers beneath the folds of her skirt. "And, because it's so different from Mr. Murray's original plans, I'll need more time." She hoped the slight tremor in her voice didn't betray her tension.

"I see." Vera's gaze sharpened. "Be candid, Miss Delaney. Does Mr. Murray think that sending a pretty face to plead for him will buy additional time?"

"No." Kate answered quickly. Heat flooded her face. It hadn't occurred to her that Vera would think Gabe sent her. "He doesn't know I've come. I wanted to discuss my idea with you first."

"I see," Vera said, settling back. "So, the apprentice comes directly to the client?"

Kate realized she'd overstepped her authority and tried to cover her mistake. "Mr. Murray and I are working very closely on this project. I'll let him know exactly what you want us to do."

"Of course you are." Vera smiled knowingly. "Mr. Murray is a difficult man to work with, isn't he, Miss Delaney?"

Kate couldn't have agreed more, yet admitting Gabe was giving her trouble didn't seem like a good idea. "He's very talented and a bit demanding," she said.

Vera returned an understanding smile. "I like you, Miss Delaney. You strike me as a clever young woman so I'm going to give you some advice. Learn to deal with difficult men. It's more important to your success than learning to design beautiful buildings. If Mr. Murray owes you instruction, hold him to it."

Obviously Vera understood the true situation more than Kate had realized.

"How can I force him to teach me?" she asked.

Hattie leaned forward, a hint of a smile lighting her eyes. "You've come this far, dear. You must have learned something about the way men think."

"Oh, yes," Kate said. "They're self-important and stubborn as mules."

Hattie chuckled softly. "And he's very handsome, isn't he?"

"Is he?" Kate felt her face flush as she pretended she hadn't noticed.

Vera intervened. "Now, Hattie," she scolded, "Miss Delaney doesn't have that kind of interest in Mr. Murray." She turned to Kate. "Do you, dear?"

Her expectant look made Kate blush. "I want him to accept me for my ability and consider me his equal," she said.

Vera laughed at that. "Impossible."

"Why?"

"The nature of the beast," Vera answered. "The condition of the world."

Kate couldn't accept that. "You're successful."

"Yes." Vera said, reflectively. "But my success was a necessity of birth. If our younger brother had lived, I wouldn't have had the opportunity to take charge of the family business. If I'd tried, I would have been considered outspoken and shrewish."

Kate's shoulders slumped as she admitted. "I've been called that and worse. But I won't give up."

"I should hope not," Vera said firmly.

Hattie reached for her hand, patting it gently. "I

think a long partnership between you and Mr. Murray would be lovely, dear.''

Kate had the distinct feeling the sisters envisioned a very different sort of partnership for her and Gabe.

''What about my idea?'' She focused on her purpose.

''I like it,'' Vera said. ''But I'm not going to extend the time. I expect you and Mr. Murray to meet your commitment on schedule.''

Kate felt the knot in her stomach tighten. Gabe was right. She did have a knack for backing herself into a corner and this time she put him on the spot with her. She could just imagine what he'd say when she told him what she'd done.

Hattie squeezed her hand reassuringly. ''With the two of you working closely, you shouldn't have any problem finishing this design.''

''No,'' Kate said, distracted by her worsening situation. ''No problem at all.'' She forced a smile, but knew she'd blundered.

''I'll see myself out.'' Drawing herself up from the chair, she started for the door, then turned to face them. ''There is one thing.''

''What's that?'' Vera asked.

''Would it be all right if I deliver the design on New Year's Day? It would be cumbersome carrying it to the ball.''

''Certainly, dear.'' The sisters agreed.

Kate gave them a gracious smile though her stomach was in knots. ''Well, I guess I'll be going now.''

She lingered for a minute, dreading her return to

the studio and the inevitable confrontation with Gabe. Hattie smiled back at her.

"Is there something else, dear?"

"No, nothing. Good day." Kate waved, turned her back and walked from the room in a daze.

Hold him to it, she thought. She left Fairweather and boarded a trolley, wondering how could she force Gabe to help her when he hadn't come within five feet of her design? She pondered her problem for the entire ride downtown, considering Vera's advice as she climbed the steps to his front door. While accomplishing it might be difficult, it was time to bring Gabe Murray to his knees. She opened the door and walked into his studio intending to do just that.

Chapter Nine

Kate found Gabe at the drafting table, pen in hand. She stopped short, her curiosity captured by his look of intense concentration. Removing her cloak, she draped it across the back of a chair.

"What are you working on?"

He glanced up, his eyes reflecting his enthusiasm as he placed the pen aside. "I made a few corrections to your design," he said.

"My design?" Kate flew to the drafting table, propelled by a feeling of impending doom. Her stomach pitched as she stared at the pen marks covering the drawing she'd intended to deliver to Vera.

"Oh, my God. What have you done?"

"I've compensated for your ornamentation," he said. "Here, I'll show you."

Clamping his hands on her shoulders, Gabe turned her to face him. Kate found herself gazing into his dark hazel eyes, momentarily distracted by the warmth of his strong hands on her shoulders.

"What are you doing?" she asked.

"Giving you a lesson on sound engineering principles," he said simply. "You badly need one. Now, raise your arm."

"Why?" She eyed him warily without making a move.

He kept his hands on her shoulders and puzzled over her reluctance. "You paid for instruction. I'm offering to show you what's wrong with your design."

"Oh, I'm sure you'd like nothing better. You thrive on pointing out my shortcomings, don't you?"

Her sarcasm soured his expression. "I should have expected that," he said. "Look, your design is good. It just needs a few adjustments."

"Adjustments?" Her indignant tone underscored the word. "You just don't like my decorative touches."

He met her defensiveness with a look of amusement. "Point taken, Miss Delaney."

He closed his fingers around her hand, lifting her arm to the level of her shoulder. "The problem isn't your use of ornamentation, it's that you have all of the weight concentrated at the end of the projecting beam."

"I see." She stood rigid as a brick wall, mindful of the fact that he still held her hand. She felt trapped and suddenly too aware of him.

"Relax," he said, giving her shoulder a slight squeeze. The intimate gesture sent a thousand tiny shivers leaping across her flesh.

Kate couldn't recall ever experiencing such an

odd reaction to a man. Nor could she remember a man ever giving her such personal instruction. She didn't know which confused her more.

"Are you listening?" he asked.

"Yes," she said. Disregarding the unusual effect he had on her, she tried to pay attention to what he was saying.

"For the purpose of this exercise let's pretend that I'm the ornamentation in your design. Your arm is the cantilever, your shoulder the fulcrum and the length of your torso and legs represents the vertical wall."

His nimble hand skipped along her arm, across her shoulder, down the small of her back, sending a warm sensation radiating through her entire body. She felt her muscles tense as she forced herself to concentrate on what he was saying instead of the enticing scent of his spicy aftershave. Finally he was demonstrating something useful and she couldn't keep her mind on anything except the startling inner stirrings ignited by his touch.

"Miss Delaney," he said with an easy smile. "I promise I'm not going to pounce on you."

Kate blushed, realizing his assurance didn't entirely please her. "I never suggested you would."

Deflecting another blow to her pride, she turned the discussion back to her design. "I thought the length of the supporting beam would counter the weight of the carvings I placed at the end."

"It would," he answered. "If the supporting beam were longer on one end than it is on the other. You see, either you have to put something back here at the fulcrum,'' his hand once again brushed her shoulder, ''or you have to exert enough of a downward force to counter the weight you've stacked up here at the end of the beam.''

He finished his explanation by taking her hand, studying her with interest. ''I'm glad to see you're thinking, Miss Delaney. You're not completely hopeless.''

Kate felt hopeless. She was behaving like a smitten schoolgirl while his stoic self-control kept him focused on the lesson. A lesson she'd paid for.

''I see what you mean,'' she said, recovering her composure.

''Good,'' he replied. ''Then you understand that I'm not faulting your use of ornamentation. I simply like economy of line. One of the most important lessons I learned came from a friend of mine, a medical student who let me glimpse the unseen world through the lens of his microscope. The simple forms of small creatures were amazing. Inherently beautiful structures formed by curves and undulating lines.''

The notion intrigued her. ''Do you mean like seashells?''

''Exactly,'' he said. ''Seashells, the veins in a leaf, the cell structure of an onion skin or even the intricacies of a snowflake. The world is filled with fantastic designs, Miss Delaney. All we have to do is be open to the possibilities. I thought if there was a material, a substance that could be used to create shapes like that in buildings, design would be limited only by the bounds of one's own imagination. Have you ever considered that?'' He looked at her.

A wavy strand of ebony hair curled over his forehead. Kate fought the impulse to brush it aside. At that moment she was too busy considering him to be interested in the microscopic world of science. She knew very little about the intricacies of a snowflake, but Lord help her, she did find his form appealing.

She was so absorbed that when Gabe clamped his hand down on hers, pushing hard, the force threw her forward, hurling her against him. For the second time she found herself in his arms. Startled, she raised her eyes. He met her surprise with a particularly engaging boyish grin.

''You see, Miss Delaney, your wall didn't have the strength to support all that ornamentation. Now hundreds lie dead, crushed beneath your decorative touches.''

In that instant she discovered just how devastating touches could be, decorative or otherwise. Flustered by the odd tingle she felt as their bodies touched, she quickly broke free of him, vigorously smoothing the front of her shirt.

She had to stop this foolishness. She was far too levelheaded to let some silly infatuation interfere with her plans. Her success, no, her future, depended on ending the hostilities while maintaining a polite distance. Besides, she thought, giving Gabe a quick look, he certainly didn't appear attracted to her. All he cared about was making his point and leaving her feeling stupid.

"Do you understand the nature of your problem?" he asked.

Oh, she understood all right. He'd made a fool of her again. "Completely," she snapped.

Her annoyance got his attention. "Have I upset you?"

"Not at all," she replied a little too curtly.

"I think I have." His voice had an infuriating smugness.

She glanced at him, angry with herself for finding him so damned appealing.

"You haven't," she insisted. "But you have ruined my drawing."

For several seconds of glum silence she stared at the scribble obliterating her design. Then it struck her. How could she have been so blind? Kate planted her hands on her hips and shot him an accusing stare.

"You did this on purpose."

"No," he defended himself. "I swear I didn't."

She wanted to believe him, but whether he was telling her the truth or not wouldn't solve her problem. She still had no design. "What am I going to do?" she said, disheartened. "It took me days to draft this."

"We'll just trace the portions that don't have to be changed," came his quick response. "That'll save some time."

"We?" She hadn't expected that. She wasn't disappointed.

Gabe tore a large piece of transparent paper from

the roll he kept beside the table and carefully tacked the corners over her drawing. Kate looked on.

"I don't understand why you're willing to do this," she said flatly.

"I ruined your drawing. Helping you fix it is the least I can do. Besides," he gave her a wink, "you've got my interest now."

He had her interest, too. Her interest and her suspicion. Once more she reminded herself that she had to remain focused on the purpose of their arrangement, which was to complete her apprenticeship and prove her grandfather wrong before he shuttled her home to a loveless marriage.

Gabe glanced up, assuring her with a smile as if he'd read her thoughts. "Don't worry, Miss Delaney. We'll have this ready for Vera by New Year's Eve."

Kate no longer doubted that. Whatever others might think of Gabe Murray, he'd proved himself a man of his word. And that made his sudden change of heart more suspect. She watched with interest as he diligently recreated her design. Their design, she thought. Perhaps, as Finn had predicted, he was beginning to like her. If that was true, the wall Gabe kept around himself might not be as impenetrable as she'd thought.

Kate considered that possibility along with the risks of lowering her defenses and trusting him. He'd fooled her before and she couldn't afford to fail. She watched him ink the pen, convinced her decision to trust him and her unforeseen attraction to him would likely rob her of sleep for nights to come.

Chapter Ten

"What you're saying is you have no confidence in me and no faith in my design." One by one Lloyd Peyton stared into the face of each partner.

Each, in turn, met his eyes steadily. Bernard McKee, with the anemic pallor of a consumptive. James Kendall, walrus-large and double-chinned. Conrad Hartford, his father-in-law, portly and full of himself.

Hartford spoke for them. "We can't take anything for granted, Lloyd. You know that."

Peyton scoffed, "Everyone can be bought, damn it. Even the pious new building commissioner." He knocked back the rest of his brandy.

The bastards didn't credit him with having any talent at all. He knew they only tolerated him because he'd married Hartford's daughter. Now the old man was losing patience waiting for an heir. Peyton eyed Hartford with contempt, pouring himself another brandy.

Kendall leaned forward, flicking the ash from his

cigar into the center of the heavy marble ashtray. "You read the article, Lloyd. The commissioner is backed by the Governor. Our people at City Hall can't vouch for his allegiance. With the new politics no one can guarantee we'll be awarded the museum project."

Peyton snarled at Kendall. "My design can win without the help of your people at City Hall."

"It better win, Lloyd." Hartford's tone held a warning. "The firm that gets that project will shape the future of architecture in this city."

Peyton narrowed his eyes on him. He could guarantee victory, but he wasn't going to ruin his moment by telling them he'd all but eliminated their only real competition. He only regretted Gabe's father hadn't lived long enough to see his precious son's final defeat.

McKee looked disgusted and stood up. "I've had enough of this for now. It's New Year's Eve. We can talk about this later." He reached for his coat, but didn't look any more in the mood for celebrating than Kendall.

The big man seconded the motion to end the board meeting. He heaved himself out of the dark-green leather chair. Crushing his cigar he gave Hartford a sober nod, took his coat and followed McKee from the room.

Peyton turned to the window overlooking Fifth Avenue. Daylight faded and the bronze wall clock ticked away the remaining hours of the year. A strained silence filled the mahogany-paneled room. He stood with his back to Hartford and watched the lengthening shadows devour the last rays of sunlight. He didn't give a damn about the situation at City Hall, but he had to play the game. He worked hard to put a look of concern on his face as he turned to face Hartford.

"Will you be attending the ball at Fairweather tonight?"

Hartford flashed an impatient look. "Of course I am," he said as he reached for his coat and scarf. "The Governor and other prominent people will be there. So I'll be there. Appearance is everything."

Peyton eyed him with distaste. What made the old bastard think he was such a saintly pillar of society? The son of a bitch had married into a family fortune just as Peyton had. They were two of kind. Hartford seemed to have forgotten that.

Peyton didn't have that luxury. He tightened his hand around the base of the brandy snifter, recalling Finn's biting words. It seemed no matter what he achieved, he would always be the orphan Gabe's father brought into his shabby home, but never legally into his family.

"I'll see you in a few hours," he replied cooley. "I have business to take care of before I leave tonight."

"Don't keep Eve waiting." It was an order.

"Of course not," Peyton replied, forcing a smile. "Appearance is everything." His voice carried a heavy note of sarcasm.

Hartford glared at him, then left, closing the door behind him. Peyton freshened his drink. Swirling brandy in the snifter, he assessed his situation. When he proposed his little wager to Gabe he hadn't realized how fortuitous it would be.

Gabe Murray's design would make the final cut in any honest competition. Things always came easier for Gabe. He was a fool, but the fool had genius. Peyton had resented Gabe from the time they were kids growing up on the Lower East Side. It seemed he had everything: talent, a loving family. Their rivalry grew while they apprenticed with Gabe's father and worsened as they fought for Eve's affection. Peyton took every chance to outclass Gabe, yet never succeeded. Until now.

The events of the past year had changed both their lives. Peyton savored his position along with his Napoleon brandy, debating how long he should wait before telling the partners and his father-in-law they had nothing to worry about when it came to winning the museum contract.

He didn't want to act too fast. It wasn't every day he saw the foundations of New York architecture jarred. He laughed aloud, thinking he hadn't had this much fun in years. He'd planned and sacrificed for the dubious pleasure of bedding Eve Hartford and the promise of a full partnership in her father's firm. The only real joy in that had been stealing her from Gabe. Now he was bored and tired of being Hartford's marionette. His life had settled into such a droning routine, his only pleasure was making sure Gabe Murray was just as miserable as he was.

His smile hardened as he considered the irony of Gabe wagering his design for a fair shot at the project when, as it turned out, he had the best chance all along.

Grinning, he sipped his brandy, anticipating the look on Gabe's face when he realized his mistake. At last he had a chance to prove his value to Hartford and the partners and he wouldn't neglect it. This year he would deliver the two things Hartford wanted most. He'd bring in the first major project of the new century and he would see to it that Eve produced the long-awaited grandchild. Preferably male. Satisfying those two New Year's resolutions would secure his position with the firm, solidify his place in the family and finally give him everything that might have belonged to Gabe.

He downed the last of his brandy contemplating the pleasure he'd take in fulfilling his second resolution. He would accomplish it tonight, even if it meant breaking the damned lock on Eve's bedroom door.

Chapter Eleven

The feeling of tension and uneasiness that plagued Gabe all week began working on his nervous system again as the evening wore on. He had to keep Kate from going off to that party to rub elbows with Lloyd Peyton. But how could he do that without flat out asking her not to go because she might find out that he had bet against her?

He absently drummed his fingers on his desk while staring at the pages of a book he had no intention of reading. What was it about the woman that made it so difficult to do what had to be done?

Logic called for one course of action, while his conscience demanded another. He considered telling her the truth, then realized she'd be angrier than all get-out. Most likely she'd leave and he really couldn't blame her. After all, wasn't that what he wanted her to do?

Gabe didn't know what he wanted her to do. He seemed as incapable of ridding himself of his confusion as he was suddenly unwilling to rid himself of Kate Delaney. If she got angry and left, he would win the bet. But he really didn't want her to be angry with him. He liked her. What had seemed at first an easy task had become more complicated with each passing day.

Gabe lay down the book and rested his head in his hands. Damn the museum bid. Damn Lloyd Peyton and damn Kate for invading his solitary life.

Slouching in his chair, he thought about her, a pursuit he'd spent too much time on lately. Why did she have to be so nice? She probably didn't have a conniving bone in her body. Admitting that about any female surprised him. He didn't like what she was doing to him, seducing him with her personality and strength of character.

Seducing him? Gabe shoved the sobering thought aside and concentrated on his problem. Short of knocking her unconscious, he didn't have a prayer of keeping her from that party.

He heard the sound of her footsteps in the hall and quickly buried his nose in his book, pretending to be engrossed. As she moved past him to get her wrap, the provocative rustling of her skirt sparked his imagination. He felt her warmth, fresh from her bath. Gabe fought to keep his eyes riveted on the pages of his book, but her nearness and the fragrance of French lavender conspired against him. He glanced up at her and his jaw went slack. All other thoughts fled as the unmistakable evidence of her femininity once more collided with his resistance.

She looked like she might have stepped from a pedestal at the Louvre. Only better. This artwork was flesh and blood. The fitted bodice of her dove-gray satin gown hugged her long slender waist, the skirt plunging to the floor like a cascading waterfall of narrow pleats. She'd drawn her hair neatly to the nape of her neck, where it erupted in a riot of soft curls.

Gabe fought his attraction, telling himself he'd simply spent too much time in her company. There was nothing special about her. The modestly cut neckline of her gown was anything but provocative. Edged in Irish lace, it revealed only the delicate scented ridge of her collarbone and hinted at the rise of her breasts. Yet, the sight of her was enough to put a hard knot in his belly, awakening long-suppressed urges. Gabe shifted uncomfortably in the chair and cleared his throat.

"Maybe letting you go to this party alone is a mistake." He regretted saying that as soon as he spoke.

Kate laughed softly. "Should I take that as a compliment?"

She slipped a pair of long white gloves over her hands and forearms. The graceful motion shattered what remained of his self-control, making him wonder how long he could continue denying the emotions clawing his insides.

"You look lovely," he said. "Take it as it's meant."

A slight blush colored her cheeks. Gabe found her naiveté refreshing. Her innocence stirred something deep within him, making him feel both protective and predatory. And here he was allowing her to go off to mingle with vipers. He wanted to warn her, to tell her to take care and guard her feelings.

Guard your own feelings, he advised himself.

She turned to him, a tiny smile playing at the corners of her mouth. "Knowing how you despise ornamentation, I can't help thinking I must be sorely underdressed for the occasion."

Gabe responded to her teasing. "If the structure is inherently aesthetic, ornamentation is unnecessary."

They exchanged glances before she turned away, moving toward the window. "What time is it?" she asked, her eyes riveted on the street.

He flipped open his pocket watch, unable to ignore the inscription, *Trust your instincts.* He could almost hear his father saying the words.

Gabe looked at her, itching to touch her. Trusting his instincts now would mean disaster. "It's nearly nine," he said.

She rubbed her hands over her bare upper arms and sighed deeply. "It looks so cold out there tonight."

He swore she trembled and his heart went out to her. Striking as she looked, she'd be out of her league tonight. In the company of women like Eve Peyton, who wouldn't?

"Will there be hundreds of people there?" she asked, turning to face him.

Gabe hesitated to answer though he knew exactly who would be there. He thought of all his former friends and colleagues, the people who had turned their backs and closed their hearts to him.

"Not hundreds," he replied softly. "Just New York's most prominent. You'll have a good time." He smiled, wishing she wouldn't.

"Maybe if you were coming with me I would." Her voice fell to a whisper as she quickly turned back to the window.

Gabe thought he'd heard wrong. It had been a long time since someone made him feel his presence mattered.

"My carriage is here." She lifted the waist-length cape to her shoulders and started for the door, carefully pulling the hood over her hair. She looked at him. His heart skipped at the way that final touch accentuated her femininity.

Stop her. He wanted to sink his fingers into those silky curls and press his lips to the soft hollow of her throat. He imagined how she would feel lying beneath him on his bed and became more aroused. He frowned when he realized where his thoughts had led him. As much as he wanted to be a gentleman and open the door for her, he couldn't stand without embarrassing himself.

She turned to him. "Good night," she said with a quiet smile.

The words *Don't leave* caught in his throat as the door closed behind her. Gabe groaned inwardly.

He pushed his chair back away from his desk and went to the window. A halo of snowflakes swirled in the streetlight. Gabe watched her disappear into the waiting carriage before turning away from the window.

The smell of French lavender lingered, and for the

first time, his studio seemed too large. A riptide of silence engulfed him as he looked around. For the most part he'd accepted his loneliness. A solitary life had been his choice. Tonight, though, the emptiness in his soul became an acute pain. Trouble was, the only antidote he knew for that pain was to trust again. To love again. To let someone into his life again.

No. It was much better to fend off the occasional pangs of loneliness and bury himself in his work. His work never betrayed him. He walked to his drafting table and noticed Kate's drawing lying there. He lifted it, recalling the sound of her soft voice, her request for him to join her. Had she purposely left her drawing? A foolish notion. She had worked too hard to finish her design. A damned good design, too. He enjoyed working with her. He enjoyed being near her, more than he cared to admit, and he regretted not telling her so before she left.

Fool. Gabe tapped the drawing on his open palm, debating what to do. Whether she had purposely left it or not, the drawing gave him an excuse to go to the party tonight, if he really wanted to. Which he didn't. He'd attended enough parties to know what he wasn't missing. The veiled glances and treacherous conversations masked in smiles and champagne. Missing one more party didn't bother him one bit. He'd sooner spend the night in hell than in the company of people like Lloyd Peyton. Then again, he couldn't let his pride cost him the museum bid. Wasn't that the purpose of this whole exercise?

Gabe placed her blueprints on his desk, walked to

his wardrobe and removed his tuxedo. No matter how he rationalized or argued with himself, the real reason for his going to that party had just walked out of his studio.

Kate's stomach churned. Her heart pounded like a kettledrum. *New York's most prominent,* she recalled Gabe's words. Despite insisting to herself that she would relax and enjoy the evening, her anxiety about arriving unescorted eclipsed her excitement.

She wondered why Gabe refused to attend, then scolded herself for wasting time thinking about him. As much as she liked him, she couldn't let his reluctance hold her back. An elegant evening at Fairweather represented the beginning of her new life. The people she met tonight could open doors to her future and speed her success. Yet, her ambivalence about the evening ahead mirrored her uncertainty over the end of the year and the start of a new century. Almost against her will, she found herself wanting to cling to the familiar while everything new and unknown beckoned to her.

The muted sounds of a string quartet drew her in. A doorman dressed in formal tails and top hat greeted her. Kate tried to relax as he took her wrap and directed her down the long hall. The sounds of laughter and conversation coming from the ballroom renewed her anxiety.

Josef stood at the entry, smiled and extended his hand as she presented him with her gold-engraved invitation. He announced her arrival and she made her way along the reception line.

The room looked different, larger than she remembered. In an instant she realized why. The wall which had separated the dining room from the music room had been removed, making one enormous ballroom. Two gilded mirrors, extending from floor to ceiling hung at opposite ends of the great hall and added to the illusion of endless space.

Kate wondered how a solid wall, complete with paintings and columns could vanish, but with so much else to look at, her curiosity soon dwindled. Spectacular gold-and-silver decorations had transformed the room into a glittering ice palace. Shimmering streamers suspended from crystal chandeliers glistened like icicles in the soft light of what must have been a hundred candelabra.

Feeling like a common sparrow in the company of peacocks, Kate lifted a brimming crystal champagne flute from a sliver tray and made her way to an inviting arrangement of blue velvet settees secluded by potted palms where she intended to spend the evening unnoticed. She inhaled the sweet scent of delicate white tea roses and snowberry sprigs cloaking the carved mantel of a cavernous fireplace. A roaring fire crackled and danced.

Sipping champagne, she watched elegantly dressed couples glide across the dance floor to the Viennese waltz. The men all looked dashing in their tuxedos, their starched shirts and ties, snowy white against black lapels. The women wore gowns of velvet and silk trimmed in fox and sable. Watching how gracefully they moved, Kate regretted not taking seriously her grandfather's urging and learned to dance.

"Trying to hide is pointless for one so lovely." A masculine voice came from beside her.

Kate tilted her head up to meet his silver-gray eyes. His thinning fair hair fell in a wisp across his high forehead.

"I beg your pardon?"

He gave her an assessing look. "You appear to have been abandoned."

Kate laughed at the obvious. "I am here alone if that's what you're asking."

"Not any longer," he smiled. "Let me introduce myself. I'm Lloyd Peyton." He offered her his free hand while balancing a brimming glass of champagne in the other.

Kate instantly recognized his name. "You're the architect Hattie Goodhue insisted I meet. Kate Delaney," she said. Placing her gloved hand in his, she stood.

His smile broadened as he looked her over. "Please call me Lloyd."

"All right, Lloyd." Kate glanced around, feeling self-conscious. "I really am happy to meet you," she said. "Except for Vera and Hattie, I don't know a soul here."

"I guarantee you won't have that problem very long."

"What do you mean?"

"Fresh blood always attracts the sharks," he said, glancing around the room.

Kate didn't know what to make of him. "Lloyd,

I'm afraid some women might mistake you for a terrible flirt.''

"Yes," he said. "My wife is constantly reminding me." He sipped champagne.

"So, how are you connected with the Goodhues?" he asked.

"I'm designing their Long Island retreat."

"Really?" His eyes sparked with sudden interest. "I thought Gabe Murray was working on that project."

"He is," Kate confessed. "I'm apprenticing with Mr. Murray. Do you know him?"

Before he could answer, Eve joined them, looking regal in a princess gown of royal-blue velvet. It fit to perfection. Peyton drew her to him, his hand settling at her slim waist with comfortable familiarity.

"Let me introduce you. Miss Delaney, my wife, Eve Peyton."

Eve smiled imperceptibly, tucking a wisp of nutmeg hair behind her ear. Her soft suede gloves brushed against her diamond earring. "Miss Delaney and I have already met."

Kate toyed with her glass, intimidated by Eve's striking beauty and cool practiced poise. "It's nice to see you again," she said, catching Peyton's interest.

"Then you know that Miss Delaney is studying with Gabe?"

His thin lips curved in a knowing smirk as if he enjoyed delivering that bit of information to his wife. "We've known Gabe forever," he added. "Haven't we, Eve?"

Kate felt the sudden chill of Eve's arctic-blue eyes. "Is Gabriel here with you?"

Peyton answered for her. "Miss Delaney is on her own tonight."

"Pity," Eve said, her eyes fixed on Kate. "It would have been lovely to see him again. You will tell him we were asking for him?"

She turned to her husband. "Will you excuse me, Lloyd? Father is waiting." Then to Kate. "You'll have to come to the house for tea, Miss Delaney. The Fifth Avenue Ladies League would love to hear all about your interesting career—" she paused "—as would I."

"I'd enjoy that," Kate replied, though she suspected Eve was more interested in hearing about Gabe.

Eve smiled and left them. Drawing her fingers along the rim of her glass, Kate watched her walk away, having mixed feelings about the invitation. While she would have liked meeting the members of the Ladies League, she couldn't see herself sipping tea with Eve knowing she'd jilted the man who was becoming so much a part of her life. That realization came as an unsettling surprise.

"Take care, Miss Delaney." The odd timing of Peyton's remark drew her back.

"Excuse me?"

He smiled as she turned. "Eve is a social butterfly. She moves from one petal to the next gathering gossip as if it were nectar. Once she spreads the word about you, every man in this room will have you branded as an ambitious woman."

"Is that bad?"

"Disastrous."

"How so?" she laughed.

"They'll lock and bolt the doors that are already closed to you. You'll have to work harder and do better than any man in your field to prove you're half as good."

"That's already true, Mr. Peyton."

He placed his empty glass aside. "It doesn't have to be that way."

"No?"

"No," he replied, shaking his head. "What you need is an ally."

"I believe that's Mr. Murray's role." Peyton's laughter put her off. "Did I say something funny?"

"Forgive me," he apologized. "Gabe Murray is a dear old friend but he's not in a position to help himself let alone you."

"And you are?" Her defensiveness surprised her.

"Perhaps." Peyton's cool eyes turned speculative. "My father-in-law is Conrad Hartford. He's president of the New York Board of Architects."

He lifted a fresh glass of champagne from the tray of a passing servant and motioned toward the corpulent gray-haired man talking with Eve. "If you're interested, I might be able to arrange something for you."

"Arrange something?" Kate returned a quizzical look.

Peyton nodded. "We feature promising young architects at our monthly meetings. Introducing a woman could be interesting, to say the least."

She didn't like the sound of that. "Mr. Peyton, I appreciate your offer, but I'm very serious about my work."

"Of course you are." He smiled, unoffended. "That's admirable. I didn't mean to imply otherwise. But, you have to admit aligning yourself with a firm like Kendall, McKee and Hartford couldn't hurt."

"No, of course not," she said, wondering if she'd jumped to the wrong conclusion. "Aligning myself with a firm like yours could help very much."

He reached into his breast pocket and removed a small leather wallet. "Why don't you take my card and let me see what I can do. I'll mention you to my father-in-law."

Kate smiled, ignoring her misgivings as she slipped his card into her small beaded purse. "I'm flattered, Mr. Peyton. Kendall, McKee and Hartford is one of the finest firms in New York."

"In the country," he corrected her. "Would you like to visit our offices?"

"I'd like that very much."

Peyton proposed a toast. "To the New Year and new friendships?"

"To new friendships," Kate replied, but as she brought her glass to her lips, she noticed he no longer seemed to be listening.

"Would you excuse me?" He touched her arm. "I'm being summoned."

She followed the direction of his gaze and saw Hartford talking with Governor Roosevelt, impatiently motioning for Peyton to join them. "Of course," she said.

"We'll talk later." Peyton smiled as he left her, but Kate doubted she would see him or Eve again for the rest of the evening.

Chapter Twelve

Gabe started down the flagstone walk, under the stony glare of Fairweather's snow-encrusted gargoyles. Their silent accusation made him question his sanity. Walking into a room full of people who already thought of him with suspicion served nothing but to further smudge his already tarnished reputation. He would have called anyone crazy had they told him he'd be here tonight.

He handed the drawing to the doorman along with his silk scarf and coat, fighting to sound at ease. "Please make sure those plans are taken to Miss Goodhue's study."

The man nodded. Gabe walked toward the ballroom, raking his fingers through his hair. He paused before the hall mirror to straighten his tie, thankful that his late arrival would spare him Josef's questioning look. It would take more than champagne and soft violin music to ease his nerves. He tried to loosen the knot in his stomach and shake off the image of Kate waltzing in the arms of Lloyd Peyton.

He stopped short, realizing he didn't have an invitation, then told himself he was being foolish. He'd come tonight on business, simply to deliver the drawing. He didn't have time for frivolous parties, champagne or pâté de foie gras.

Gabe lifted a glass of champagne and stood at the entry searching the room. Who are you trying to kid, he thought, catching sight of Kate. She was his reason for being there, and not because he feared he'd find her in Peyton's arms. Gabe wanted her in his arms and, until tonight, he hadn't realized just how much.

Kate placed her champagne glass aside and made her way toward the buffet line. Austrian crystal sparkled. Sterling silver gleamed and French Limoges sat regally upon the finest linen. She took a plate, eager to sample the delicacies spread out before her in a multitude of sterling chafing dishes.

She surveyed the mountains of hors d'oeuvres deciding whether to try pâté, cracked crab or something from the enormous platter of assorted cheeses. Her interest settled on the Viennese pastries topped with whipped cream and powdered sugar that surrounded glazed pears and cocoa truffles.

Turning up her nose at the oysters poached in white wine and cream, she was about to try the cracked crab when something made her glance up. From across the room Gabe's eyes met hers.

Kate nearly dropped her plate. He wore a tuxedo as if he were born to it. She wasn't the only one noting his late arrival. Everyone in the room seemed to turn in his direction.

He raised a delicate fluted glass in salute and started toward her. Kate felt a rush of warmth flood her face. Why was it that every time he came near her he upset things? He upset her.

She stepped back away from the line, still holding her plate. She looked around and saw everyone staring. "What are you doing here?" she said in a hushed voice, lowering her eyes.

Gabe took the plate from her, placed it aside and drew her away from the table. "I was going to ask you to dance, but if that's the reception I can expect, I'll spare myself the rejection. Good night, Miss Delaney." He turned to walk away.

"Oh, no you don't." She caught his hand. "You're not going to leave me standing here with all of them gawking."

Realizing how tightly she held his hand, she quickly released her grip. "I'm surprised to see you, that's all."

"Too surprised to dance?"

Her eyes shot up to his. Panic lodged in her throat. "I can't dance with everyone watching."

Gabe looked around as if he hadn't noticed there was anyone else in the room. "Sure you can."

"You don't understand." She looked away, mortified. "I don't know how."

He smiled, threading his fingers through hers. "Why not let me be the judge of that."

His touch set off a familiar tingle, making it impossible to refuse. Kate looked at him, longing to feel his arms around her. Yet she hesitated, knowing if she made a fool of herself on the dance floor, it would only draw more attention to them. Once more she glanced around.

"Why are they all looking at us?"

"Probably my tie," Gabe replied in an offhand way. "I couldn't find the white one."

Even his disarming cavalier attitude couldn't shake her from her preoccupation. Gabe slid his hand beneath her chin, lifting her face to his. "We can dance and really give them something to talk about. Or, you can slap my face and I'll leave. That, I promise, will make the evening for them. It's up to you."

Kate smiled, admiring his ability to find humor in the most awkward situation. "I have no intention of slapping your face," she said. "We'll dance. But remember, you've been warned."

He squeezed her hand as the orchestra began a slow waltz. "Ready?" he asked.

"Ready."

In spite of her misgivings, she found herself hoping Eve Peyton was watching them as Gabe whirled her around the dance floor sprinkled with gold and silver confetti. One by one other couples joined them. Kate tried to relax, concentrating on her steps to keep her mind off the blatant stares of the other guests.

"So far so good," Gabe said in a soothing tone of voice.

Kate began to relax at last. "I'm really glad you're here."

"So am I."

She smiled up at him. "What changed your mind?"

"You."

Her heart tripped, but she managed to keep in step. "Really?"

Gabe nodded. "You left your design at the studio. I thought I should deliver it."

"Oh, how thoughtful," she said, struggling to hide her disappointment. She changed the subject. "Fairweather is full of surprises, isn't it?"

"Surprises?" His brow knitted.

Kate smiled, enjoying his puzzled expression. "Yes," she said. "The last time I was here I noticed a wall that separated these two rooms. Now it's gone. Vanished. Where is it?"

"Miss Delaney, you're the first woman I've ever held in my arms who wanted to discuss houses."

"Really?" Did she detect disappointment in his eyes? "A woman does have to find her own way of standing out in a man's mind."

Gabe twirled her to the music, pulling her closer. "Believe me, Miss Delaney, you have no problem."

His remark took her by surprise and broke her concentration. She stumbled, the heel of her shoe coming down on his foot. Gabe cringed. She pressed her hand to her lips, a violent flush burning her face.

"I'm so sorry."

He forced a smile. "I was warned."

Kate glanced around at the arrogant stares shot in their direction. Gabe made a noble attempt to appear indifferent, but she had the feeling he shared her embarrassment.

"This might be a good time to show you how that wall operates," he said.

"Now?"

Gabe confessed, "My feet would fare better."

"Your feet and my pride."

He took her by the hand and quickly led her from the dance floor out into the hall. Gabe lifted a small candelabrum from a marble-topped table. They passed the entrance to the palm house, continuing on to the stone archway that led to the basement. He turned the knob and the heavy wooden door groaned open. Gabe descended the stairs first, holding the light high and in front of them. He reached back with his free hand.

"Stay close," he said, his voice echoing off the damp granite walls.

Silken webs brushed her cheek. Kate could see only a few inches beyond the flickering candlelight and held tightly to his hand until they reached the landing.

He placed the candelabrum on the bottom step and in the shimmering light their shadows danced. Kate chuckled, succumbing to her nerves and a little too much champagne.

"My shadow is better coordinated than I am."

Gabe responded to her giddiness with a lazy smile as he reached into his breast pocket to remove a small matchbox. "Dancing takes practice. Your interests obviously lie elsewhere."

Striking a match, he turned the key on one of the

gas jets, lit the lamp affixed to the wall and replaced the painted opal glass shade. Kate watched him, wondering if he knew just how much of her interest he had at that moment.

He shook the match, extinguishing the flame. "Come here and I'll show you how this operates." He motioned for her to move closer.

She stood beside him, her arm brushing his. He gave her a quick look then explained. "The wall is lowered to the basement on cables. A counterweight makes for ease of operation from above."

"Fascinating," she said, shifting her gaze from him to the narrow gauge through which the wall had been lowered. A thin sliver of light seeped from above, carrying with it the faint sound of violins.

She glanced back at Gabe, catching a glint of mischief in his eyes. "What are you thinking?" she asked.

He answered with a sheepish grin. "We could cause an uproar by raising the wall right now."

"You wouldn't," she said.

"Are you daring me?"

"No," Kate laughed.

So did Gabe. She liked the sound of his laughter. She liked him and wondered if it had been more than her drawing that brought him to Fairweather tonight. The possibility jolted her. She turned away from him, pretending to study the intricate system of pulleys and metal cords while fighting to put her feelings into perspective. What she was experiencing was simply caused by the music, the champagne, the magic of the moment.

''This construction is truly amazing,'' she said.

''Yes, truly amazing.''

His thoughtful tone made her turn. Gabe stood very close to her with one hand flattened on the wall panel directly above her shoulder. The nearness of his body sent renewed shivers up her spine. The heat of his gaze fell on her lips and she realized just a slight tilt of her chin would position her perfectly for a kiss. She closed her eyes and tempted fate.

His lips brushed hers, the soft touch releasing a swarm of butterflies in her stomach that left her weak-kneed and wanting more. As their lips parted, he regarded her with uncertainty. Kate wondered if he would kiss her again. She wanted him to kiss her again and let her eyes convey her desire.

Gabe lowered his mouth to hers once more and she abandoned herself to the pleasing rush of sensations sweeping over her. She draped her arms around his neck as his hands dropped to encircle her waist.

The kiss deepened. The warmth of his mouth startled her. She had spent so many years battling men she hadn't stopped to think how good it might feel to let one touch her. To kiss her. To love her. She was doing that now and she liked it.

From what she could tell, he liked it, too. She responded to his coaxing tongue, mimicking, seeking. A soft groan caught in his throat and he pulled her closer, flattening her against him. The warmth of his body sent a liquid heat racing to her limbs. Kate kissed him back, shyly at first, then with growing hunger that blossomed into something at once exciting and frightening.

He made her feel things she had never felt and forget things she had no business losing sight of. Realizing where they were heading, Kate pulled away, leaving cold emptiness where warmth had been.

Gabe searched her face as the muffled voices from the ballroom rose in a chorus of "Auld Lang Syne." Frightened by the strength of her emotions, she retreated to the steps, the feel of his lips still searing her.

"Wait," he called. His voice, no more than a whisper, had the power to stop her.

Kate dared not turn, afraid the longing in her eyes would betray her. She needed time to sort out what had happened, to understand what made him act so impulsively and her respond so willingly.

She took a deep breath, the obvious reason for his behavior already plaguing her. "Was that meant to scare me off?" she asked without turning.

"Kate, no." He touched her arm, restoring the warm sensations she hadn't yet subdued.

Her eyes slid shut and she found herself longing for the safety of their initial animosity. With one kiss Gabe Murray had awakened her untapped passion and she knew he could also break her heart.

"It was just an innocent New Year's kiss," he said.

Was it? She turned to face him. His tone was convincing, but the look in his eyes was not. There was nothing innocent about that kiss and they both

knew it. Yet, for some reason he was offering her
an excuse, giving them both a way to move beyond
this and go on.

She didn't understand what was happening between them and rational thinking at that moment
was impossible. One thing she did know, if she allowed her feelings for Gabe to come between them
and drive her away, she would fail. Her grandfather's threat became a menacing presence as she saw
its power to rob her of what might be her one chance
to know love. Her throat tightened with unshed
tears, making it impossible for her to speak. Kate
nodded slowly in response. Lifting the hem of her
gown, she turned away from him and climbed the
stairs.

Gabe could still taste the sweet warmth of her
mouth. What the hell had he been thinking? Innocent? How inane. Innocent or not, what amazed him
was the way she kissed him back. In that kiss he'd
felt the passion she kept bottled inside her like a
genie. A genie powerful enough to loosen the reins
of his restraint. She shared his desire. He was sure
of that now and it was hard not to see the promise
of more in her response.

Gabe shook himself, certain her response was
nothing more than the result of too much champagne
and soft candlelight. Hell, a woman like Kate
wouldn't fall for a loser like him. She had talent and
ambition to match. She deserved more. Much more
than he could give her.

Gabe wrestled with himself as he watched her

walk away. A woman like that comes along only rarely and he'd be a fool to let her go. He raced up the stairs, hoping to catch her in the hallway. The sight of Eve stopped him cold. His body tensed as he braced himself for the moment he'd dreaded for over a year.

Eve moved closer, candlelight illuminating her exquisite face. She stood before him like a dream. "It's good to see you, Gabriel. Miss Delaney said you wouldn't be here."

Gabe glanced at Kate who stood watching them from the vestibule. Peyton waited just outside the ballroom. The way they looked at him made Gabe uncomfortable.

Eve didn't seem to mind having an audience. She always managed to make any situation work to her advantage. Why should this time be different? She reached up to straighten his tie, drawing his gaze back to her.

"If you insist on wearing a black tie to a formal affair, you should at least make sure it's straight."

Her fingertips brushed his jaw as she adjusted his tie, rekindling unwanted memories. Gabe recalled how he'd loved Eve and how like brothers he and Lloyd had been. *Fool.* If he could be so wrong about them, how could he trust his instincts about Kate?

Sure, she'd kissed him, but it was probably just her way of getting what she wanted. They were all alike. He ground his teeth, thinking he'd almost fallen for more female deception. The sound of the door closing got his attention. He looked up. Kate was gone.

Let her go, he thought. Curling his fingers around Eve's wrists he pulled her hands from his lapels. "Good night," he said, his eyes fixed on Peyton's face. "And Happy New Year." He turned his back on them and left.

Once outside, it took him a few minutes to regain his composure. He started down the noisy street, pushing his way through the swelling number of New Year's revelers. Shouting and laughter competed with the clangorous sound of carriages and church bells that filled the frosty night. Pushed along by the crowd, he felt trapped in a nightmare where everyone but him had something to celebrate. Flares and skyrockets exploding above the city turned the snowflakes to colored pieces of confetti.

He knew finding a carriage would be impossible and as the champagne started to wear off, he shivered from the bone-chilling cold. *Damn.* Gabe wrapped his arms around himself, realizing he'd left in such a hurry, he forgot to pick up his coat. Well, he sure as hell wasn't going back to get it now. He'd send for it in the morning. A long walk on a cold night might be just the thing he needed to forget Eve, to forget Lloyd and, damn it, to forget the way Kate's kiss had sent him reeling.

It occurred to Gabe that he did have something to celebrate. Seeing Eve with Peyton had put things back into perspective and doused the flame of his desire. He'd never leave himself open to be hurt like that again.

Someone in the crowd thrust a champagne bottle into his hand. Gabe brought it to his lips, taking a long pull before passing it along. He would make Kate believe his kiss was meant to run her off. It was time she went back where she belonged. At last he'd come to his senses.

He freed himself from the throng of people when he noted a coachman beckoning to him. He sprinted to the carriage waiting beneath the streetlamp and opened the door, eager to get out of the cold and snow. He saw Kate seated inside and it felt like a skyrocket burst in his chest.

She sat back, her face half in shadow. "Would you like to share my carriage?" she said.

Gabe nodded, unable to squeeze a word past the huge lump that had lodged in his throat. He climbed into the carriage and sat opposite her, knowing he was lost.

Chapter Thirteen

Tension filling the carriage settled as a tightness in Kate's chest making it difficult to breathe. For the entire ride she fought not to stare at Gabe, but the memory of their kiss drew her gaze to him again and again.

The tenderness had left his face, replaced by an expression of anger. Knowing how seeing Eve must have hurt him moved Kate. Her own irrational emotions moved her even more. She couldn't recall ever being jealous of another woman and she had no logical reason for resenting Eve; except for the tormented look now etched on Gabe's face. Kate could think of only one explanation for her odd reaction to a woman she hardly knew and though she hesitated to admit it, she knew she was falling in love with Gabe.

She glanced at him as the streetlight flickered through the carriage windows to define the strong contours of his handsome face. She would have scoffed at the possibility that she could ever long for a man's touch. She told herself that without the glow of candlelight and the warmth of champagne to cloud her judgment, her thinking would clear. She hoped then her foolish heart would realize their kiss meant nothing to him.

They rode on. The effect of the champagne soon faded and it seemed they'd left Fairweather hours ago, yet her heart remained captured by the sensual promise of his kiss. Her newly discovered yearnings left her feeling vulnerable and unsure. Dormant insecurities surfaced to claw at her, telling her she was being foolish. No one had ever given her reason to consider herself a beauty. How could she think a worldly man like Gabe would find her desirable?

The carriage came to an abrupt halt. Kate looked up as shouting and the shrill sound of police whistles broke her reflections. Gabe sat forward in his seat, his gaze fixed on a long line of row houses just ahead.

She peered from the window at policemen pushing back the crowd of people lining the street. Carriages and wagons snarled the avenue and drivers strained to calm their skittish teams. As Gabe slid open the window, the acrid smell of smoke filled the cab.

"Stay here," he said, stepping from the stalled carriage out into the crowd.

Kate ignored his cautioning and followed him out to the street. The narrow strip of sky between tenements was barely visible through the black billowing smoke.

Gabe stood beside Kate in the midst of the crowd

and chaos, feeling helpless. He knew how the tin-derbox tenements were built and how fast a fire could move. If one building went, the entire block followed.

A hysterical woman broke through the police line, darting across the street. Tripping over the hem of her soiled skirt, she stumbled on the wet cobbles as she ran in the direction of the burning building. An old man tried to stop her.

Gabe took off after them, his long stride easily overtaking her.

"Let me go," she shouted into his face, battling to free herself. "My baby. Mary is up there. My baby."

She wrestled in his arms, surprising Gabe with her strength. Trying to free herself, she lurched forward. Gabe tightened his hold. The hard toe of her boot met his shin and he lost his grip.

She bolted, knocking the old man out of her path. Gabe caught her again. She pummeled him with her fists, fighting with all she had.

He held fast as the old man tried to make her see reason. Her desperate cries tore at Gabe as she continued to struggle until, at last, her strength gave way to remorse and she collapsed in his arms.

Kate raced to them in a futile attempt to console the sobbing woman. There was nothing she could say. Gabe stared at the oily smoke pouring from the building, knowing his chances of rescuing the child were slim. Yet, he had to try. If he could save one life, in some way, it might make up for the life he'd taken.

"Which floor?" he asked before he could change his mind. The woman didn't respond.

Kate shot him a terrified look. Gabe ignored the fear and disbelief in her eyes. He asked the woman again, raising his voice. "Which floor?"

Her hand trembled as she pointed to the third-floor window.

"Stay with her," he said, removing his jacket and tie. He handed them to Kate.

The old man pressed his arm. "God help you."

Gabe wasn't sure he believed in God, but the admiration and fear he saw in Kate's eyes gave him absolution. He carried her image with him into the burning building.

Smoke closed around him like a shroud. He fought not to breathe until he thought his lungs would explode. His eyes watered. Unable to see through the stinging smoke, he groped along one wall until he found the narrow staircase. He bounded up the steps, dodging flames.

Reaching the landing, he felt his way down the dark, narrow corridor. He tripped over a trash barrel, flattening his palm on the floor to break his fall. Fast-moving flames closed in on him, igniting the corridor with an eerie glow. The walls began to smolder. Gabe wondered what the hell he was trying to prove. He almost turned back when the faint sound of a child crying urged him on. The heat increased, and the smoke.

Bending low to gasp what air he could, he staggered ahead, using his arm to shield his face. Disoriented, he followed the cries that seemed to come from behind every door. Yet each room he checked was empty. When he came to a locked door he kicked it in. The screaming toddler stood at the railing of a shabby crib.

He lifted her into his arms and turned, retracing his steps through the dark back to the stairwell. His lungs burned. He squinted his eyes, fighting to find the way out. The loud crack of a splintering beam brought his head up sharply as a burning timber fell across their path.

Gabe spun away, smoke clawing at his throat. Protecting the child from the flames, he backtracked to the room where he'd found her. He kicked the door shut behind them to keep the flames out and give himself a few more priceless minutes. Placing her on the floor, he fought to open the window. It wouldn't budge. He tried again. Again he failed. His heart pounded like thunder as he realized thick layers of paint had sealed the window. The noxious smoke grew blinding, the heat scorching. Gabe searched for something to break the glass.

A toppled chair lay on the floor beside the crib. He tripped over himself to reach the chair, raised it above his head and swung hard.

The glass shattered. Icy air sucked the choking smoke through the opening. He felt a slight tremor, a rumbling in the floor. The smoke cleared. He saw firemen in the street holding a canvas net. They shouted for him to jump.

He lifted the screaming child. Her body stiffened with fear, causing him to nearly drop her as he hoisted her above the spikes of glass jutting from the window frame. He held her tight, praying they would catch her, then let her go.

Again he felt the rumbling beneath his feet, followed by a low, almost human moan. The coal furnace, he thought. Gabe wedged one foot on the windowsill, groping for a secure handhold on the outer brick wall. Before he could boost himself up, the weakened floorboards gave way beneath him.

His hand shot out. Blindly he grasped for something to keep from falling back into the inferno. The jagged glass sliced his flesh. He cried out, hanging on, his anguished cry swallowed by the roaring flames now snapping at his heels. Burning debris fell through to the floors below.

He was going to die and there was nothing he could do about it. His folly mocked him as he thought of Kate, of dying before he'd really lived, before he had the chance to make things right. He couldn't let it end like this. Not yet. With a strength that could come only from desperation, he pulled himself up, bracing his shoulders against the window casing. Blood soaked his shirtsleeve and dripped from his fingertips. He felt his consciousness ebbing as he fell forward into darkness. His stomach lurched to his throat and the deafening rush of air closed his ears, silencing the world.

Kate screamed his name as she broke from the pressing crowd. Trembling and struggling to catch her breath she watched the firemen lower Gabe's limp body onto a stretcher. In the dim light of the streetlamps his face looked as gray as a granite funeral urn. Heart hammering, she fought hard to control her fear and panic. She moved toward Gabe and felt a firm hand close around her arm. Kate turned with a start.

The man relaxed his grip. "I'm from the *Tribune*," he said. "Do you know him?" He pulled a pencil and small notepad from his coat pocket.

Kate stared at Gabe, her senses dulled by shock.

The reporter persisted. "Is he your husband?"

She didn't know what was happening. Her ears rang with the clanging commotion of bells, police whistles and people shouting. She didn't hear the approaching police wagon until it nearly backed into her. The reporter pulled her out of danger as two men jumped from the wagon hurrying toward Gabe.

"Look, lady," he said. "Your husband just saved the New Year's baby. What's his name? What's your name?"

She stared at Gabe's bloodstained shirt not knowing if he was alive or dead. "Murray," she muttered, pressing his bundled jacket close to her breasts. "Gabe Murray."

She watched half-dazed as the reporter scribbled something on his pad. He looked at her. "What's your address?"

"What?" Kate couldn't think. They were lifting Gabe into the back of the wagon. "I have to go with him."

She took a few steps, but the reporter stopped her again. "Just give me your address."

Kate blurted out the address of Gabe's studio as she lifted the hem of her gown, trying to climb onto the wagon when a policeman stopped her. The reporter stepped forward, moving between them. "She's his wife," he said. "Let her go with him."

She gave the man a puzzled look as he helped her up into the wagon. "I'll be in touch, Mrs. Murray."

Chapter Fourteen

Across town, Peyton drew the rich brocade drapes, closing off the world from the elaborate dressing area adjoining Eve's private bedroom. He returned from Fairweather early, intent on being ready when Eve arrived. She'd had her way too long. Things were about to change. He adjusted his silk robe over his lounging pajamas, then reached for the lamp on the dressing table to lower the flame.

At the sound of the door, he turned, accidentally brushing his hand against the heated globe, burning himself. Growling a curse, he jerked his arm away, massaging his hand.

Eve looked on indifferently. Removing her gloves one finger at a time, she walked to her vanity and slid onto the velvet chair, her back to him. As she glanced up, he met her gaze in the oval mirror. Eve looked away.

"I don't recall inviting you to my room," she said, dismissing him. She tilted her head to remove first one diamond earring, then the other.

Peyton flexed his fingers, anger and desire building. He stared at the diamonds he presented her with on their wedding anniversary. The earrings were the most extravagant item to be found at Tiffany's and he didn't recall waiting for an invitation that night.

"A husband doesn't need an invitation." He leaned to press his lips against the lilac scented curve of her shoulder. Eve shifted in the chair, shrugging him off.

"I'm tired, Lloyd."

His temper flared and he spun her chair around to face him. "I don't care," he ground out. "I will not tolerate this arrangement any longer. Do you understand?"

Eve didn't flinch. Her icy indifference enraged him further. The memory of her fawning over Gabe burned a hole in him. He flattened his palms on the vanity, pinning her in the chair. The muscles of his jaw tensed as he fought to keep his voice down and avoid rousing the household.

"Do you think I'm blind?"

"I think you've had too much to drink, Lloyd. Now let me up." She tried to move.

He planted his hands more firmly on the dressing table and leered at her. "I didn't drink enough to miss your little show at Fairweather."

Something flickered in her eyes. Was it fear? "What are you talking about?"

"I saw the way you looked at him. The same way his father used to look at him. You act as if he's some kind of god. He's a man. Like me. Nothing more."

"You're being foolish, Lloyd."

"Am I?" Rage brought him within inches of striking her. Peyton refrained, fearing bruises would bring about questions from her father.

He tempered his anger and spoke through clenched teeth. "I've worked too hard designing my future and I refuse to live in Gabe Murray's shadow any longer."

"I won't listen to this." She turned away. Peyton squeezed her face in his hand, forcing her to look at him.

"You will listen. You're my wife, damn it, and you're going to behave like it. I'm the man who will inherit your father's firm and I'm the man who will father your child."

Her cold stare confirmed his fear that he would never be anything more than the man her father had decided she should marry. Her silence cut deeper than anything she could have said. Now he knew she still loved Gabe.

Incensed, Peyton closed his hands around her arms and tore her from the chair. He knew she wouldn't cry out. "Appearance is everything, isn't it, Eve?"

"You're hurting me."

He tightened his grip on her bare arms until red marks surfaced on her flesh. "You don't know anything about hurt," he snarled at her. "I've lived with the pain of rejection for too many years and it's going to stop now."

He pulled her to him. Clamping his hand at the base of her skull, he lowered his mouth to hers. Eve clenched her teeth, yet her resistance only aroused him more.

Drawing back he searched her face and saw neither fear nor anger, but the infuriating contempt he had known his whole life.

"You're not turning me away tonight." He swept her up into his arms and carried her toward the bedroom. "Pretend I'm him. It doesn't matter. You're the prize I won for destroying Gabe Murray. Now I have everything he wanted."

"Put me down." Eve pounded his chest with her fist, struggling against his forceful hold.

Peyton kicked the door shut behind them. Tonight he would have what he'd bargained for.

Chapter Fifteen

Kate shifted uncomfortably on the hard wooden bench located just outside the door of the small surgery room. It seemed she'd been waiting for hours and still had no word about Gabe. Curious immigrants stared at her from the sepia light of the adjacent room where ragged, gaunt-looking people occupied rows of narrow cots. The stench of festering sores, carbolic acid and sweat nearly made her retch.

A repugnant man watched her from a nearby cot. Kate turned away, feeling conspicuous and out of place dressed in her ball gown. Her nervous fingers worked over the wrinkled sleeve of Gabe's jacket as she willed him to be all right. Exhaustion pounded at her temples and she leaned her head against the wall, but couldn't rest.

She'd lost track of time. The gray light of dawn now tinting the windows came as a surprise. At last the door to the surgery room opened. Anxiety squeezed a knot between her shoulder blades. She stood as the doctor approached. She held her breath, her eyes riveted on his gaunt face. He looked tired and worn, little better than his patients. As she took a step forward, the doctor returned a feeble smile.

"He's going to be all right," he said, reaching for a towel to dry his hands.

"Thank God." She exhaled a prayer, her eager gaze darting to the nurse who wheeled the gurney from the surgery. Kate stared at Gabe, struck by his stillness and waxen appearance. The sight of his bandaged hand renewed her fear and doubled her concern. She turned to the doctor and the anxiety in her eyes drew his response even before she spoke.

"His hand required a lot of stitches, but it should heal just fine."

Kate nodded, trying to take some comfort in his assurance. She forced herself to think about what had to be done and nothing more. "How much do I owe?"

Surprise sparked his weary eyes. "I charge whatever a patient can pay."

Kate reached into her purse, for what little money she had. She offered it to him. Once again she became aware of people watching her. She felt apprehensive about leaving Gabe alone at the clinic, helpless to defend himself.

"Can I take him home?" she asked the doctor.

He looked reluctant, then seeing the way she was dressed he seemed to understand. "He's going to be in a lot of pain when the ether wears off. Let me give you a bottle of laudanum."

He left her there and returned a few minutes later

with a small lapis bottle. "Follow the instructions and keep him quiet for the next few days."

"I understand." She dropped the bottle into her purse and cinched it tight. "I'll come back for him with a carriage," she said, noticing the doctor had already turned his attention to another patient.

Kate stepped from the clinic into the hushed stillness of falling snow. The street was deserted, not a carriage in sight. She took a deep breath fighting the feeling of panic tightening her chest. She needed help and knew the Green Harp Tavern wasn't far away.

Feeling at risk, she walked as fast as she could, her dress shoes sliding on the icy sidewalk. She hurried past narrow alleys, tripping over the torn wet hem of her gown. Keeping her eyes forward she closed her ears to the lewd remarks shouted at her from dark hallways. The idea that Gabe had risked his life for the likes of such people angered her, making her want to shout back, shaking her fist. She kept walking, picking up her pace until she reached the Harp.

Kate pounded on the tavern door with her fists, calling out to Finn. The commotion she created unleashed the barking of neighborhood dogs. Trembling, she pulled her cloak around her shoulders and noticed the satin had been stained with blood. Frightful images of the evening assaulted her and she pummeled the door even harder.

At last a light shone from the upstairs window. She waited, counting the seconds, listening for the sound of the heavy bolt sliding from the lock. Finn opened the door, wearing an old gray union suit and a coarse woolen blanket slung over his shoulders. His eyes wide and alarmed, he stared into her face from beneath an unruly mane of snow-white hair.

"What's wrong, lass? You look like the ghost of a shipwreck."

She caught her breath as Finn brought her inside and she told him what happened to Gabe. "I need your help. I can't leave him at that dreadful place."

"I agree," Finn said. "Just give me a minute to dress and harness the old nag to the supply wagon, then we'll be off."

Draping the blanket over the bar, he disappeared up the stairs. He returned a few minutes later, one arm already stuffed into the sleeve of his threadbare jacket.

Kate followed him out the back door, through the snow to the stable. The sway-back horse nickered, annoyed at being roused so early on such a cold morning. Finn gave the horse a soothing pat on her neck, then hitched her up to his flatbed wagon. He helped Kate onto the seat before climbing up beside her.

Arriving at the clinic, they made their way quickly down the hall to the narrow cot where Gabe lay half-conscious. He mumbled incoherently as Finn struggled to get him out of the bed and onto his feet. Kate draped the blanket around his shoulders, helping as best she could. With her on one side of Gabe and Finn on the other, they finally managed to keep him on his feet, get him out of the clinic and into the wagon.

She climbed onto the flatbed, pulling another blanket around Gabe. His bleary eyes stared up at her but she doubted he knew who she was. Finn clicked at the horse, moving slowly trying to keep the motion from jarring Gabe. On the empty street, they made good time back to the studio.

Kate ran ahead to hold the door. Finn maneuvered Gabe up the slippery steps. Securing one arm around Gabe's waist, he slung Gabe's arm around his shoulder. His head bobbed forward and his feet dragged up each stair. Kate locked the door while Finn lowered Gabe onto the bed and started to remove his soot-and-bloodstained clothes.

She stood with her back to them, arms folded around herself. A painful groan escaped Gabe as Finn carefully tucked the blanket around his shoulders. She remembered the bottle of laudanum in her purse and hurried to the kitchen to get a spoon.

She stopped on her return, confronted by the pile of bloodstained clothes and the realization that Gabe might have died. Her pent-up fear began unraveling all at once and she couldn't keep from shaking. Closing her eyes she took several deep breaths trying to get hold of herself. She removed the bottle from her purse and held it out to Finn, her hands trembling so she couldn't steady the spoon.

Finn lifted Gabe's head from the pillow, holding the spoon to his mouth. His vacant eyes opened a slit and he mumbled to Finn, "I didn't realize how much I loved her."

Jealousy stabbed Kate's heart and she turned away, certain he spoke of Eve. She caught Finn watching and tried to hide her feelings, but knew she wasn't fooling him. She couldn't keep the love she felt from showing in her eyes. She left the room as Finn placed the spoon and bottle on the bedside table.

He moved behind her and she turned, trying to mask her embarrassment. "I felt like a helpless fool tonight. I don't know what I would have done without you."

"You're far from helpless, lass. Besides, what are friends for if not to be there when you need them?"

She hoped Gabe knew what a good friend he had in Finn. "He means a lot to you, doesn't he?"

"Aye," Finn said, holding her gaze. "And you?"

She pressed her lips together, fighting an onslaught of emotions and nodded her reply until she found her voice.

"Coming so close to losing him made me realize just how much."

Tears spilled over and she let them flow. Finn folded her in an embrace, wrapping her in the deep secure warmth she'd never received from her grandfather. Drawing back, she wiped her eyes.

"Would you stay and have a cup of coffee?"

"No," he said, a smile crinkling the corners of his eyes. "But the bottle of Scotch I sent over for Christmas should be in the bottom drawer of his desk. I wouldn't mind a bit of that."

"Of course." Kate went to the desk, opened the drawer and found the sealed bottle of Scotch, nestled beside a bulky leather-bound notebook. On the cover of the book the words *Liquid Stone* were written in Gabe's hand. Recalling what he said about a substance that could free her designs to soar to the heights of her imagination, she lifted the bottle from the drawer, making a mental note to look through the book at another time.

She walked to Finn and handed him the bottle. "I'll get a glass," she said. She started for the kitchen.

"Get two glasses," he called to her. Kate paused, surprised by his request. It wasn't often a gentleman invited a lady to share in a drink. Yet, they had weathered a crisis tonight so his invitation seemed natural.

She returned with two glasses. Finn snapped the seal from the bottle. He took one glass, splashed a small amount of Scotch into it and offered it to Kate. She sipped slowly, unaccustomed to the fiery taste. He poured a tumbler for himself and swallowed a mouthful, exhaling with contentment.

As the tension eased from her body, Kate began to relax, a thousand questions crowded her mind. She'd experienced so many new feelings she needed to explore she didn't know where to start. It didn't seem possible her life could take such a turn. She shuddered with a chill of uncertainty.

Reaching for the andiron, she stooped down to coax a flame from the weary embers. She added kindling, taking care not to choke the budding fire while trying to smother the emotions she knew would cause her grief. She lingered before the fire, staring at the flames, trying to come to grips with her disconcerting emotions.

"Are you all right, lass?"

She nodded thoughtfully as she straightened, keeping her back to Finn. "It's funny, but I've always known exactly what I wanted and thought I knew exactly how to get it."

The soft clink of the bottle touching his glass filled the silence after she spoke. "Well, learning that love doesn't play by our rules is a hard lesson, isn't it?"

She turned and looked at him. "Is it so obvious then?"

Finn laughed softly. "It is to me. But don't concern yourself, lass. Your secret is safe. Young men like Gabe don't develop full vision until they're too old and bent to do anything about it."

Thoughts of her unwise bargain with her grandfather returned to haunt her. Kate dropped onto the straight-backed chair opposite Finn and sighed deeply, wondering what she would do.

"Foolishness isn't exclusive to men." She looked at Finn, feeling she could speak freely.

"You said that Gabe was afraid. I'm afraid, too."

"Of your feelings for him?"

"No," she said, shaking her head. "I know the risk of letting myself love him. What frightens me is failure. If I can't convince my grandfather that I can be as successful an architect as any man, I'll be penniless. Dependent. Poverty doesn't scare me, but I've agreed to marry a man of his choice."

Finn wrinkled his brow. "Have you told Gabe that?"

She drew a deep breath and allowed her gaze to

return to the fire. "When I agreed to my grandfather's terms I didn't anticipate falling in love with the very man who threatened my future. I made a bad bargain." She turned to Finn again.

He shook his head, running his callused thumb along the rim of his glass. "Wagering with lives isn't like playing the ponies."

Something in his tone made her think he'd say more. When he didn't she asked the question that had been gnawing at her since her visit with Hattie. "Do you know why Gabe went to fight in Cuba?"

Finn studied her for a moment before he answered. "It wasn't a sudden bout of patriotism, I can tell you that."

"Why, then?" She waited, but he disappointed her.

"Oh, lass, as much as I like you, telling you that would betray his trust and friendship."

Kate understood. She hoped Finn would keep her confidence, as well.

He put his empty glass aside and pushed himself out of the chair. "It's getting late. You need some rest." He squeezed her shoulder, put on his jacket and adjusted his cap.

Kate walked with him to the door. "Thank you for everything." She kissed his wrinkled cheek.

Finn drew back, smiled at her then turned and left. Kate closed the door, lingering for a while at the entry. Left alone, she confronted her feelings. She glanced toward the bed. Gabe looked so peaceful. She envied his unconsciousness, wishing she had a magic elixir that could end her confusion.

Her logical mind went in one direction while her irrational heart took off in another. She was torn between what she had always wanted and these upstart feelings that nudged her common sense aside.

As much as she craved the independence of a career, she longed to one day know a husband's soft kiss and to have children of her own. She didn't want to meet the closing years of her life never having known love or to have had a man look at her the way Gabe looked at Eve. She mustn't torture herself and tried to put her mind on something else.

She remembered the notebook, walked to the desk and took it from the drawer. She pulled a woolen blanket around herself and pushed the cushioned chair beside the bed. Settling back, she leafed through his notebook and soon lost herself in his fanciful designs. Steel towers encased in glass seemed to scratch the sky. Some so tall they pierced the clouds, emerging on the other side, sunlight glinting off their crystal windows.

Instinct seemed to guide his hand. Ideas flowed from his pen without hesitation. The basics were so ingrained he was free to bend rules and explore possibilities. Explore he did.

She studied an entire city block of *liquid stone* structures that looked like they might inhabit the landscape of the moon, or the pages of a Jules Verne novel. Kate realized that his ideas could transform architecture and change his life. Why, she wondered, did he keep them hidden?

Gabe stirred, groaning her name.

"I'm here," she whispered. She placed the book

aside and leaned close to him. His rhythmic breathing told her he was still asleep. Did he dream of her? Kate doubted that. She brushed a wisp of hair from his forehead, recalling the excitement she felt in his arms, wishing she could know if he felt the same. Finn was right. Learning that love didn't play by her rules was a hard lesson.

The hours passed. Her thoughts grew hazy, her eyelids heavy. Unwilling to leave Gabe's side, she pulled the blanket around herself, curled up at the foot of his bed and slept.

Chapter Sixteen

Gabe drifted in and out of consciousness, body and senses tethered by slim threads of sound and smell. The distinct aroma of licorice pipe tobacco cut through the half-tone curtain of unconsciousness as his father's voice penetrated the fog.

"How are you doing, son?"

Gabe watched the shadowy figure move toward the foot of his bed. He studied the apparition, his logic battling his senses. He knew his father was dead, yet seeing him there seemed as natural as the sunrise.

He tried to move, but the sluggishness that had invaded his body coiled around him like a binding steel cable. When he opened his mouth to speak, his voice came from somewhere deep within his groggy brain. Dad? Is that you?

"Who did you expect?" The familiar sound of his laughter made Gabe smile.

He sat at the edge of the bed, inviting conversation just as he had countless times when Gabe was a boy. "I'm proud of you, son. You did what you thought was right. Trusted yourself. Now, what about her?"

You mean Kate? *Gabe thought of her and the fragrance of French lavender instantly filled his nostrils. The feel of her cool tapered fingers on his brow came and went like snow in the desert.*

He called her name, straining to get one more look at her before sinking back into that half-light world of murmuring strangers.

The image of his father sharpened. He freshened his pipe while eyeing Kate. "So, what do you think, son?" *He winked at Gabe.* "Your old man wasn't as far gone as you supposed, was he?"

Gabe shook his head. He'd suspected his father's hand in this mess all along. Still, he couldn't be angry. It felt so good to see him. Dad, do you realize what your meddling has done to me?

"I think so," *he said. His sheepish grin faded to a wistful smile.* "I kind of miss that part of it, though."

He looked Gabe over. "I'm worried about you. You should be enjoying yourself. Life goes by so fast."

Gabe knew his father was right. He shuddered, recalling the quickening footsteps of death at his heels. There was so much he still had to do. So many questions he needed answered.

Just tell me one thing, Dad, will you?

"Sure son. What is it?"

Do you think she has real talent?

They both looked at Kate, old Murray smiling qui-

etly. *"What I think doesn't matter anymore, Gabe. Trust your instincts."* He rose to leave. His image began to fade.

Dad, wait. Gabe willed his father to stay.

"What is it, son?"

Gabe looked at him, wanting so much to talk. But until he could get past his guilt and remorse and set things right, there was nothing he could say. *Never mind, Dad. It was good seeing you.*

His father smiled as if he understood. *"Let your footsteps follow your heartbeat, son. You'll never go wrong that way. Now get up, out of this bed and on with your life."*

When Gabe finally woke it took all of his concentration to pry his eyes open. His world solidified and the familiar scent of French lavender penetrated his grogginess. Blinking his eyes, he swept his tongue over his parched lips. He felt Kate's presence and turned his head to meet her smile.

"Welcome back." She leaned close, fresh linen bandages in her hand.

Her hair fell across the front of her crisp white shirtwaist like a fiery sunset spilling color on a field of snow. Gabe couldn't recall ever seeing anyone look so lovely. He opened his mouth to tell her, but his throat was too dry to form the words.

Kate poured a glass of water and held it to his lips while lifting his head gently from the pillow. He drank deeply, swallowing one last mouthful before she put the glass aside and eased him back.

"How do you feel?"

"Like hell," he croaked out.

"Actually you look a little worse," she laughed. The soft musical sound filled his studio, making him glad to be alive.

He reached for her hand, but a stabbing pain stopped him. The image of knife-edged glass shot through his brain. Turning his hand over, he stared at a railroad track of dark sutures crossing his palm.

When he tried to close his hand, his swollen fingers wouldn't respond. He knew he was finished. Panic drummed in his chest at the thought of never again being able to work.

He pushed himself up, then wished he hadn't. The room tipped, shoving his brain sharply into one side of his skull. His head felt like it had been used to sink pylons. Squeezing his eyes he lowered himself back onto the pillow.

"God, what hit me?"

Kate pressed an assuring hand on his shoulder. "You'll be all right. The doctor gave you laudanum for the pain."

Details of that evening were coming back fast. Gabe remembered the party, the fire, their kiss. He looked at Kate and felt a twinge of desire. "Is the little girl all right?" he asked, trying to force his attention on something else.

"She's fine," Kate told him. "You were very brave."

Her admiration crept up on Gabe to sock him in the gut. He'd used her and for what? He didn't have a prayer of winning now. He wasn't even sure that mattered. His gaze shifted to his drafting table and his unfinished design, then back to his hand. The purple swollen flesh might have belonged to Mary Shelley's monster and he wondered if his thoughtless deeds had darkened his mortal soul as much. He groaned, feeling more confused than ever.

"You just need time to heal," she insisted.

Her attempt to soothe him only made Gabe feel worse. She sat at the edge of his bed and took his hand onto her lap to replace the dressing.

The feel of her weight on the mattress gave him the odd sensation of having shared the bed with her before. That wasn't possible, he thought. If she'd been in his bed, he'd know it. Or would he? He was so perplexed he couldn't tell what was real, let alone how he felt.

She raised her eyes to meet his gaze. "Is it very painful?"

Gabe shook his head, the throbbing in his hand not half so painful as the clash of emotions tearing at him.

"Can I get you something?" she asked as if sensing his turmoil.

"No, thank you." Her caring made him feel like a bastard. He hadn't thought of her as the nurturing type. Of course, until a few days ago, he hadn't thought of her as anything but a means to his end. In her kiss, he'd discovered a warm desirable woman, a woman who roused feelings in him he found hard to ignore.

She rested his hand back on the bed. "You might feel better if you get cleaned up. Do you think you can manage?"

She lifted the water jug from the bedside table and turned to leave him. She paused, looking back at him. "If you need anything, call me."

"Sure," he said. He waited for her to leave the room before attempting to stand.

He pushed himself up, sitting at the edge of the bed until the room stopped spinning. As he stood, the floor heaved and he stumbled against the chair for support. Straightening slowly, he took one step, then another, testing his balance like a toddler. He was glad she couldn't see him. He felt old and unsteady and thought he must look like his father had before he died.

The image renewed his guilt. Remorse over the part he'd played in his father's decline came back to haunt him. As much as he cared for Kate, he hated Peyton more. While he might not be able to finish his design, he could still prevent Peyton from submitting one. If Kate left before bids were due, neither of them would win. Yet Gabe stood to lose much more and he knew it. He wondered what kind of man he'd become that he could want her so badly and still want to win at her expense. He couldn't think with his mind so muddled so he concentrated on simply crossing the room.

He staggered over to the wardrobe like a drunken sailor, the floor rolling beneath him. He pulled a clean white shirt off the nearest hanger, then hugging the wall, made his way to the bath on shaky legs.

Resting against the door opposite the chipped porcelain sink, he stared at the mirror, cringing at his

reflection. Three days' growth of beard darkened his
jaw. Gabe glanced at his shaving kit, but dared not
take a razor to his throat with his left hand. He
washed as best he could, dragging a comb through
his tangled hair. He reached for the shirt he'd left
hanging on the doorknob. It smelled of laundry soap
and he realized she'd done the wash. Everything had
a clean, polished look. He couldn't remember the
last time someone had done anything for him without expecting a favor in return.

After struggling to button his shirt and wrestling
down his conscience, he turned to the kitchen, heed-
ing the loud protests of his empty stomach. The tan-
talizing aroma of crisp bacon, eggs and fresh biscuits greeted him at the door.

"Smells good," he said.

Kate turned from the stove, wooden spoon in
hand, shirtsleeves rolled to her elbows. Her unexpected domesticity made him smile.

"I thought you didn't cook."

"I never said I didn't know how." The slight
smile that tipped the corners of her mouth brought
to mind the soft warmth of her lips on his. Even
though he could hardly walk he found himself toying with the idea of what they might have done that
night if he hadn't been sedated.

"What else can you do that I don't know about?"
he asked.

She gave him a quick once-over as she placed a
basket of warm biscuits on the table. "I can button
a shirt properly."

He followed the direction of her gaze down the

front of his shirt and frowned, noting one side hung lower than the other. Kate stepped around the table, looking very proper in her starched white apron. She stood in front of him and started opening his shirt. Her cool teasing fingers ruffled through his chest hair as she aligned the button at his throat and adjusted his collar. An unwanted sensation shot to his groin even as his stomach growled.

Her eyes met his, her palms resting comfortably on his shoulders. "You must have quite an appetite after three days."

Gabe groaned. If she only knew. He might have brought a three-day appetite to her table, but a year's worth of hunger dictated to his weak-willed body. He wrestled down the urge to pull her against him and sample her kiss once more.

She lifted her hands from his shoulders as if she knew what he was thinking. "I'll get your breakfast," she said, moving away.

Only God knew what she saw in his eyes. Her hasty retreat back to the stove made him wonder if she recalled their kiss with the same longing. Standing barefoot in the kitchen he contemplated the possibility while she placed his breakfast on the table.

"Don't let it get cold," she said.

If only his desire for her would cool as fast as the biscuits. Gabe slumped into a chair thinking he could at least satisfy the needs of his stomach. He thought again as the perfectly poached egg sitting at the center of a piece of toast dared him to try.

Gripping the fork with his left hand he held it awkwardly above the plate. Concentrating mightily, he tried to cut into the toast with the dull edge of the fork, feeling as if the fragile connection between his brain and hand had been severed. Every labored movement was backward, like navigating through a mirror. A simple task that he'd taken for granted suddenly became impossible. When he caught Kate watching, what little coordination he had slipped and the toast shot to the far side of his plate.

''Do you need some help?'' she asked.

''I'm fine.'' Gabe managed just barely to keep the building frustration out of his voice.

It seemed the universe had conspired against him. Here he was sitting opposite the woman he ached for and after the way he'd treated her, his chances of having her were as remote as his attempt to feed himself.

Grumbling, he slammed his fork on the table, reaching instead for a biscuit. He dropped it onto his plate, snatched up the knife and plunged the blade into the butter crock. He watched disheartened as he withdrew the knife and the creamy dollop slipped onto the table cloth.

''Oh, jeez.'' He rolled his eyes.

A loud scraping sound got his attention. He glanced up as Kate dragged her chair around the table and sat beside him. Without a word, she took his fork and knife and began cutting his breakfast into bite-size pieces. It took him a second to realize what she was up to.

Oh, no, he thought. He wasn't going to sit back and be spoon-fed. He opened his mouth to protest when she slid the fork gently over his tongue.

A dribble of egg yolk dropped onto his beard. Kate lifted the napkin, dabbing his chin clean. The intimacy of her action threatened to shatter what remained of his waning control. Gabe swallowed hard as one kind of hunger replaced another. Was she really so innocent that she didn't know what she was doing?

His gaze roved freely over her face as she lifted the fork from the plate to offer him another bite. He took the food into his mouth, chewing slowly, his eyes holding her, wondering how much more he could take.

Lowering her lashes, she scooped up another forkful and held it before his lips. "I hope you don't mind that I read one of your journals," she said.

That shook him from his brief fantasy. He didn't like anyone snooping through his notebooks, but he supposed he couldn't keep her nose out of his business forever. Hell, she'd probably washed him and changed his clothes while he was unconscious. *Wait a minute.*

It dawned on Gabe that while he was having some half-baked dreams about his father, she might have actually seen him naked. The possibility made him smile. He wondered if she'd made as detailed an account of him as he'd previously made of her.

He couldn't resist asking, "Are you the one who undressed me?"

Her eyes flashed to his as she lowered the fork to the plate. "No. Finn did," she said with a defensive edge. "You don't think that I could lift you up the stairs and into bed on my own?"

The deep-crimson flush that colored her cheeks had him visualizing the scene as it might have been. Oh, she could easily get him into bed, he thought. He didn't have long to contemplate the possibility before she steered the conversation back to safer ground.

"Your ideas are very interesting," she said. "Why do you keep them a secret?"

His spirits crumbled as his thoughts returned to his unfinished design and the wager he'd made with Peyton. "I was going to use some of them in my museum design but I can't finish it now."

"Why not?"

Gabe looked at her, puzzled. "My hand, remember? I can't draw."

"But I can." She smiled sweetly.

He stared at her, momentarily stunned. What would he do now?

Kate couldn't keep from laughing at his expression. It seemed to her that finishing his design would solve both their problems. So, why was he staring at her as if she'd suggested they jump off the Brooklyn Bridge for an icy swim in the East River?

She didn't wait long for an answer. "You can't finish my design."

"Of course I can," she said, chuckling at his stunned expression. "I'm capable of following instructions and I'm sure there are no rules that prevent an apprentice from assisting."

Before she could say anything else, there came a knock on the door. "I'll get it."

Kate pushed her chair back and went to the door to find Finn Hurley, cap in hand and a copy of the *Tribune* tucked beneath one arm.

"Good morning, lass." He walked in. "How's our lad today?"

Kate motioned toward the kitchen table where Gabe sat stone-still. Finn made a face, taking a few steps toward him. "Hell of a way to start the new year." He put a deliberate touch of sarcasm in his voice.

Even his goading couldn't get a rise out of Gabe. His failure to respond troubled Kate and she wondered if the laudanum had permanently muddled his mind. She hoped that Finn's visit might help shake him from his depression.

"Would you like some coffee?" She didn't give Finn a chance to refuse before she had a steaming mug in front of him.

"Thank you, lass." He placed his newspaper on the table and cupped his hands around the mug. He looked at Gabe, trying for a reaction. "So, how does it feel to be a hero?"

"What are you talking about?"

"The news, you lunkhead." Finn laughed. "You've been in the headlines for days now. Even the Fifth Avenue Ladies League has jumped on the bandwagon. They're collecting food and clothes for the victims of the fire. All because of what you did."

"I didn't do anything," Gabe said.

Kate glanced at the photograph on the front page, catching a glimpse of Eve Peyton standing among the other well-turned-out ladies of the Fifth Avenue

League. Fighting the brackish taste of jealousy, she tore her gaze away and turned to Finn.

"We hadn't seen the papers," she said.

Finn swallowed a mouthful of coffee and replied. "Well, I more than saw the papers. I helped write this here story. Day after the fire this reporter waltzes into the Harp, wearing fancy duds, asking questions about Gabe. So, I says to him, no one knows Gabe Murray better than me and commence telling him all about how you were a hero down in Cuba with those Rough Riders."

"You didn't," Gabe said.

"'Tis God's truth. Why deny it?"

Kate watched Gabe scan the front page, noting his expression change from one of mild irritation to full-blown anger.

"Why did you tell the reporter we were married?"

His accusation caught her by surprise and put her on the defensive. "I didn't tell him anything. He must have assumed."

"You didn't correct him."

Her emotional temperature shot up several degrees. "Well, excuse me. I had my mind on other things at the time."

She snatched the breakfast dishes from the table, turned her back and mumbled under her breath on her way to the sink, "As if being his wife is such an elevated state."

Finn cleared his throat, rising to her defense. "It was a natural assumption, lad."

"Why would it be?" Gabe snapped.

Kate met Finn's eyes, praying he'd keep her confidence and remain silent. She turned away, annoyed with Gabe and with herself for caring so much. What arrogance, she thought. Wasn't it he who kissed her? She vigorously scrubbed the dishes as the tense silence dragged on.

"Well," said Finn while pushing his chair away from the table. "I'd best be going. I only stopped by to see how you were doing and I can see things are just as they should be."

He started to see himself out, then paused, reaching into his pocket. "I almost forgot," he said. "I stopped by the post office. There was a letter for you, lass."

"For me?" Kate let the dish she was washing slip from her hand and sink beneath the soapy water. Only one person would be writing her here. She turned, trying not to think the worst, but the Elmira return address confirmed her fear.

"Thank you," she said, wiping her hands. She took the envelope from Finn and shoved it into the deep pocket of her apron. "I'll see you out."

She walked beside him to the door. Finn paused, glancing back at Gabe. "Don't let him discourage you, lass. You're doing just fine." He gave her shoulder a gentle squeeze.

Kate nodded, but she was too distracted by the letter to reply. She closed the door behind Finn and absently dropped onto the soft cushioned chair beside the fireplace. Pulling the envelope from her pocket, she held it between her thumb and forefinger, wondering why her grandfather was writing her now.

There was only one way to find out. Pressing her thumbnail beneath the wax seal, she pried open the flap and removed the buff-colored paper. Her hands trembled as she read and she focused all her attention on every word, unable to believe what she was seeing.

"Oh, good Lord." Her eyes slid shut as her hand fell to her lap.

It didn't seem possible that her grandfather would get so worked up over something he'd read in the New York paper. He'd made no secret of his disdain for the press after the way they had slandered her mother.

"Bad news from home?" The sound of Gabe's voice startled her.

Kate glanced up and found him leaning against the doorjamb, watching her with the intensity of a hawk. She resisted the temptation to confide in him, reminding herself that his sympathy wasn't what she wanted.

"Everything is fine," she lied. Her voice sounded tight even to her and she doubted he believed her.

Forcing a smile, she put the letter back into her pocket. Any other time she would have welcomed his attention. Right now she had to think and she couldn't concentrate with him standing so near.

She stood while untying her apron, then folded it over the chair, aware of his gaze. It took all of her control to hide her simmering nervous tension beneath a calm expression. She turned to him, knowing she needed time alone if she was going to collect herself.

"You should rest now. I'm going for a walk."

Eager to extricate herself from the studio, she reached for her purse and cape and started for the door. Gabe staggered after her.

"Kate," he said. "I'm sorry I lost my temper. What happened wasn't your fault."

The sincerity in his eyes tugged at her heart, making her once more fight the urge to tell him everything. "It's all right," she said. "Now, go and lie down."

Closing her hand around the doorknob, she let herself out. She crossed the street, her thoughts spinning like the dry leaves cartwheeling down the alley. She turned the corner, heading in no particular direction, walking several blocks unaware of her surroundings. If her grandfather hadn't sounded so serious, she would have laughed at the idea of him barreling down to New York to annul a marriage that didn't exist.

Not paying attention to where she was going, she collided with a street vendor's cart. The impact sent a small avalanche of roasted chestnuts tumbling onto the sidewalk. Mortified, Kate met his angry scowl. "I'm sorry," she said.

The man growled at her, shaking his fist.

Kate stooped down, scrambling to collect the chestnuts, carefully returning them to his cart one handful at a time. "There," she said. "No real harm done."

He mumbled a curse under his breath as she

backed away, then picked up her pace. What was happening to her? Tears welled up in her eyes and she turned away, trying to hide from the curious stares of a couple on their way to Woolworth's Five and Dime.

Kate had never felt so confused or alone and didn't know where to turn. She'd always known exactly who she was and where she was headed. Somehow she had to find her way back to the sane person she'd been before she ever laid eyes on Gabe Murray. Sniffling, she dug into her purse for a handkerchief. As she removed it, Lloyd Peyton's calling card fell onto the sidewalk. Kate picked it up, staring at the embossed letters through watery eyes. A tiny bud of hope unfolded in her heart as she recalled his offer. His promise to help her seemed the answer to her prayer, yet she had misgivings. She'd always shied away from calling attention to herself and while being the first woman to present a paper to the New York Board of Architects would be an honor, doing so would also put her in the spotlight, making her ripe for more ridicule. She didn't relish that. Of course, she didn't look forward to the prospect of facing her grandfather, either.

She considered her options and saw none. Gabe's reluctance to let her help with his design and her grandfather believing she'd reneged on their agreement left Lloyd Peyton her only chance. The more she thought of the alternative, the more his idea appealed to her.

Pushing aside her doubts, she dropped his card back into her purse, dried her tears and boarded the first trolley heading up Fifth Avenue.

Chapter Seventeen

A short ride brought Kate to the offices of Kendall, McKee and Hartford. She stepped from the noisy street into the quiet lobby. Sunlight streamed through the glass panes of the bronze-encased doors. Kate stood at the center of the immense lobby admiring the elaborate marble-and-bronze fixtures when she noticed Lloyd Peyton step from the shadow of a newsstand.

He wore a black suit and a fleeting look of surprise as she caught his eye. He crossed the onyx tile and headed in her direction.

"Miss Delaney, how nice to see you." He glanced at his newspaper then with a sly grin, back at her. "Or is it really Mrs. Murray?"

Kate swore her face turned the color of his flamboyant red silk cravat. "It's Miss Delaney," she answered, lowering her eyes.

"Forgive me," he said. "I didn't mean to embarrass you. I guess we can't believe anything we read in the papers these days."

"No," came her emphatic response. "Unfortunately, my grandfather has seen that article and it's causing me a lot of trouble."

Peyton returned a sympathetic smile and slipped the paper into the leather folio tucked beneath his arm. "How's Gabe doing?"

"Recovering," Kate said, slowly regaining her composure.

"Good to hear that." He looked her up and down in a way that made her very uneasy. "What brings you here?"

"If you have a few minutes, I'd like to talk with you."

He flashed a perfect smile, motioning toward the bronze Otis birdcage elevator. "For a lovely lady friend of Gabe, I have all the time in the world."

They crossed the lobby together. "Have you given more thought to my suggestion?" he asked, allowing her to step into the cagelike car ahead of him.

"Yes, I have," she said. She glanced up at the bronze relief of Hercules, capping the lattice grillwork above the door as she moved to the rear of the car.

Peyton stood beside her, making room for others to board. Kate watched with interest as the man operating the lift pushed a lever to one side, setting the car in motion. It seemed only minutes and they arrived on the third floor.

"We'll talk in my office," Peyton said.

They stepped from the elevator and he directed her to a suite of rooms beyond mahogany double doors. Watercolor washes of Newport mansions, bridges and other projects adorned the walls of the reception area.

Peyton ushered her down a long corridor, past a dozen or so young draftsmen who worked at tables. His fast pace made her wonder if he was embarrassed to be seen with her.

"Here we are," he said, unlocking the door to his office.

Kate walked in, immediately taken by the panoramic view of Fifth Avenue visible from the corner window. "You can see Saint Patrick's Cathedral," she said. "This is lovely." Turning, she caught his surveying stare.

"It suits me." Peyton smiled, offering to take her coat.

"Make yourself comfortable," he said. "Would you like some refreshment?" He motioned toward a small table where a bottle of brandy and a porcelain teapot sat beside an arrangement of red roses.

"A cup of tea would be wonderful, thank you." She sat in one of the soft leather chairs adjacent his desk.

Peyton hung her coat, handed her a cup of Darjeeling and took the chair beside her. Her fingers tingled as they began to thaw.

He crossed his legs and studied her from behind his cool gray eyes. "I'm glad you've decided to let me help you."

He set his cup aside. "Still, I sense uncertainty."

"A little," she confided, lifting her eyes to his.

"It's understandable, but you've made a wise decision. This could really make a future for you."

Kate placed her cup and saucer on the table. "Exactly what is it I'll be doing, Mr. Peyton?"

"It's simple," he said. "I'll schedule you for one of our Board meetings where you'll present a short thesis paper on your work. Your theories of design."

Simple for him, she thought. The one thing she had learned over the past few weeks was that she didn't know half as much as she once thought she did. She wet her lips nervously, wondering what she would talk about.

"I have to confess, the prospect of standing before a room full of skeptical men is very intimidating."

Peyton laughed. "Don't be silly. I'll be there to help you."

"I appreciate that." She managed a weak smile, thinking she'd be a fool not to take him up on his offer.

"Are we in agreement?" Peyton asked, drawing her back.

"Yes." She nodded. "I'd like to invite my grandfather. He's financing my education and this would mean a lot to him."

Peyton smiled. "I don't see why not. Inviting him might help explain yourself out of the situation the press has put you in."

"I hope so," she said.

"Then I'll take care of everything as soon as the partners get back from their New Year's holiday. That'll give you some time to prepare."

Kate felt a stitch of anxiety. She hadn't the slightest idea what she would say. "I think I will need time to prepare for this."

"You'll do just fine." Peyton assured her.

She met his gaze, hoping he was right. "I should be going now. I've kept you from your work long enough."

Peyton rose as she stood. "It's been my pleasure and I look forward to our big day. It'll be an exciting moment."

"Yes, it will," she agreed.

He helped her on with her coat. She left the office to return to Gabe's studio feeling good about herself for the first time in weeks. She'd made a decision, regained control of her life. She would never surrender that control again. Nothing and no one was going to keep her from realizing her dream. All she had to do now was come up with an idea for her presentation. Not an easy task.

Apprehension surfaced as she considered the critical audience she would face. She agonized over what would make an interesting enough topic to hold their attention and allow them to see her potential rather than dismissing her for being a woman. Still puzzling over it, she walked into the studio, took one look at Gabe seated in the armchair, and made her decision.

Of course. He'd make the perfect subject. She admired his ideas and respected his talent even if his annoying stubborn streak drove her to distraction. Kate smiled, her problem solved. Her relief turned to renewed concern for Gabe as she noticed the deep stoop of his shoulders.

He looked as though some fierce turmoil raged inside him and the all-consuming depth of his depression made it impossible for her to stand by and do nothing. Kate thought she knew just how to get him out of that armchair and back to working on his design. She removed her coat without saying a word and walked past the chair where he sat with a book in his lap. She proceeded toward his drafting table, feeling him watch her every move. Lazily drawing her fingers along the paper's edge, she studied his design for the new museum.

The unique circular structure rose from a spacious atrium to a large domelike ceiling. A spiraling maze of concrete ramps hugged the curve of the wall, leaving an open area at the center of the building. Natural light flooded the galleries, enhancing the flowing form, making a spectacular open interior.

His idea was ingenious, but not perfect and that's what she'd counted on. Drumming her fingers on the table she considered her approach. She knew how it felt to work for weeks on an idea only to have it bashed by a callous remark. She hoped his fierce dedication and his present vulnerable emotional state would make her job easy. Anticipating his response, she put a dose of arrogance in her voice.

"You're probably right not wasting any more time on this. The design really doesn't stand a chance of winning."

Her criticism catapulted Gabe from his chair,

shaking him from his lethargy. He strode across the room to her side. "What do you mean it doesn't stand a chance?"

His defensiveness had a familiar ring that made her smile. "Now don't get so angry," she said. "I just don't think people will want to climb this steep ramp to look at paintings. What about poor Vera with her cane?"

He wasn't in the mood to be challenged and his voice had a sarcastic bite. "Well, unless they sprout wings, it's either the ramp or stairs."

"Why not an elevator," came her quick response.

"An elevator?" His brow furrowed.

"Yes," she added. "It's convenient, would add a little elegance and could be the one decorative touch in your stark design."

"It's not stark." His boyish protest drew another smile.

"It is," she argued. "And I think I understand what you're trying to do. But if you really want to make your building a part of the aesthetic experience, I have a suggestion."

"I'm listening," he said, his curiosity piqued.

She hesitated, than began. "Instead of people walking into the gallery, why not lift them to the uppermost level in a beautiful bronze elevator? They could descend by the inner ramp back to the atrium. You could create a garden or even a café to greet them on their return. They would be enticed to linger, discussing the art they've seen. That would make your building design an integral part of every exhibit it houses."

Gabe studied her with new interest. Hearing her put the concept into words made him feel like a fool. "An elevator," he mused, rubbing his jaw. "I hadn't thought of that."

"Obviously." An impish smile accompanied her playful jab.

"Don't push your luck," he replied in a good-natured way.

He became more interested as he saw the possibilities of her idea. "Where would you place the elevator?"

She looked at him, surprised. "Do you really want my opinion?"

"Yes," he said, growing impatient. The thrill of creativity shot through him and he felt excited about his work for the first time in months.

She gave his design a cautious look. "Well," she said, circling her index finger above the drawing. "I think right here at the center of the atrium, don't you?" Her eyes met his.

Gabe simply nodded as she went on. "The cage could be made of polished brass with wide decorative doors. And," she added with a delightful coltish look, "I have just the design for the doors."

"I thought you might." His eyes swept over her as she hurried to fetch her portfolio.

"Don't push your luck," she quoted.

He laughed, enjoying the fact that she didn't know he'd already seen and liked her drawings. He kept his opinion to himself, taking her in as she removed four large art posters from her portfolio and leaned them against the chair. Stepping back she placed her hands at her waist and assessed her work.

"If we cast these female figures in bronze and use them as part of the door panels, they could represent the muses."

She looked at Gabe as if measuring his reaction to her concept.

"Why don't you sketch it out?" he said.

Her amazed expression made him laugh. "Well, I sure as hell can't do it." Gabe raised his injured hand as if she hadn't noticed.

Kate didn't waste a minute. She rolled up her sleeves and tacked a fresh sheet of drafting paper to the table before he could blink an eye. The quick precise movement of her hand captured him as she sketched the elaborate elevator and incorporated the four figures into the design for the doors.

They laughed, debated and exchanged ideas. The hours passed like swift-moving clouds, pushed by a creative breeze. Gabe watched her ink the pen to apply the final strokes. She'd captured his heart as well as his imagination.

She placed the pen aside and looked at him. "It's finished."

"I like it," he said and realized the design truly was finished.

She threw her arms around him, swept up in her enthusiasm and his approval. Gabe caught and held the scent of her perfume. He closed his arms around her, feeling her excitement, sharing the intoxicating thrill of accomplishment. Their creative effort spanned the chasm of their differences and he found himself wishing time could leave them as they were. She was beautiful, intelligent, everything he could ever hope for. Instead of happiness, indecision filled his heart.

The moment passed. Kate drew away and the sobering reality hit Gabe hard. She'd completed his design. *Our design,* he thought. How easily that word slipped into his vocabulary. Her additions to his plan made it a winning concept. But the blueprint for their museum would never see the light of day if she remained.

He couldn't recall ever feeling so miserable and elated at one time. His injury had given him a valid excuse for not working and letting her stay. She was the best thing to come into his life at the worst possible time. Their wonderful idea might just as well remain buried in his desk unless he could forget he'd fallen in love with her.

Chapter Eighteen

Gabe didn't know what to do. He lost track of time as his confusion deepened with each passing day. He didn't want to lose the bet, but how much he still wanted to win nagged at him constantly. Trying to make a decision, he stared at the street through a thick forest of hoarfrost.

The tinkling of milk bottles followed the slow clip-clop of a horse-drawn wagon as street vendors jockeyed for the best location from which to sell their wares. The city was waking up. Men were going about their business. Gabe felt useless. His hand was healing, but guilt over the way he'd deceived Kate plagued him day and night.

Unable to submit their design and unwilling to tell Kate the truth, he felt the walls of his studio closing in around him, every inch pushing him closer to her. A few weeks ago he wouldn't have hesitated to do whatever it took to defeat Peyton. But Kate had made him lose sight of what mattered…or put him in touch with it.

She had rearranged his soul, swept the cobwebs from his heart and thrown open his eyes to let in the fresh air of promise. He was in love with her and, damn it, he couldn't be. Gabe had to get out or go mad.

Grabbing his coat, he left the studio. He crossed the freight yard where vagrants huddled around trash barrel fires to warm themselves and walked on to the waterfront, stopping when he reached the end of the pier. A brisk wind whipped riggings, twisting flags around tall masts. Gabe stared at the choppy gray water searching for an answer he wouldn't get.

Knowing how much hurt the truth would cause Kate chilled him more than the icy spray kicked up by a passing tug. How could he repay her kindness and caring by confessing he'd bet against her? Could he bear having her think her feelings meant so little to him? No matter how many times he asked himself those questions, his answer was always no.

While he would have liked nothing better than to unburden himself, he couldn't betray her trust and wouldn't be the cause of her disillusionment.

Raking his fingers through his hair, he watched stevedores loading cargo onto a ship and thought how easy it would be to board that ship and turn his back on everything. But where could he go? He'd run from trouble before. He wouldn't run again. Like it or not he was trapped. Boxed in by his inability to choose between the woman he wanted and the man he wanted to destroy.

He kicked a stone from the edge of the pier and returned home feeling no better than when he'd left.

He barely slipped his key into the lock when, from the corner of his eye, he saw Hattie and Vera Goodhue's old victoria roll to a stop in front of his studio.

"What the devil..." A tingle of suspicion wriggled up his spine as he scratched his head, wondering what had brought them out on such a cold blustery morning.

Whatever the reason, Gabe didn't like the looks of it. They stepped from the carriage with purpose in their stride, making their way single file up the steps to his front door.

"Good morning, Mr. Murray." The stiff wind caught and carried away their wispy voices.

"Ladies." Gabe fixed a smile on his face as he held the door. They marched ahead of him into the vestibule.

"Let me take your coats," he said, raising his voice to get Kate's attention. He looked at her from over his shoulder as he hung their heavy overcoats.

Kate glanced up from the desk, obviously taken aback by their unexpected visit. She hurried to greet them. "What a surprise."

She flashed Gabe a puzzled look as he ushered the old sisters into the front room. "Please make yourselves comfortable."

He motioned toward the small settee near the fire. The Goodhue sisters took their seats, Kate and Gabe standing side by side, facing them. The arrangement gave him an uncomfortable feeling. As the two old sisters stared up at him, he wondered what they wanted.

"So, what brings you here?"

"You do, dear." Hattie studied him, a little too intently, he thought. Gabe glanced at Kate who looked just as baffled.

Vera hooked her cane over one arm, removing her gloves. "We're very disappointed," she said.

"I see." Gabe rubbed his jaw, mulling over the events of the past few weeks, trying to figure out what he'd done. He remembered the design he'd delivered to Fairweather. They probably hated it.

"I'm sorry you felt you had to come all the way over here to tell me that."

Vera fixed her gaze on his face as she replied. "Hattie and I have always considered you family and we believe in the courtesy of a personal visit when major decisions are made."

"Major decision?" Her scolding tone left Gabe at a loss. He'd always been summoned to Fairweather when Vera wanted to give him a good dressing-down and he couldn't understand why today was different. Unless they had come to fire him. He opened his mouth to defend himself, but Hattie cut him off.

"You really have surprised us, Mr. Murray, and we've come to give you our thoughts on the matter."

Gabe glanced at Kate, who stood beside him, hands clasped in front of her. "Would you like some tea?" she asked the sisters.

Vera replied. "No, we don't want anything."

"Oh, I insist," Kate said, turning to Gabe. "Would you help me in the kitchen?"

"Of course." Glad for an excuse to make a hasty

exit, he followed her from the room. "We'll be right back," he called to his guest from over his shoulder.

Kate drew him off to one side of the cramped kitchen. "What's going on?"

"I'm not sure," he said, keeping his voice down. "Maybe they've come to fire us."

"Fire us?" Her voice rose to a squealing pitch.

"Shh." Gabe gently covered her mouth with his hand. "Keep your voice down."

Her wide, puzzled eyes locked on to his as he slid his hand from her lips.

"Why would they fire us?"

He didn't know the answer to that. "I guess they just don't like the design."

"My design?" Her pained expression moved him and he tried to console her.

"Well, they don't really need a reason."

Kate looked close to tears. "I can't believe I'm being fired."

He sympathized. Her complete devastation reminded him of the first time he'd been dismissed. Just how routine that had become in the last year came as a sobering realization. He didn't have long to ponder the downward slide of his career before they were summoned by the impatient tapping of Vera's cane on the wood floor.

"Will the two of you come back here now?" she called out. "We don't want tea but we do have something to say."

"Oh, dear," Kate sighed, nervously wringing her hands. "What do we do?"

"There's nothing to it," he said as he slipped a

comforting arm around her shoulder and pulled her close to his side. "Being fired isn't the end of the world. Believe me, I've had experience."

Somehow the fact that he was about to lose his sole means of support didn't upset him as much as he thought it would. They were leaving the kitchen when Gabe noticed the old newspapers still lying on the table. He recalled the article referring to Kate as his wife.

So that's it, he thought. Now it all made sense. No wonder the two old things were so peevish. He could just see the pair of them sitting over a game of whist, sipping port and fuming because they thought he'd eloped without saying a word to them.

Well, he'd set them straight. But not before he enjoyed this a little longer. Putting a scare into Kate might do her good. Besides, he couldn't deny he liked having her look up to him for a change. She hesitated at the door, so he walked into the room ahead of her.

Kate stood stiff-backed in front of the Goodhue sisters, looking like Saint Joan facing the flames. Gabe managed to keep a sober expression and control himself enough to speak.

"Now Vera," he said in a serious tone of voice. "Before you say anything you might regret, I want you to know that we have a new design."

He gave Kate's arm a nudge and just as he'd hoped, she followed his lead.

"We think you'll like it," she added.

Hattie turned to Vera. "What did they say?"

"Nothing, dear. They think we've come because we don't like the design."

"Oh," Hattie chuckled. "We don't. But that's not why we're here."

"It isn't?" Acting confused, Gabe looked at them. "Then why are you here?"

Hattie appeared ready to explode from excitement. "Oh, sister. Let me tell them now."

"Tell us what?" he asked. His suspicion piqued as he noted the mischievous glint in Vera's eyes. He'd seen that look before whenever Finn got the notion to match him up with some unattached female. "What's this all about?" he said at last.

Hattie and Vera beamed. "We have a little wedding gift for you two rascals."

"Wedding gift?" Gabe and Kate exchanged glances. "But we're not—"

"Hush up." Vera silenced them with another loud thump of her cane. "Learning about your nuptials through the newspaper was bad enough. At least have the courtesy to hear us out."

"You don't understand," Gabe tried to explain.

"Oh, yes we do," Hattie interrupted with a blissful expression. "And to show you how excited we are, we've arranged for you to spend a honeymoon weekend in the country."

Kate's mouth dropped open. "We can't."

"She's right," Gabe added. Sharing a studio was one thing, but playing newlyweds for a weekend in the country was too much to ask of any man.

"You must." Hattie insisted. "You should enjoy

yourselves now. It won't be long before you're tied down with the responsibility of a family.''

Vera sat back, looking very content. "I think I'm going to enjoy being called Auntie Vera."

Kate's eyes widened with alarm and Gabe decided this had gone far enough. "Look," he said, seeing no way to be tactful. "The truth is, we're not married."

Hattie turned to Vera, confused. Vera gently patted her hand and informed her, "He says they're not married."

Disappointment clouded Hattie's eyes. "You're engaged?"

Kate shook her head. "I'm afraid it was a misunderstanding."

Vera turned to Gabe, grasping at a fragile remaining hope. "Premature perhaps, but you'll be announcing your engagement soon, won't you?"

This time Gabe shook his head.

"Oh, dear." Vera settled back in her chair, looking glum.

The foursome exchanged uneasy glances. At last Hattie leaned over, whispering something to her sister. Vera looked first at Gabe, then Kate. "You might have a point," she said to Hattie.

Gabe smelled trouble. "What are you thinking?"

"Well," Vera said, "there's no reason to waste a nice weekend in the country. It's paid for, so you and Miss Delaney might as well go."

"Why?" he asked.

To his dismay Vera had a ready answer. "The property lines need to be surveyed again before we move ahead with our project. Isn't that right, sister?"

"Absolutely," Hattie added, a spritelike smile lighting her face. "The last storm blew the fences down. Besides," she said to Kate, "your design really does need work, dear. Seeing the property might help."

"And who knows," Vera added, "far away from the stresses of the city the two of you might get ideas."

Gabe already had too many ideas and he didn't like where this was heading. "I don't think it's necessary."

"We do." Vera dismissed his objections.

Kate quickly pointed out the obvious problem. "But we can't share a room."

"Of course not," Vera chuckled softly. "It's an inn, dear. They have other rooms."

"I suppose they do," Gabe said, feeling cornered.

"Good," Hattie concluded. "You'll leave this weekend."

He gave Kate a sidelong glance, felt the familiar spark ignite and looked away before she caught his reaction. He had the uncomfortable feeling that he was about to find out just how much his restraint could be tested.

Chapter Nineteen

The Plumbush Inn stood on an island of uninterrupted saw grass, sand dunes and windswept pine. A two-story colonial saltbox, the inn had a rustic charm that enchanted Kate and raised her expectations for a quiet weekend away from the city.

She stepped from the coach, took a deep breath and tasted the salty freshness. Exhaling slowly, she delighted in the prospect of spending two nights wrapped in the privacy of her own room. How refreshed she would feel once the quiet of the country eased weeks of tension from her body and a spacious room removed her from the source of her distraction.

Gabe followed her from the coach, stretching the kinks from his back as she looked on. Her eyes traversed the lean arc of his hard-muscled body, made more apparent by the denim trousers, flannel shirt and sheepskin jacket he wore.

His rugged appeal distracted her so she spent the

entire train and ferry trip trying to concentrate on a dime novel to keep from staring at him.

An icy gust of wind blew over them and swept her from her preoccupation. She held fast to her hat, fighting to keep it from sailing into a puddle. The driver placed their bags adjacent to the white picket fence surrounding the inn.

Gabe dug into his pocket, tipped the man and swung open the gate for Kate to pass through. Side by side, they started up the flagstone walk, each toting a large leather valise.

They crossed the threshold. The lanky innkeeper glanced up from behind his desk. He took one look at them and announced with a grin, "You must be Miss Goodhue's guests. I've been expecting you."

Gabe set down his valise and acknowledged their host with a smile. "Did she arrange for the extra room?"

The man looked puzzled. "Why?" he asked. "Is someone joining you?"

Kate choked down her apprehension and stepped toward the innkeeper. "Didn't Miss Goodhue say anything about our accommodations?"

"Of course," he said, his smile restored as he looked her over. "She gave me specific instructions. I think you'll find the bridal suite very nice."

"What?" Gabe's outburst drew curious stares from other guests.

Kate glanced around. Her face flushed. "There's been a misunderstanding. This gentleman and I are colleagues. The second room would be for him."

"I see." The man was sympathetic, but offered no solution. "I'm afraid we're full."

Her stomach twisted into a knot. This couldn't be happening. The bridal suite was a special place, reserved for intimate moments between husband and wife. Moments she'd probably never know.

"You must have something else," she pleaded.

The innkeeper eyed Gabe. "Perhaps the gentleman would consider staying in the stable."

"Oh, no," Gabe said. "Not this gentleman. I didn't want to be here in the first place. We'll have to work out something else."

Kate nervously wrung her hands. She'd counted on this weekend, hoping the change of scenery and a little distance would help her to see things clearly and put her wild emotions back into perspective. She couldn't speak for Gabe, but remaining alone in her loft night after night with him so near had frayed her nerves beyond repair. She couldn't keep the mounting tension out of her voice.

"We're not sharing the bridal suite."

Gabe looked hurt. "You didn't mind sharing my studio."

His wounded expression took her by surprise and she wondered if he might care for her. The possibility sent a new rush of color rising to her cheeks. She quickly looked away.

By now their conversation had the interest of everyone in the room. Kate wanted to crawl beneath the large counter and die. Eager to escape prying eyes, she made a snap decision.

"You take the room. I'm leaving." She picked up her valise and headed for the door.

She didn't get far before the innkeeper called to her. "I'm afraid the ferry from the mainland doesn't run again until noon tomorrow, miss."

Kate stopped short, her shoulders rigid, as exasperated she spun on her heel. "Then what do you suggest?"

Her voice held an edge, leaving no doubt someone would be without a bed tonight and it wasn't going to be her. The baffled innkeeper scratched his head and angled a glance at Gabe. "The suite has a sitting room and sofa."

Gabe didn't look happy. Kate suspected if the ferry were running he'd be heading back to the city to give Hattie and Vera a piece of his mind. She stared at him, waiting for his response.

"It'll have to do for one night," he grumbled. "But we're riding out to look at the property today. The sooner we get this over with and get back to the city, the better."

He spoke as if this whole mess was her fault. "Fine," she snapped. "But I'll have to change my clothes."

"I'll wait right here." Gabe turned to the innkeeper. "Do you have a wagon we can hire for the afternoon?"

Again the man shook his head. "The axle is broken, however, I have some fine saddle horses you're welcome to."

Kate grasped at what seemed one bright spot in

her worsening situation. "A ride in the country sounds like fun."

Obviously, Gabe didn't share her enthusiasm. Determined to salvage something of the weekend, she trifled with him, goading him in the presence of the old innkeeper, suspecting a challenge to his pride was more than he could resist.

"Unless, of course, your poor hand is paining you too much."

Gabe glanced at his hand, then at the nosy innkeeper. "Not at all," he said forcing a manly smile. "I have two hands. A little exercise might be just what the doctor ordered."

"Are you sure?" Kate waited.

"Absolutely." Flexing his fingers, Gabe turned his attention to a rack of picture postcards resting on the counter.

The innkeeper walked from behind the desk, took their bags and led her up the stairs. He opened the door, allowing her to precede him into the room. Her prayer that the suite would be a dismal little place with shabby furnishing went unanswered. The room was perfect.

The walls were painted a soft Wedgwood-blue and colorful braided oval rugs softened the wide slats of the polished oak floor. Lacy eyelet curtains covered the windows. A painful sigh escaped her as she wondered how many marriages had been consummated in the enormous four-poster bed.

The innkeeper placed their valises on the floor. "If there's anything you need, just let me know."

"Thank you," Kate replied as he left the room.

Removing her hat and gloves, she walked around, checking the layout of the suite. Noting the close proximity of the small sofa to the bed, she sighed deeply, anticipating another restless night with the man she longed for sleeping just out of reach.

She tried to put her mind on something else, but every detail of the cozy room invited a romantic interlude. A tidy little table was set with white linen, creamy petaled roses and scented candles. It nestled beside the fireplace, awaiting newlyweds with a bottle of chilled French champagne.

Something undefined awakened within her as she drew her fingers across the ivory crochet tablecloth. She felt like an intruder, the solitary member of some species on Noah's ark. There were two of everything: crystal champagne flutes, linen napkins, lace pillow shams. She stared, transfixed, at the overstuffed bed that seemed to fill the entire room.

Her skin prickled pleasurably as her imagination wandered and she fantasized about what it would be like to really spend her wedding night in a room like this.

There was no point in thinking along those lines. Until Gabe Murray knew his own heart, she would not admit to losing hers. All of this was wasted on them. They were impostors sharing this suite tonight. With that reality firmly implanted in her head she prepared for their ride.

Slipping out of her tailored travel suit, she lay it across the bed and unpacked her full-skirted dress. She changed quickly, then brushed out her hair, catching it at her nape with a green velvet ribbon.

She paused before the large cheval glass, comparing her pale skin and fair hair with Eve's striking features.

Something had happened to her since meeting Gabe. She stared at her reflection and felt plain. Ordinary. She'd never given much thought to her looks and had always considered herself adequate. Now, she longed to be pretty as well as intelligent. It seemed every time Gabe looked at her, he loosened the bow that bound her heart and released feelings she never had before.

"Foolish vanity is a waste of time."

No matter how much she wanted it to be so, she was not the kind of woman a man like Gabe dreams of carrying off to his bed. Unless he wanted to spend the night debating design. Turning her back on the mirror, she put on her fleece-lined jacket, slipped on her leather gloves and hurried down the stairs to meet him.

She stopped on the landing, feeling her pulse race when he glanced up at her. Gabe looked her over then glanced away. He could have no way of knowing how his subtle gesture stung. Kate felt a pang of sadness for the old sisters' romantic intentions.

"They have our horses ready," he said.

"Then let's be off." She fought to hide her feelings. They crossed the yard to the stable. The sweet smell of hay filled her nose and she recalled the enjoyable hours she'd spent riding across the fields flanking her grandfather's orchards.

Her disappointment vanished as the stable lad walked a chestnut mare out of the stall. He handed

Kate a riding crop and gave her a leg up. She hooked her knee into the sidesaddle and draped the folds of her skirt gracefully across the mare's withers.

Another stableman led a large coal-black gelding from a stall farther down the aisle, tacked up and ready to ride. Gabe took the reins, giving Kate a cursory glance.

"You look right at home." He turned his attention back to his mount.

She was surprised he noticed her. He seemed much more interested in his horse. "My grandfather insisted I learn to ride," she said, amused by his distraction. "I spent hours at the Elmira Riding Club."

"Wish I had," he mumbled.

She pretended not to hear but wondered if he really couldn't ride. The gelding snorted impatiently as Gabe looked it over, checking first the saddle then the bit.

Kate couldn't resist an opportunity for some playful heckling. "Is something wrong with the cinch?"

"No," he said, regarding her across the animal's wide back. He took a deep breath, exhaling with a look of consternation. "All right," he said at last. "Where the devil is the saddle horn?"

Kate barely managed to suppress a smile. "Haven't you ever seen an English saddle before?"

"No," he admitted, swallowing his pride. "I don't have much experience with horses."

"I would never have guessed," she chuckled.

"How did you manage with Teddy Roosevelt's cavalry?"

A smile played at the corners of his mouth as he gripped the ridge of the gelding's neck with his left hand, slid his boot into the stirrup and clumsily swung himself into the saddle.

"Well, now you know where the name Rough Riders comes from," he said, turning his horse.

Kate laughed as they rode from the inn. His teasing broke the earlier tension. Feeling at ease, she took in the surroundings. The scent of pine laced the salty air and the low winter sun played hide-and-seek from behind leafless trees. Fog nestled in low places. A comfortable quiet settled between them. Kate found herself watching Gabe, thinking he wasn't as bad a horseman as he pretended to be. He caught her gaze and smiled with nostalgia.

"I almost forgot how much I enjoyed being out here."

"It is beautiful." Her eyes swept the countryside, returning to Gabe as he spoke again.

"When I was a boy, the Goodhue family allowed my father to hunt on this land. I'd always planned on buying a parcel from them one day, building a place of my own." He paused, reflectively. "I even had the location picked out."

Her interest sharpened as he went on.

"It was always a treat to get away from the old neighborhood."

"Yet you went back," she said. "Why?"

Their eyes met for a moment before he returned his gaze to the trail ahead. "When I got back from the war, my father was ill and needed me. Being home gave me a sense of belonging.''

"I can understand that," she said, recalling her unhappy childhood. "I never knew my father. My mother suffered a breakdown just after I was born. I was raised by my grandfather."

Gabe glanced at her. "Being widowed with an infant must have been hard for your mother."

Kate shook off a moment of hesitation, softly adding, "My father didn't die."

"I see," he said.

"No, you don't." She became defensive. "You can't possibly understand. I've spent my entire life trying to convince my grandfather that not all women are alike."

Her words, rife with double meaning, hung between them. Kate realized she was defending herself not only against her mother but Eve and every other woman whose dependence had made her own ambition harder to attain. Disturbed by the depth of her resentment, she looked away, toying nervously with the reins.

Gabe spoke softly. "I never assumed things came easily for you."

His eyes were unguarded, steady on her face. For the first time in her life she believed she could trust a man. "Were you and your father close?" she asked.

"We were once," he said as if her openness had moved him to talk about himself. "He wanted me to go into business with him. But I thought his ideas were old-fashioned and being full of myself and youthful impatience, I turned him down. I wanted to be richer and better than anyone else.'' His story faded into silence and Kate sensed regret in his voice.

The unexpected exchange left her pensive, as well. They rode on. The sun disappeared and the deepening weather reflected their somber moods. The wind kicked up clouds heavy with mist. Kate felt the chill of an ominous presence between them. Hoping to shake off the tension, she playfully challenged Gabe to a race.

''Last one to reach that stand of trees cooks dinner next week.'' She applied the quirt to the mare's hindquarters and shot forward, leaving him anchored in the sand.

''Come back.'' He called for her to stop.

''Catch me,'' she shouted back at him from over her shoulder. Her horse shared her eagerness. The wind whipped through her hair, snatched the ribbon and carried it away. She galloped on, feeling free and alive for the first time in months and handily beat Gabe to the mist-shrouded pines.

He reined in beside her, laughing. As she pushed her damp hair from her face, their eyes met and held. His laughter died. The heat of his gaze made her heart skip. She looked away first, hoping he would think the cold had brought the sudden blush to her cheeks.

''We'd better get moving,'' he said.

The tightness in his voice made her wonder if he felt the same invisible cords that seemed to bind her heart whenever their eyes met. She turned her horse, telling herself she was being foolish. His insistence came from his concern over the deteriorating weather, not his desire for her.

They had gone only a short distance farther when the sky broke and the squall hit them like a gray wall of rain. Kate tightened her hold on the rain-slick bridle to control her nervous mount and strained to see through the downpour.

"Follow me," Gabe shouted, urging his horse forward.

Kate fought to see through the soaking rain that plastered her hair to her face. She rode blind, plodding through mud. The cold fabric of her drenched skirt clung to her like a second skin that made her shudder.

Gullies swelled into rivers and tidal pools flooded their boundaries. She struggled to stay close, following Gabe's shadowy outline, wondering where he was leading her.

"We'll wait it out here." He reined in suddenly, shouting above the fury of the storm.

She glanced up, the wind slapping her face with icy sheets of rain. Through the dull light she saw the vague and welcome shape of a windmill. Its long wooden sails rotated wildly.

Gabe dismounted. He struggled to keep a firm grip on the reins of the frightened horses. Kate wrestled with her wet skirt, frantic to free her foot from the stirrup before the mare reared up. She jumped from the saddle, her shoes sinking in the mud. Rain pelted them as they hastily tied their horses to the

low-slung branch of a nearby tree and dashed for
the shelter of the windmill.

She lost her footing on a steep embankment and
tripped over the hem of her dress. Gabe caught her,
closing his arm protectively around her waist before
she fell to her knees.

Regaining her balance, she glanced up at the
windmill. The creaking wooden sails spun danger-
ously close to the door. Gabe held her back. He
squinted through the rivulets of water dripping from
his hair and tried to gauge when they could run
safely between the rotating blades.

Bending low, he pulled her with him as he darted
ahead, avoiding the deadly sails by inches. He
yanked the wooded bolt from the door and fought
the gale to hold it open. The forceful wind pushed
her into the darkness. Swirling dust made her
sneeze. She trembled, shaking like a leaf. She
couldn't see and reached for Gabe with her icy hand.
His wet fingers closed reassuringly around hers.

"We'll be safe here." He squeezed her hand
gently, then released her.

"I'll stable the horses in the granary."

He left her alone in the dark, listening to the rum-
ble of the rotating shaft. The measured bump of the
grinding stone resounded like a dull heartbeat in the
dark cavity of the windmill.

Kate folded her arms tightly around herself and
cast a short glance at the wavering shadows. She
swallowed her fear trying not to think of what might
be sharing their refuge. Even inside the cold rain
sought her out through cracks in the roof. Pulling

her collar close around her neck, she thought of the cozy room awaiting them at the inn.

Gabe returned in a splash of watery light that spilled across the floor as he shook the rain from his hair. He touched her shoulder, pushing her gently forward away from the draft. Her wet clothes chaffed her skin and the complaining wind grated on her already frayed nerves. The door flew open, slamming against the wall. Kate gasped, her heart pounding.

"It's all right," Gabe assured her. It took all his strength to push the door closed. Leaning against it, he secured it with the wooden bolt.

Once more he disappeared into the deep shadows. Kate held her breath, listening to the sound of creaking hinges followed by his returning footsteps. She strained to see as he handed her what felt like woolen blankets. In the quick flare of a match, she saw him light a lantern and began to relax within the comforting circle of amber light.

"You've b-b-been here b-b-before." Her chattering teeth clipped her words.

Gabe nodded. Water dripped from his hair over his forehead to the tip of his nose.

Wiping his face, he crossed the room again, this time returning with an armful of kindling. He arranged it in a makeshift fire pit formed by a circle of large stones. Crouching, he struck a match and cupped his hands around the flame. A sulfurous curl of smoke rose to the top of the windmill as he coaxed a fire from dry twigs.

He straightened. She handed him a blanket. Gabe

spread it out on the ground before the fire, sloughed off his wet jacket then sat to remove his sodden boots and socks. Kate speculated on whether or not he'd stop there. As his hands fell to his belt buckle, she looked away, glancing around the windmill as an excuse to avert her eyes.

A low heavy sigh followed the rough sound of wet denim trousers coming off. She bit her lip in anxious confusion, trying to decide what she should do now. She couldn't stand with her back to him all night. But she hesitated to confront what her vivid imagination had already conjured up. She gave him a moment, listening to him shift around on the blanket.

"Are you decent?" she said at last.

"I like to think so." She sensed a smile in his voice and turned, relieved to find his flannel shirt and long johns still intact.

He stretched out, comfortably resting on his elbows, bare feet near the fire. His wet tousled hair glistened in the orange glow.

He returned her steady gaze. "You'll feel better if you take your clothes off."

The idea of stripping down in front of him sent a hot flush to her cheeks. She looked away, wiping her face with her jacket sleeve.

"I'm fine." Her blush must have been visible even in the soft light.

"You won't be if you don't get dry," he said.

She knew he was right. She'd be a fool to risk catching pneumonia for the sake of propriety. She put the blanket down and slowly removed her jacket, shoes and socks. Her defensive posture slipped as the fire warmed her icy feet. The urgency to get out of her wet clothes soon replaced any feelings of modesty she had. She started loosening the buttons of her dress, then caught Gabe staring at her. His gaze dropped to her breasts then veered up to her face. She clutched her wet bodice, pulling it closed, feeling her heart pound beneath her hand.

"Would you mind turning around? I'm not accustomed to disrobing in front of a man."

"I would never have guessed," he said. A sardonic grin curled his lips.

Kate glared at him and he shifted around, duly censured. He sat with his back to her, staring into the darkness, listening to the sound of drenched clothing being peeled away from her damp skin. The smell of wet wool, rain and earth was primal. His playfulness turned to lust as a corkscrew tightness wrenched his gut and he imagined her naked body sculpted in firelight.

The image burned in his brain. He swallowed hard, trying to concentrate on the sound of the rain, the fact that this entire episode was keeping him from the most important project of his life. Any subject but her. It didn't work. The throbbing beat of the grinding stone drummed in his ears like the metronome of his desire.

"I'm decent now." Her voice was an invitation.

As Gabe turned, water dripping from the cap of the windmill splashed on the hot stones with a sputtering hiss.

She sat near the fire, the coarse woolen blanket

covering her like a tent from shoulders to feet. Clearing his throat he reached for a twig and poked carelessly at the flames.

"That's more comfortable, isn't it?" His voice sounded anything but comfortable.

Kate worked hard to avoid eye contact and scooted closer to the fire. The fluttering of wings overhead reminded her they were not alone. She tried to think of something else, but that only drew her attention to Gabe and her awkward condition of near nakedness. What she wouldn't give to be back at the inn, soaking in a hot bath, lounging on that warm bed. Her refusal to share the room with him seemed foolish in light of their current situation. She ventured a quick look his way.

"Do you think the rain will stop soon?"

Gabe shook his head, fighting to keep his eyes off her. He added a piece of wood to the blazing fire, cursing himself, thinking if he hadn't insisted they ride out here, he would have had a full stomach and been curled up on a warm sofa back at the inn. Vera would have provided them with a feast of champagne, Delmonico steaks and angel food wedding cake. The idea seized him. His gaze shifted to Kate, his wayward thoughts turning to images of wedding nights and marriage beds. He swallowed hard.

"I'm afraid we won't be sampling the pleasures of the bridal suite."

Her eyes met his across the flames. The moment held a disquieting beat as if they each knew what the other was thinking. The fire cracked. So did his voice.

"Was it a nice room?"

"Very…" she sighed. Her voice trailed off like the smoke curling up to escape through the cracks in the roof.

He turned his attention back to the fire, thoughtfully poking it with a stick. "You do intrigue me, Kate."

She extended her feet, warming them near the fire, taking a moment to mask her surprise. *Intriguing* was not a word she would have expected him to use when describing her.

"In what way?"

He captured her sober gaze and answered. "For one thing, you ride like a Russian Cossack, yet you can't dance. Why is that?"

Kate nervously ran the tip of her tongue over her lower lip and pushed the wet strands of hair from her forehead. At the moment, not knowing how to dance seemed the least of her problems. She tried to hide her uneasiness by trading barbs in a flippant tone.

"How is it you can hurl yourself from a burning tenement yet shy away from horses?"

Gabe assessed her with an easy smile, but before he could answer, something scurried in front of her. She jumped with a squeal that brought him to his feet and her into his arms. The blanket sailed from her shoulders.

"It's just a mouse," he said.

His hands splayed across her back, the feel of her in his arms provoking the desire he'd fought so long to keep in check.

The harmless rodent disappeared beneath a pile of burlap sacks. Kate felt like a fool. Worse. She wore only her flimsy camisole and damp linen shift. Face flaming, she tried to free herself to reach the blanket, but Gabe tightened his hold, keeping her flush against him.

His forcefulness drew her eyes to his. The way he held her sent a wave of heat from the tips of her bare toes to the crown of her head.

With his thumb he traced the delicate curve of her jaw. "Don't run."

His low, tight voice made her heart beat wildly. He lifted her chin, lowered his lips to hers and captured her mouth. If she had any intention of running, it was lost in the overpowering need he stirred in her. She draped her arms over his shoulders and parted her lips, inviting more.

He deepened the kiss, eager to taste her, tunneling his fingers into her wet hair. His hands dropped from her shoulders, to her waist, to her back, holding her, molding her to him.

The heat of his body, the warmth of his probing tongue made her feel faint. She swayed on her feet like a blade of grass caught in a gale. Slowly he released her lips and drew back to look at her in the dimness of the windmill. His eyes, dark as jet in the firelight, reflected her own longing.

A nervous thrill shot through her as he gathered her close once more, whispering, "I want you," against her parted lips.

She trembled with excitement and fear. He desired her and she longed to know him in all the ways a woman could know a man. Yet she hesitated, fearing he'd find her inexperienced and lacking. She thought of her mother and how one moment of pleasure had caused so much shame. Her body tensed.

Gabe drew a deep hard breath, searching her face. "Kate, do you want me to stop?"

She didn't know what to say. Her mouth dried even as a restless heat pulsed through her.

"Kate?" He framed her face with his hands, waiting, eager for her answer.

She was never so confused. Reason warned her, but her heart wouldn't listen. Holding his gaze, she whispered, "I want you."

He kissed her then, kissed her hard and deep. A kiss that evolved into sensual exploration that shook her to the depths of her soul. All her vows and oaths returned to taunt her only to be shattered by wave after wave of sensation. She tilted her head allowing him access to her neck, the soft curve of her bare shoulder. His lips left a fiery trail along the slender column of her throat.

She'd longed to be with him this way, wrapped in satin and candlelight with whispers of forever. Her eyelids fluttered and for an instant the dinginess of the windmill closed around her, but their surroundings didn't matter. Gabe held her in his arms. Everything centered on him. The moment.

She strained against him, holding him tightly, as clinging to each other, they dropped to their knees. He lowered her gently onto the blanket, soft wet kisses brushing her forehead, her eyebrows, her nose.

Like an exquisite form of torture he drew one finger along the curve of her collarbone, dallying at her lacy neckline, each touch sending a ripple of excitement to her limbs. Sensations exploded within her as she gave herself up to the wonder of him.

The delicate satin ribbon yielded to his touch and she felt the searing heat of his fingers sliding beneath the slender straps of her camisole. His gaze shifted from her face to follow the film of fabric as it fell open, revealing her pink-nippled breasts.

"You're so beautiful." His heated murmuring made her quake as his warm breath flowed over her skin, following his fingertips.

Gently he traced the curve of her shoulder, to waist, to hip, his warm fingers delicate on her moist skin. He filled his palms with the weight of her breasts, his worshiping, caressing hands, drawing her deeper into a lush maze of sensation she hadn't thought possible.

She arched to him, shamelessly begging for delights she'd yet to know. He gave what she desired, dipping his mouth to her breasts, leisurely rolling each rigid nipple between his lips, until the sound of her moaning filled the dark.

When he withdrew from her to shed his clothes, she whimpered a soft protest, opening her eyes in time to see his shirt fall away and the bottom of his union suit slide across his narrow hips. The flickering light danced along the swelling muscles of his dark chest, the planes of his taut abdomen, the rampant evidence of his masculine desire. Her heart pounded harder.

He lay beside her, pulling her close, crushing her against the firm wall of his body. Nothing separated them except the gossamer fabric still clinging to her torso. He kissed each fluttering eyelid, the tip of her nose, distracting her as his skillful fingers slipped beneath her waistband and slid the shift from her heated flesh.

Her body came to life in unimaginable ways. She'd never believed she could feel like this. Never imagined giving herself so completely. As he stroked and caressed her, she watched his face, relishing the pleasure he took in her nakedness. It was pleasure shared. Her tentative fingers traced the shadowy ridges and valleys of his body.

"Kate," he groaned. Her name came as a raspy whisper as his body covered hers fully for the first time.

His arousal throbbed between them, a thick hot weight against her thigh. She sighed as the overwhelming need engulfing her deepened with each bottomless kiss. He caressed her inner thigh, stroking her in unspeakable ways, his warm sure fingers seeking her moist sensual core.

She tensed, startled by the sudden intimacy. The brief moment of modesty fled as his gentle probing lifted her to the heights of never dreamed of ecstasy. She closed her eyes, disbelieving the luscious feel of his exploration. Her body quickened and she let herself fall into the spiraling warm darkness, yearning for things she had no knowledge of.

He turned his attention to her mouth, his quick hot breath meeting hers, mingling as their tongues sought each other. She was sweet, so sweet. The wet heat of her, the eager innocent way she moved beneath him, her soft sighs, conspired against him nearly making him forget the necessity to go slow. Restraining his own overpowering need, he pressed himself against her slick moist body, promising forbidden delights.

The exquisite urge to feel him inside fueled her eagerness. She wanted this. She hadn't realized for how long. He drew his open mouth along the creamy curve of her shoulder as their bodies joined in a quick lightning bolt of pain that made her gasp.

He held fast and still, poised above her as her moist warmth closed around him. He cupped her face in his palms, brushing her lips with his. "I'm sorry," he breathed against her open mouth. "It won't be like this again."

She was afraid to move. Afraid to breathe. He shifted slightly, making her more aware of him within her. At last she relaxed, growing used to the feel of him, clutching him tightly.

He responded with a slow delicious thrust of his buttocks. She felt every inch of him coming inside, then pulling away. She thought she didn't know how to love a man but her body moved instinctively, undulating beneath him as the pace of their lovemaking increased.

He withdrew, returning again, like the tide, filling her, taking her deeper and deeper into that mysterious liquid ocean of pleasure. Each time they came together pushed her closer to the precipice of a cresting wave. She wanted the driving need consuming her to end and she wanted it to last forever. Moaning, she wrapped her legs around him, pressing him, arching to take him deeper.

"I want it to be like this every time."

Her breathless words filled him with something more profound than he'd ever known. He lowered his lips to hers as if to take the sound within himself and return it as a deep feral groan. He craved her like he'd never hungered for anything before and the satisfaction she gave him was more than he deserved. He wanted to please her, to take her soaring as high as she was able to go this first time.

He held back, restraining his own excruciating need. When he thought he couldn't stand it any longer, he felt her body quake. Her breath came in long surrendering moans. She cried out, her voice like the wind closing around them. Only then did he drive into her with the power of a man's urgent need until everything within him collapsed and he lost himself inside her.

In the stillness that followed, his slick body lay on hers, covering her. He felt her racing heart beating with his own and softly kissed her.

His weight came as a welcoming crush against her tingling flesh. Slowly, awareness threatened to pull her from this mysterious new place. Reluctant to think about tomorrow, she closed her eyes, shutting out the world, holding on to the feelings that were fading fast.

He brushed her lips with his as he rolled onto the blanket beside her. He pulled the other blanket over them, kissing her forehead, feeling the heat of her body curled close to his chest. There were secrets he could have told her now, things she deserved to know. But with each icy blast the walls of the old windmill creaked and reality intruded.

She nuzzled close, her breathing taking on the peaceful rhythm of sleep. Gabe listened to the sound of the rain. The howling wind turned his own thoughts inward. He'd never known pleasure like this and it wasn't because of all the celibate months he'd spent steeped in hate. The emotions she stirred in him went far beyond the physical, making what he'd had with Eve seem trifling and childish.

Slowly he drifted off in her arms. He knew he couldn't deny the depth of his feelings for her. Yet, even sleep didn't free him from the nagging sense of doubt.

Chapter Twenty

Lloyd Peyton despised uncertainty and lately it seemed he'd had more than his share. He rested his elbow on the mantel and waited for Hartford, wondering why the older man had insisted on a private breakfast meeting. Sliding the cigar from his lips, he took in the study with its leather chairs and oiled furniture. The plush surroundings reminded him that these temporary annoyances with Eve and her father assured him a comfortable future. He mentally reviewed the events of the past year, contemplating his next move. His conniving had skillfully convinced Hartford it was his genius that drove his fledgling partnership with Gabe. He knew his early boasting had lost its luster and he needed some way to reassure Hartford of his worth. Winning the museum project wasn't enough.

The butler arranged a breakfast tray on the maple credenza. "Coffee, sir?"

Peyton declined, shaking his head. He could already feel acid building in his stomach and he didn't need coffee adding to his discomfort.

Eve had been more high-strung than usual and he suspected her behavior was the reason for this meeting. He didn't think she would take their marital problems to her father, but he couldn't be sure. Exhaling a stream of smoke, he prepared himself for possible questions as Hartford walked in.

He acknowledged Peyton with a slight nod while the butler poured him coffee. "That'll be all," he waved the man off and waited for him to close the double doors.

Peyton tried to appear indifferent as Hartford settled into his chair. Slowly he sipped his coffee. He admired the older man's mastery of timing. His technique reminded Peyton of a spider, allowing his adversaries to dangle from a strand of paranoia until they tied themselves into knots with their own stupidity.

Peyton was smarter than that. Silence had paid off for him in the past and he wasn't going to volunteer information until he knew exactly what they were talking about.

"You wanted to see me?"

Hartford placed his cup aside, delaying his response for a heartbeat longer. "I know this isn't what you want to hear, Lloyd, but the board has rejected your request."

His blunt announcement stunned Peyton and he responded more sharply than he'd intended. "What do you mean?"

"Just what I said. Sponsoring a woman is absurd. There's no point. The board refused."

"You are the board."

"And don't you forget it." Hartford raised his voice.

Peyton tempered his anger. "I don't believe it. This is the twentieth century. For God's sake, Conrad, William Hearst has women reporters working on his newspaper."

Hartford sniggered, unimpressed. "Hearst thrives on sensationalism. We have a reputation to uphold. What's wrong with you, Lloyd? You sound like a suffragist."

Peyton swallowed his anger, realizing he tread on dangerous ground. "What am I supposed to tell the girl?"

"Tell her to find herself a husband and raise a family. You can't encourage this kind of woman."

Peyton couldn't do that. He'd look like a fool. "Conrad, listen to reason."

Hartford put his cup aside. "Enough said about it. There's another matter I want to discuss."

Peyton braced himself. "What's on your mind?"

Hartford flipped open the lid of his mother-of-pearl inlaid humidor and lit a cigar. Shaking the match, he dropped it into a marble ashtray. "Eve has been a little distracted and her mother and I are hoping it's a sign that we might expect a grandchild this year."

Unsure of what Eve might have told them, Peyton carefully chose his words. "You know how women can be at times."

Hartford nodded without shifting his gaze. "Has she been to the doctor?"

Peyton answered, with a guarded smile, "I don't think she has."

"Well, see that she does."

The conversation ended as Hartford pushed his bulky frame out of the chair. "That's all," he said. "I have an appointment." He left the room

Peyton ground his teeth. Who the hell was he to be giving orders? "Son of a bitch." He tossed his cigar into the fire and stormed from the study.

He caught Eve in the vestibule. "Where are you going?"

She tightened her fingers around the doorknob. Her whole body tensed at the harshness in his voice. Her heart pounded and she fought to regain her composure.

"I asked you a question, Eve."

She felt him move behind her and closed her eyes, schooling her features into an expression of aloof indifference. Her veiled hat hid her puffy, red-rimmed eyes, but disguising her growing contempt was becoming more difficult with each passing day.

She turned to face him with a lie. "There's a meeting of the Ladies League this morning."

He studied her, skeptically, but thankfully didn't press her. Her body stiffened as his arm brushed hers when he reached for his coat.

"We'll share the carriage," he said. "I have a meeting uptown."

She managed a weak smile as he opened the door and she stepped into the cold sunlight. He helped her into the carriage, putting on a show for any of the neighbors who might be watching from adjacent windows.

She sat opposite him, eyes downcast. She could feel him watching her, certain he sensed her fear. She risked a quick look at him, caught his smug expression and knew what he was thinking.

Eve prayed she hadn't conceived. But he'd taken her during a fertile time and she suspected that even now she might be carrying their child.

He shifted in his seat, placing his attaché case beside him. "Your parents are concerned and suggested you see a doctor."

She turned to the window to hide her surprise. She hadn't realized anyone had noticed. Obviously her distraction was more evident than she'd thought. For days now she'd been consumed with the idea of leaving, but facing poverty without family or friends frightened her almost as much as the prospect of remaining with Lloyd.

"I could make an appointment," she said. "But there really is no need for it."

"Your parents think there is."

"And you?" She looked at him, searching his eyes for one thread of compassion.

She found none. His expression remained as hard and cold as the granite outcroppings in the park. "I have a right to know if you're carrying my child."

My child, she thought. His typical self-centered attitude confirmed her feelings. Anger and resentment choked her. He might use her to satisfy his lust, but he couldn't get an heir without her. If only she had some way of denying him that. Everything within her recoiled at the idea of harming her innocent unborn child.

Her long, thoughtful silence drew his speculative stare. "The condition isn't something you can hide for very long, Eve."

She met his gray eyes straight on and decided to plant a seed of doubt. "But the details of paternity are easily masked."

His look of loathing pleased her. At least he would always question whether or not the child was his.

A snarl of traffic slowed their progress. "What's holding things up?" Peyton shouted his impatience to the driver, rapping his walking stick against the ceiling of the carriage.

Her moment of defiance dissolved as his temper flared. Eve turned away, peering from the window and saw what had caused the commotion and delay. "A horse has fallen just ahead," she told him.

Peyton slid open the window and shouted at the policemen crowded around the injured animal. "Damn it, just shoot the miserable beast and let's get moving."

Eve gave him a repugnant stare.

"Why are you looking at me that way?" He reached for the door handle. "I'm walking," he snarled.

He shoved the door open and stepped from the stalled carriage. "Take Mrs. Peyton wherever she wants to go," he instructed the driver, slamming the door behind him.

Eve watched him disappear into the crowd walking up Fifth Avenue. Relieved to be left alone, she closed her eyes, drawing a deep breath. Her hands were moist, her whole body trembled. Fearful of the retribution awaiting her that evening, she pressed her back firmly against the leather seat cushion and clamped her hands over her knees to stop her shaking.

It seemed hours had passed before the carriage finally moved forward. Her nerves calmed. Eve debated what to do now. She refused to go home. Knowing her mother might be watching her every move would make her feel like a prisoner. She surrendered to the overpowering need to breathe fresh air and to hear the sound of laughter. Eve slid open the window to speak to the driver.

"Please take me to the park," she said. "I'd like to watch the skaters for a while."

Chapter Twenty-One

Kate drowsily blinked her eyes open as pale threads of daylight wove a pattern through the cracks in the roof. A few cold embers were all that remained of the fire, but the feel of Gabe curled close against her back warmed her against the early morning chill. She smiled, content, feeling his arm slung loosely across her waist.

Slowly, she became aware of aches in places she didn't know could hurt. She felt him stir. He brought his hand to cover her breast, fondling her, causing her body to respond in the same delightful ways she thought she'd only imagined last night.

She was only beginning to understand the wonders of lovemaking yet she reveled in the way his body reacted to her, making her feel desirable and desired for the first time in her life. Her intimate knowledge of him and the delicious things he could do to her increased her pleasure and anticipation of what would follow. More than ready to share that intimacy again, she turned to face him. He smiled, half asleep, as she curled her fingers through the mat of ebony hair covering his chest. She traced the tapering swirl to his navel, lower still. Closing her fingers around him, she held him there.

With a sharp intake of breath, he pulled her close, gently pinning her beneath him. Her awareness heightened and she savored every sensation rippling through her; the coarseness of the woolen blanket against her back, the warmth of his plundering tongue delving deeper into her mouth, the prickle of the surgical stitches in his palm as he closed his hand over her breast. A spiral of heat radiated to the very core of her until the unbearable ache inside made her beg for the extinguishing rush of his throbbing flesh.

She strained to him, impatient for him. This time his entrance was slow and given without pain, his provoking presence like a burst of ecstasy pulsing inside her. She folded him in her arms, her legs holding him to her as she arched to meet each solid thrust of his virile body. His slow deliberate movements made her quiver and ache for more.

She thought she knew what to expect, then with one fluid motion, he shifted their positions, rolling her on top of him. For a startling moment she found herself astride him, not knowing what to do. Her surprise gave way to sighs of delight as he filled his hands with her breasts. A delirious warmth overtook her and she relaxed, letting him guide her, following the rhythms of his body, testing her own as they moved in tandem.

Waves of heat enveloped her. She moaned mindlessly, the world shattered and flowed from her consciousness. Her hair fell across his face as she leaned forward, riding him, holding tightly to his broad shoulders. The sinuous movement of their bodies quickened and her pleasure grew with each rise and fall as she took him deeper.

He gripped her buttocks, slowing her movements until she thought she would die from the exquisite friction. Her hands slid from his shoulders to grip his biceps, holding on as she felt him tense with a final thrust that ended in surrender. Her head hung back, the last waves of pleasure shaking her body with deep fulfilling spasms.

Kate fell forward, melting into his arms, the blissful feelings shimmering within her. She hadn't thought that she could feel like this, that she could remain herself yet be so bound to him.

"I love you," she murmured on a sigh.

She felt his body tense. In the shattering silence that followed, doubt assaulted her, leaving her words an embarrassing echo. She'd spoken her heart and given herself in love. His unmistakable reaction to her words made her wonder if she'd given too much, too freely.

She slipped from his slack embrace onto the blanket. Unable to accept that he didn't return her love and unwilling to once again suffer for the sins of another woman she blurted, "I'm not Eve."

The warmth of their lovemaking ebbed quickly then. Gabe propped himself up on one elbow. He looked at her, his gaze intense. "What do you know about my relationship with Eve?"

His voice held an edge that made her aware of her nakedness. Her vulnerability. She turned away. Before answering, she pushed herself up and nervously fumbled for her camisole. She slipped her arms through the sleeves, then returned his steady stare.

"I know that she broke your engagement," she said. "Should I know more?"

"No."

In the finality of that single word, she understood that hearing him say he loved her meant nothing if he didn't trust her. A feeling of abandonment grew like a dark void in her heart. In spite of his earlier tenderness, the pleasure they'd shared, she realized she would never know what he thought or felt unless he told her and obviously he had no intention of telling her anything. She felt used.

She quickly got to her feet, turning her back to him. She'd behaved foolishly, impulsively. Just as her grandfather had predicted. Shuddering from the icy sting of rejection, she gathered up her clothing, dressing as quickly as she could. She fumbled with buttons and snaps while fighting to hold back tears. She refused to look at Gabe even when she heard him hurrying to dress. She felt his hand on her shoulder and tensed at the brief contact.

"Kate, listen to me."

She closed her eyes, trying to keep the angry tremor from her voice. "It's too late. Your silence has made your feelings clear."

He lifted his hand from her rigid shoulder. "There are things you wouldn't understand."

His voice was soft enough to pretend she didn't hear, but his words cut too deeply to ignore. Kate turned to confront him, her face, her whole body burning with rage and shame.

"How dare you?" She grabbed her jacket and punched her arms through the sleeves, making no effort to hide her tears. "I don't take what I feel or what happened between us lightly."

"Neither do I," he said quickly.

"Don't you?" Her tearful eyes impaled him.

Gabe felt the truth clawing its way up his throat and saw the hurt in her eyes. He wanted to take her in his arms and tell her what she needed to hear, what he wanted to say. God help him he tried, but the words wouldn't come. Admitting he loved her meant offering hope and promises. He couldn't give her either without telling her the truth and the truth had already cost him so much.

Kate backed away from him to widen the distance his silence had already put between them. "You gave me reason to believe you loved me." Her voice trembled.

"Damn it, Kate. I'm sorry."

Raking his fingers through his hair, he half turned, unable to come to grips with the conflicting emotions tearing him apart. Until he found the courage to confess the terrible things he'd done, he had no right to love her. He stood there for a long agonizing minute torn between the opposing forces of fear and desire. Her last hope died in his silence.

She turned from him, eyes filled with tears as she hurried for the door. "I'll send for my things when we get back to the city.'' She flung the words back at him as she pulled open the door.

The slamming sound jolted Gabe from his stupor. He had to stop her. ''Kate, wait,'' he shouted, struggling to get his boots on.

He raced from the windmill in time to see her ride off in the direction of the inn. He'd won the bet. That stark realization chilled his heart with an emptiness that matched the bleak winter landscape.

Chapter Twenty-Two

A few days later at Fairweather Kate felt as if she'd awakened from a long sleep to find her senses. The tang of lemon oil clung to the heavy dark furniture and beeswax candles scented the air. She glanced around the bedroom, becoming aware of her surroundings. With awareness came the hornet sting of reality. She had always believed she was different from her mother, stronger and more levelheaded. Now she realized how naive and deluded she'd been. Given the chance she made the same mistake. How could she have been so blind to think the man she'd fallen in love with was different or that she was immune to heartbreak? She was no better or worse than anyone else who had loved unwisely.

Gabe Murray may have been an unwilling teacher but she had learned a great deal from him, including how easily one can deceive those who care for you. She cast a quick glance at Hattie, who swept into the room, directing two burly men as they hauled Kate's heavy steamer trunk inside.

She felt ashamed for lying to Hattie and Vera, but claiming a shortage of cash had forced her to vacate her rooms at the midtown hotel for women drew fewer questions. If only she could deceive herself and spare her soul the painful truth. The sound of the trunk hitting the rug resounded like a death knell in her heart. She'd managed to get through the past few days by clinging to the hope that Gabe would stop them from collecting her things and send a carriage for her.

Hattie placed a few silver coins into the palm of each man. Kate felt the piercing sword of rejection cleave her heart. She realized with painful certainty that she'd allowed her youthful romanticism to weave fruitless dreams. Life didn't turn according to her wishes no matter how hard she willed it to.

It didn't seem possible that love could bloom and fade so fast. Except for the ache deep inside her, their night of passion might never have happened. She never imagined how much the heart could hurt and for the first time she understood her mother's pain. Pent-up tears filled her eyes as thoughts of her mother flooded her head and heart. Kate now felt she shared a sorrowful bond with her mother that could never be severed. Her new understanding filled her with shame and remorse for allowing the opinions of others to color her impression of the woman she'd never known.

She brushed her fingertips across her collar and searched for the filigree shamrock only to find it missing. An overwhelming feeling of loss and abandonment settled deep within her.

She willed a spark of anger to flare up and cut through the hurt, certain if she could hate Gabe she would be free of the pain. Her hope faded fast as she admitted to herself that he was only partly to blame. She had made a choice and her only regret was that she'd allowed her heart to rule her head.

The soft feel of Hattie's hand on her shoulder drew Kate back. "Are you feeling all right, dear? You look a bit pale."

Kate nodded, reaching deep inside to summon a smile for Hattie's sake. "I'm all right," she said.

Hattie looked doubtful. "You've been cooped up inside for too many days," she said. "A little fresh air will do you good."

"Maybe you're right," Kate agreed halfheartedly. She'd wasted enough time on self-pity. She had to concentrate on the future, pull herself together and get on with her life. She didn't know how she would do it and her mind seemed so muddled she could hardly think about the next few hours, let alone the next several weeks. Or years. Yet she couldn't let one mistake drag her down and destroy her. She was like her mother, but that didn't doom her to the same fate. She vowed never to let gossip or what others thought make her regret loving Gabe. If what they shared proved to be just one night of passion, she would carry the memory of that passion with her forever.

Drawing a deep fortifying breath, she squared her shoulders and held her head high. Her grandfather would be arriving soon, expecting to hear her make a presentation and she intended to go through with her plan. Whatever success life brought her, she would share with her mother's memory. There was still one man in the city of New York willing to help and it was time she called on him again.

"I think I will go for a walk."

Hattie gave her an approving smile before leaving the room. "I'll see you at dinner?"

"Of course," Kate replied. She locked the door behind Hattie, dropped to her knees beside the trunk and rummaged through her clothes, searching for Gabe's journal containing her notes. An unexpected yearning swelled within her as she took the notebook into her hands. Drawing it home to her breasts she traced her fingers across the supple leather binding, recalling the sweetness of their lovemaking. She couldn't have been so wrong. There had to be an explanation for his cruel rejection. Yet, if she allowed herself to believe his uncaring grew out of some reason she'd never know, she'd go mad. She prayed that time would toughen the layer of indifference around her heart and spare her these tormenting memories.

Drawing herself up, she placed the journal gently on the coverlet and turned to the mirrored vanity. She took a long assessing look at herself and wondered how she could appear unchanged when she felt so different. Her youthful innocence and ignorance had been taken from her. She would never again view life and love through a golden haze of idealism. The loss saddened her, but would not stop her.

She dressed carefully, selecting a tweed tailored

skirt and a soft pastel-rose blouse with full sleeves. After coiling her hair neatly at the nape of her neck she stared back at her reflection, pinching color into her drawn pale cheeks. Satisfied with her appearance, she carried the notebook downstairs, donned her coat and hat and left Fairweather.

Bright sunlight stung her eyes as she stepped out into the world. She found it odd that life had gone on in spite of her misery. Spring teased the air with the promise of flowers yet the leafless trees that lined the cold gray concrete better suited her mood. Kate walked to the trolley stop, paid the driver and took a seat near the front. Lost in thought, she barely noticed the passing scenery.

It was late afternoon when she arrived at the now familiar Fifth Avenue office building. She stepped from the streetcar into the lobby and took the elevator to the third-floor reception room. She waited while a young clerk walked to Peyton's office. He returned a moment later and motioned for her to approach.

Peyton stood behind his desk when she entered the room. "Miss Delaney," he said. "How nice to see you." He seemed momentarily flustered by her unexpected arrival.

Kate felt awkward. "I hope I haven't interrupted."

"Not at all." He smiled on cue. "In fact, I've been thinking about you. You never did say where you were staying."

Kate lowered her eyes to hide her hurt. "I'm staying at Fairweather," she softly replied.

"With the Goodhues? How nice." He offered her a chair.

"Thank you." Kate sat, knees pressed together, clutching the notebook in her lap. She went straight to the point.

"My grandfather will be arriving any day now and I was anxious about our plans for the presentation."

Peyton returned a tight smile. In an instant Kate knew what had happened.

"They've refused, haven't they?"

"Well, yes," he faltered, his confidence shaken.

The unexpected setback hit her hard. Her shoulders slumped and she stared blankly ahead, anticipating her grandfather's reaction.

"I'm sorry," Peyton apologized.

Her eyes shot up to his, anger and frustration tightening her voice. "You're sorry?"

She started to get up, then dropped back into the chair, reminding herself that none of this was Peyton's fault. She'd been a fool to think the men on the board would be different from any of the others she'd encountered.

She lowered her eyes ashamed for her outburst. "I should have expected this." She took a moment to regain her composure.

"Tell me truthfully. If I were a man, they would have allowed me to speak, wouldn't they?"

He remained silent.

Kate looked away, filled with helpless anger. She fought back choking tears and took a deep breath. "They must have enjoyed a good laugh." Her voice broke as she went on. "To them my dream will always be just a hobby. I've worked for nothing."

She looked at him. "I'll be going now, Mr. Peyton. Thank you for your help."

She stood to leave. The notebook slipped from her lap, papers scattering as it hit the floor.

Peyton hastily retrieved them. Stooping down he held the notebook, studying it with interest. "This belongs to Gabe." He glanced up, meeting her eyes.

Kate nodded, wondering why that surprised him. "I was going to use his work as the subject of my talk."

She extended her hand to take the book. Peyton straightened, clutching the journal, keeping it from her. "Let's not give up so easily."

Kate didn't understand. "I don't see any point in pursuing this."

"I do." His quick response came without warning. He smiled, thoughtfully tapping his fingers on the supple leather notebook.

"Mr. Peyton, what are you thinking?"

She waited, the abyss of silence filled only by the hollow ticking of the bronze wall clock. When at last he spoke, she found she'd been holding her breath.

"You've done all this work. It seems a shame to abandon the idea. It takes daring people like us to change things and accomplish the unthinkable, don't you agree?"

Kate felt a new stirring of anger. She couldn't have agreed more, but frustration and rejection had worn her down. "Mr. Peyton, I'm tired of trying to change things. The board has said no and I'm not about to force my way into that meeting hall, march up to the podium and lecture a bunch of clay-footed men.''

He smiled at her anger. "Of course you're not. I am.''

"You?''

He returned to his desk where he sat, hands folded, staring back at her from across the rich leather blotter pad. The notebook lay between them, his manicured fingernails skirting one frayed corner.

"It makes perfect sense,'' he told her. "I owe Gabe and we both know he's not a man who sings his own praises. So I'll do it for him,'' he paused to smile. "I'll do it for you.''

Kate studied him, considering his offer and the terms of the agreement she'd made with her grandfather. His proposal did make sense. She had nothing more to lose and everything to gain.

"I suppose you're right.''

"Of course I am. We can't disappoint your grandfather.''

He rose and walked around the desk to where she stood. Placing his hand on her shoulder he led her toward the door. "Rest assured, I have your best interests at heart, Miss Delaney. Just leave everything to me.''

What choice did she have? She placed her future in Peyton's hands and left his office.

Chapter Twenty-Three

Gabe poured a glass of Scotch, toasting his empty victory. He moved around his studio, lingering here and there, going over every detail of the past few weeks. The unbearable silence thundered in his ears and the scent of Kate's perfume filled him with regret and longing. He should have told her everything before allowing himself the pleasure of her body. She had a right to know the harsh reality of the man she thought she loved.

A shimmering object lying on the floor beside his table caught his eye. He reached for it, taking the tiny filigree charm into his hand. Another reminder of Kate. Everything about the room whispered her name, mocking him.

He dropped the pin into his pocket and brought the glass to his lips. "What shall it profit a man?"

He swallowed another mouthful, but the Scotch tasted of regret. Kate had become his reason for living and without her it made no difference if he designed every building in New York City. He would still be miserable and incomplete.

"Damn it."

He flung the glass at his drafting table splattering whiskey and ink across his fresh blueprint, sending pens careening to the floor.

The sound of someone knocking at the door brought him around. Thinking Kate had returned to find she had no key, he shot across the room. He pulled open the door to find himself, instead, face-to-face with Eve. His disappointment turned to shock, momentarily silencing him.

"May I come in?" she asked, her nervous fingers working over a well-used lace handkerchief.

Gabe stepped aside, studying her warily as he closed the door. "What are you doing here?"

Eve gave him a slight smile that lacked her usual poise. "You've become quite a celebrity."

He didn't think she'd come all this way to give him a compliment. Her drawn face and shaky voice defeated her attempt at cheerfulness and further raised his suspicion.

"That's not why you've come."

"No," she replied, shaking her head. Her eyes filled with tears, reflecting puzzlement as if she couldn't quite comprehend the hand fate had dealt. "I need your help," she added softly.

That took him by surprise. Gabe stifled the impulse to be sympathetic, forcing indifference into his voice. "Why me?"

Her eyes held him, her perplexity genuine and

profound. "You're the only one I can turn to." She paused. "The only one I can trust."

"Trust?" His voice hardened as he became more defensive. "You didn't trust me a year ago. Why should I care now?"

Eve looked at him, her eyes wide and wounded. "I'd hoped after a year you might have forgiven me."

He set his jaw, cursing himself for feeling anything but contempt. "Forgiving and forgetting are two different things."

"Please don't turn me away," she said. In her tearful expression he saw Kate's face and felt the pain he'd caused her. His intended harshness backfired. Regret tore at his heart and he took pity on Eve as she broke down sobbing.

"I won't send you away." His voice returned to its normal tone.

He helped her to a chair, sat beside her, holding her in his arms. Almost against his will he tried to comfort her. She rested her head against his shoulder and the fragrance of carnation recalled pleasant memories of the love they once shared. He stroked her hair, felt the soft vulnerability of her in his arms. How many times had he imagined Eve coming to him this way? Now, he was only too aware that the woman he held was not the woman he loved.

She straightened, as if sensing at the same moment that instead of sharing love they now shared pain. She took a deep shuddering breath and wiped her eyes. "I'm leaving Lloyd."

Gabe looked at her in disbelief. "You're doing what?"

"I'm running away," she told him. "I'm nothing but a prisoner, a wealthy captive in my own home. I can't go on like this."

The words spilled from her as quickly as her tears had a moment before. "I've thought about leaving until it's nearly driven me mad. I have a little money of my own, some jewelry I can sell. I can live well enough on that for a while."

Surprise gave way to confusion as he tried to make sense of her motives. "Have you told your parents about this?"

"No," she said.

"Why not?"

"Because they'll talk me out of it. Just as they talked me out of our engagement."

He knew that was true, but he questioned her emotional state, doubting she'd given this idea enough thought. "Do you know what you're doing, Eve?"

She hesitated, twisting the damp handkerchief between her fingers. "I only know I have to get out and they'll never let me go through with a divorce. Father would never tolerate the scandal. But I'm terrified Lloyd will hire Pinkerton's to find me, especially if what I suspect is true." She paused, debating whether or not to say more. "I think I'm carrying his child."

Gabe leaned back in his chair. He found the role of confidant uncomfortable and glanced away, sorting out a disquieting mix of emotions. What Eve did with her life wasn't his business. She'd made her choice when she married Peyton. He shouldn't give a damn about what happened to her, but he did and his caring angered him. It kept him bound to a part of his life he wanted to forget. He couldn't keep the bitterness out of his voice.

"Why do you come to me? If you're unhappy in your marriage, go to your priest."

Her response was swift and filled with resentment. "I can't. Don't you see? He would blame me just as my own father would blame me. Marital problems are always the fault of the wife, aren't they?"

Gabe looked at her and knew she was right. He felt like a fool, only now grasping the complexity of her problem.

"Lloyd doesn't know about the baby, does he?"

Eve lifted her chin, an uncommon look of defiance lighting her eyes. "And he never will. Not if I can help it. No child should be exposed to his kind of brutality."

Her words hit him with the stark realization that if Kate had conceived as a result of their lovemaking, he might never know. The possibility distracted him as he saw himself as no better than Peyton.

"Will you help?" she implored. "I've taken the first step and with it a great risk. But I can't do this alone."

The desperation in her voice brought his wandering thoughts up short. Gabe looked at her staring back at him like a wounded fawn waiting for the merciful bullet that would end her suffering. He couldn't refuse.

"I'm not sure what it is that you're asking of me."

She reacted quickly. "I need help selling my jewelry. I can't risk being followed. I plan to go to South America, Australia, any place where Lloyd can't find me."

Gabe stared at her, stunned by her determination. She had always been so dependent. He couldn't fathom her managing on her own. She must have sensed his doubt for she pressed his hand.

"At least tell me you'll think about it. Please."

The desperate tremor in her voice rent his soul as her need pulled him one way and his concern took him in another. He recalled the steaming jungle heat and menacing flies he'd endured while in Cuba and tried to picture Eve alone in a place even worse. The image was absurd.

"I am thinking about it and I'm concerned. Eve, listen to what you're saying." He planted his hands firmly on her shoulders. "How will you get by in a place like that? Especially in your condition."

"Women have babies every day," she said. Her casual attitude fell before a nervous laugh.

Gabe acknowledged the logic in her argument but couldn't ignore reality. His hands fell from her shoulders as he said, "And many die in the process."

"Don't you think I'm scared." Her voice broke as tears spilled across her pale cheeks. "Nothing could be worse than staying with him." She struggled for composure, her eyes downcast. "He beats me."

Gabe ground his teeth and his hands balled into tight fists as he fought the urge to find Peyton and tear him apart. She wasn't his wife and he had no right interfering. Still, at that moment he would have shoved Peyton beneath the wheels of an oncoming trolley if he had the chance.

Eve lifted her eyes and turned to face him. "I made one mistake. I'm not going to allow fear to ruin what's left of my life."

Gabe understood that. Hadn't his own fear allowed a coil of circumstance to tighten and give Peyton power over him? Reaching into his pocket he absently fingered the tiny gold shamrock and in the amount of time it took for him to decide to help Eve, he knew he had to tell Kate everything about himself, about his past.

"I'll sell your jewelry."

"Thank you." Eve sighed deeply. Her whole body seemed to relax. She pulled a small black velvet pouch from her purse, then handed it to Gabe. "I brought the jewelry with me tonight, hoping you'd agree."

He took the purse from her, hefting it in his hand. "I'll get as much as I can for this. But how will I get word to you when I've sold it?"

"I haven't thought it through that far." Her eyes clouded with confusion, convincing Gabe he'd have to make the decisions for her.

"All right," he said, thinking it over. "Give me a few days. I have a friend who owns a tavern. We can trust him and he knows people who might be able to help. This is his address."

He took a slip of paper from his desk and scribbled the address of the Green Harp Tavern. "Go there a week from tonight. He'll be expecting you. I'll take care of everything else."

She nodded, grateful tears filling her eyes as she closed her trembling fingers around the slip of paper he placed in her hand. "Thank you," she said, slowly drawing herself to her feet.

She placed her arms around Gabe, kissing him tenderly on the cheek. "You've given me another chance and I'll never forget you."

Gabe held her, hoping he wasn't making a mistake that she would regret. As she drew back, he saw hope in her eyes. He started toward the door, but she stopped him, brushing her fingers gently across his sleeve.

"I can show myself out." She managed a weak smile. "I'll be caring for myself from now on, won't I?"

She left him as quietly as she'd arrived.

Chapter Twenty-Four

Kate returned to Fairweather, removed her hat and adjusted her hair. Looking in the mirror above the parlor mantelpiece, she caught Hattie and Vera observing her from the corridor. Their anxious expressions made her wonder what they must think of her behavior over the past few days. She turned to face them as they walked into the parlor.

Vera smiled. "You have a visitor, dear. He's waiting for you in the conservatory."

Kate's first thought was that her grandfather had arrived early to surprise her. Her stomach churned at the idea of seeing him. "My grandfather is here?"

The sisters glanced at each other, then back at her. "No, dear. It isn't your grandfather."

Kate returned a puzzled look. "Who, then?" she asked, thinking she had no other friends in the city.

Hattie hesitated, turning to Vera, who gave Kate a sympathetic smile. "It's Mr. Murray, dear. Do you want to see him?"

"Do I want—?" Kate stopped short. She hadn't

fooled them with her woeful tale of financial distress. She drew a deep breath, embarrassed yet relieved at not having to pretend any longer.

"Am I so transparent?"

The sisters nodded in unison.

Vera spoke up and took Kate's hand in her own. "We're very fond of Mr. Murray, dear. But we will ask him to leave if you wish."

"No," she replied. "That won't be necessary. I'll speak to him."

She left them and headed toward the winter garden. Pausing at the etched glass doors she took a moment to prepare herself. She walked in, by sheer force of will managing to keep her face impassive.

Gabe paced the room nervously raking his fingers through his hair. He turned when he heard the door open. Their gazes collided and held. Kate felt her defenses crumble, replaced by the unexpected desire to have him hold her, touch her, kiss her. Her body's traitorous response came as a stunning blow.

Gabe swallowed. "I have to talk to you."

She forced herself to speak over the wild beating of her heart, summoning feelings of rejection and hurt to get her through.

"I think we've said all there is to say."

Gabe glanced away as if she'd slapped his face. "Please." He motioned toward the wicker chairs.

Kate walked to the chair and sat down, her hands clamped tightly in her lap. He stood before her, his face tense with anxiety. She waited for him to speak until she could wait no longer and finally she broke the silence.

"What is it you want, Gabe?"

His eyes met hers, his gaze deepening until she felt she was drowning in a pond fed by rapid currents. "I love you."

He spoke in a near whisper, his voice soft with the tenderness she'd longed to know in the moments just after they had first made love.

"Why do you tell me this now?" She looked at him, feeling the pain of lost minutes they could never recapture.

"I was afraid before," he admitted.

His candor and unguarded expression took her breath away.

"Afraid of what?" She waited for him to answer.

"There are things you need to know about me. Things I'm ashamed of."

He sat beside her, reaching for her hand. She pulled away not wanting him to feel her trembling.

"Kate." He whispered her name as if a prayer. "I'm sorry. I was afraid of losing you, but I realize now that by holding back I've hurt you deeply. Please, hear me out."

She fought the hot sting of tears welling up in her eyes. "I'm listening."

He reached for her hand again. This time she didn't resist. She felt the moisture on his palm and knew how hard this was for him. He began slowly at first, holding her gaze.

"Lloyd and I were partners, trying to make a name for ourselves. I trusted him with the business matters. I had no reason not to trust him," he said with a slight shrug. "We were like brothers. He had the grand plan all worked out. A vision of greatness, he called it. But I guess things weren't happening fast enough for Lloyd Peyton,'' he said.

His words held a note of regret for knowledge gained too late. Kate listened, apprehension roiling in her stomach as he went on.

"I found out that most of our projects didn't come to us because of our talent. Lloyd has a knack for digging up things about people, information they don't want known.''

"Blackmail?" The word escaped her.

Gabe's eyes shot to hers and she knew it was too late to hide her shock.

"You knew?'' she added.

"I suspected. But I was enjoying the success so I didn't confront him. It's hard even for me to believe now, yet at the time, our reputation was growing and with it all the possibilities for the future. Everything I thought I wanted was there for the taking and for doing nothing more than what I loved doing most.''

Kate interrupted him. "A future that included Eve, I suppose.''

Again he nodded, becoming very quiet.

"Go on,'' she said. He looked at her, then looked away as if he could avoid the terrible vision already forming in her mind.

"Lloyd pushed the wrong man a little too far. He was a Tammany Hall official. We were designing his new town house. The man was having an affair. Lloyd knew about it.'' Gabe shook his head in disbelief, then continued.

"The ironic thing is, so did the man's wife. Of course, none of us knew that at the time. The night we delivered the plans, Lloyd asked me to wait outside, insisting he'd only be a few minutes. He'd gotten the job so I saw no reason not to let him handle things. I didn't realize he intended to squeeze more out of the man.

"It started raining. The front door was unlocked so I walked in to wait in the vestibule. That's when I heard them shouting at each other. Lloyd called out. I burst into the study as the man leveled his pistol on Lloyd. I dove at him, trying to wrench the gun from his hand. The pistol discharged. I was on my knees, bending over the man—blood everywhere. I shouted for Lloyd to get a doctor, but when I looked up, he was gone. The parlor maid stood at the door with an accusing stare...." His words trailed off.

"What happened then?" Kate asked. Her pulse beat wildly at her throat.

Gabe swallowed hard before going on. "Lloyd was the only one who knew the truth and he wasn't about to incriminate himself. He left me to face the jury alone. Everything was stacked against me. I knew I was going to hang. Then, at the last minute Lloyd came forward with a story that he'd been there, that he saw the man draw the pistol on me because I was having the affair with his wife. She apparently thought her husband got what he deserved for his philandering because she corroborated the story. I got off on a charge of self-defense."

Kate felt him watching her, gauging her reaction

and fought to hide her turmoil as she turned to meet his anxious eyes. "That must have caused quite a scandal."

"My father suffered most," Gabe replied softly. "Losing all of his clients, except Hattie and Vera. I believe it killed him and I've never forgiven myself."

"So you left for Cuba no longer caring what happened to you?"

Gabe nodded. "You know the rest. Lloyd Peyton has no scruples, Kate. He will use anyone and take any means necessary to further his own gain. I let my need for revenge drag me down with him. I had to win just once. You offered me the opportunity. I wagered my museum design that I could make you quit. When you left, I won the bet but lost a lot more. There's no victory without you," he paused. "Or happiness," he said. "Can you forgive me?"

She no longer heard him above the hammering of her heart. She stared straight ahead, his every word deepening the labyrinth of her comprehension. Now she understood Peyton's eagerness to get his hands on the notebook. Realizing what she'd done, she pushed herself out of the chair, taking a few steps away from Gabe. She stood with her back to him, absorbing the implications of her act. It didn't seem possible that a few minutes could make such a dreadful difference and she wished she could turn back the clock just one hour to undo what she had done. She could not and every second she delayed telling him the truth made confronting it more painful.

''Why didn't you tell me?'' She turned to him, feeling her body tremble.

''I was afraid you'd hate me.''

''Oh, God.'' She pressed her hand to her lips, tears filling her eyes. ''Gabe, I—'' She tried to speak but couldn't get the words out.

''What is it?'' He went to her, placing firms hands on her shoulders, searching her face.

Kate looked into his eyes, seeing everything she'd hoped for dissolve in the aftermath of her mistake. ''I've done a terrible thing. I'm the one who needs forgiving.''

Confusion clouded his eyes. ''What could you have done that's so awful?'' he asked.

Drawing a deep breath, Kate told him. ''I gave your notebook to Peyton.''

His face turned the color of ash as he stared at her in disbelief. ''Why would you do that?''

Kate shook her head, tears blurring her vision. ''He offered to help.''

''Help?''

She flinched at the anger in his voice.

''He'll help himself to my ideas just as he's helped himself to everything else I've worked for.''

His torment was more than she could bear. ''There must be something I can do.''

Unyielding rage contorted his face. He pushed her aside. ''You've already done enough. Get out of my life. I don't need you. I don't need anyone.''

Gabe stormed from the room, leaving her to agonize over her mistake.

* * *

An hour later Gabe sat opposite Finn at a small table in the Harp's back room. He emptied the jewelry from the velvet pouch, assessing the older man's reaction. He tried to keep his attention focused on Eve instead of the feelings of betrayal eating at him.

"Can you sell it?"

Finn nodded. He fingered the gold link chain of a shimmering diamond pendant. He raised his eyes and met Gabe's steady stare. "Where did you get this?"

Gabe answered simply. "From a lady in need of quick cash."

"And does the lady have a name?" Finn asked, his tone implying he already knew.

"Eve came to see me. She's leaving Lloyd."

Finn's surprise turned to concern. "Does that make you happy?"

Gabe shook his head. "Not really. She shouldn't be the one who's leaving."

"Why is she?" Finn leaned forward, resting his arms on the table, angling a stare at Gabe.

His first instinct was to keep Eve's confidence. But Gabe knew he needed Finn's sympathy if he was going to get his help and decided to tell him. "She's pregnant and doesn't want him to know."

Finn didn't blink. "Is it yours?"

The question caught Gabe off guard and he replied with an edge. "No, it isn't mine."

"Then what brought on this sudden concern for the wife of the man you hate?"

Finn knew him too well. "She needs my help. That's all that matters."

"Aye." Finn's eyes narrowed. "Are you sure you're helping her and not yourself by using her to strike a blow at Peyton?"

Gabe fought a pang of shame. Damn it, he was only human. Sure, he'd seen helping Eve as a way to hurt Peyton. But that was before he'd had time to think. With his moral balance restored he realized whatever pain losing Eve might cause Peyton wouldn't compensate for the theft of his designs.

"I'm the only one she can turn to," he said. "I just wish I knew how best to help her."

Finn leaned back in his chair, folding his arms, mulling it over. "She's going to need people she can trust when her time comes."

"I know," Gabe said. "That's what complicates things. I don't know anyone far enough away from here who I can trust."

"I do," came Finn's reply. "My cousin and her husband tenant farm a small place outside Dublin. Nothing lavish, mind you, but I could wire them. Make arrangements. They owe me a favor for helping his brother out of a—" he paused smiling "—shall we say, a legal entanglement."

Gabe lifted an emerald brooch, thoughtfully running his fingers over the lustrous surface. "I'd feel better knowing she was with your people." He looked at Finn.

At length Finn asked, "Do you still love her?"

"No," Gabe said and meant it. The admission

was painless. Odd after so many months of carrying the weight of resentment.

He put the brooch aside and shifted his attention back to making the necessary arrangements. "The jewelry has to be sold quickly and discreetly."

Finn nodded. "I assumed that's why you came to me. So, you won't be booking first-class passage for the lady."

"No." Gabe shook his head, his own scattered emotions threatening to distract him once again. "We talked about that. Eve understands the hardships she's facing. I did promise I'd find a freighter with a captain she could trust."

"Admirable," Finn said. "But not an easy task." Then glancing at the array of high-quality jewels he added, "Though I suppose for the right price anything can be bought."

Gabe paused, then took his gold pocket watch into his hand and laid it on the table. "Add that to the take. It might bring a good price."

He went on to explain the plans he and Eve had already made. "She'll come here to meet with you next week."

That raised Finn's eyebrows. "She's coming down here alone?"

Gabe nodded. "I wanted to see how serious she was."

"And she agreed?"

"She agreed," Gabe told him.

"Well, then," said Finn. "I guess we have some plans to make."

They worked out details into the early hours of

the morning and when Gabe left at dawn he knew
at least for the next few days his restless hours
would be occupied with thoughts other than those
of Kate.

Chapter Twenty-Five

Kate knew Gabe might never forgive her. But she couldn't live with herself if she didn't try to stop Peyton. She left Fairweather without any explanation and hurried uptown, hoping to catch him as he left his office for the evening.

She entered the lobby, saw the elevator ascend and started toward the stairs. Thinking they might cross paths if he were riding the elevator down, she decided to wait in the lobby. She scanned the area and tried to control her edginess.

Three businessmen stepped from the nearby corridor. Kate smiled at them as they tipped their hats. Their ease and casual conversation contrasted sharply with the turmoil raging inside her. They exited the building. The sound of traffic momentarily flooded the quiet foyer.

Kate wrung her hands and once more fixed her eyes on the bronze elevator. She waited, praying she hadn't missed Peyton. She caught her breath when the sharp metallic ring of the cable signaled the arrival of the car. The door slid open. Lloyd Peyton stepped from the cage.

"Mr. Peyton." She called to him.

He glanced up at the sound of his name and stuffed loose papers back into his leather case. Kate crossed the tile floor, quickly closing the distance between them. Peyton turned as the elevator rose again, leaving them alone.

Kate glanced around the empty lobby and fought off a chill of apprehension. She was being foolish. She'd been here before and there was no reason to fear Peyton now.

"I must talk to you." She forced the words past the tightness in her throat. "I've changed my mind. I want the notebook."

His steely eyes narrowed into a cobralike stare as he seized her by the arm, hurrying her into a shadowy alcove.

"You're hurting me." She cringed, struggling to free herself from his grasp. He held fast with one strong hand while slamming his briefcase onto the polished walnut ledge beneath rows of shiny brass mailboxes.

She tensed, fearing he would strike her. He loosed his grip and pinned her with a cold stare. "What's this? Are you backing out on me?"

She spoke over quick rapid breaths, fighting to keep from panicking. "It's just that I—" Her courage fled, her sentence remained unfinished as he moved closer and cornered her against the cold marble wall.

Kate trembled. His hot breath brushed her cheek.

She blinked her eyes, unable to move enough to turn away and avoid his leering face. His lips curled in a menacing way.

"Why would I return the notebook? It gives me everything I want. The woman Gabe loves is my wife and, now, I also possess his genius. No, Miss Delaney. The presentation will take place and you're going to be there to help me."

Kate squirmed, desperate to put some breathing space between them, wondering what he expected of her.

"Are you afraid?" he asked.

"No." She forced defiance into her voice, but failed to escape the pressing heat of his body as he inched closer. She couldn't take even a shallow breath without feeling the pressure of his chest.

"You should be afraid, Miss Delaney. New York is a dangerous city. Things can happen to a woman alone. What would become of you if you met with an unfortunate accident? Who would know to look for you? Not Gabe. Surely you've told him about the notebook. Otherwise you wouldn't be here pleading with me now." He laughed. "Gabe won't miss you. I know him. He'll crawl beneath some rock to lick his wounds."

Beads of perspiration dotted her brow, but she forced herself to look squarely at him. "There's my grandfather," she reminded him. "And the Goodhues."

Peyton laughed rudely. "Your grandfather will turn his back on you when the sordid details of your disappearance surface. So will Hattie and Vera. You're all alone, Miss Delaney.''

She could scarcely breathe. The sound of footsteps echoed through the lobby. Kate saw her chance. She opened her mouth to cry out, but Peyton reacted fast. He pressed his mouth hard against hers. His invading tongue gagged her. She tried to slap him away. He caught her wrist and wrestled her arm down. A muffled cry escaped her as he twisted her arm behind her back. He pressed himself against her, making them appear lovers to the passing stranger. The door closed. They were alone once more.

Peyton backed off. Kate wiped her mouth with the back of her hand. ''You vile pig. How can you think I'd do anything to help you?''

The demonic gleam in his eyes made her blood ice in her veins. ''You don't have to do anything. I've taken care of all the details. Every man attending the program knows you're Gabe Murray's apprentice and your quiet presence will validate my claim to his ideas.''

Her chin inched higher. ''I won't go.''

''Yes, you will,'' he said. ''Your grandfather is expecting you to be there. I don't know what hold he has on you, but I sense it's much more than financing your education.'' He looked her up and down. ''And I don't think he'd like hearing Gabe has been tutoring you in more than design. You'll be there or I swear I'll drag you through the mud.''

She fought for control. ''I'll tell my grandfather the truth. You can't blackmail me.''

Peyton smirked. ''Go on. Tell him. I'm sure he'd

be interested in hearing what's been going on be-
tween you and Gabe. If you were my granddaughter,
I'd kill Gabe for the liberties he's taken. Tell him.
See if I'm right.''

The impossibility of her situation closed around
her. Kate shut her eyes. There was nothing she could
do. Peyton stepped aside so she could pass. ''Now
go back to Fairweather and don't ever come here
again.''

Chapter Twenty-Six

Peyton's threat haunted Kate through the long stretch of aimless hours that turned into a week of tortured inaction. She moved through each day as if in a trance, immobilized by shock and overpowering fear. Her preoccupation became so consuming that this morning the simple task of dressing to meet her grandfather at the station had drained her.

Reality blurred against the backdrop of her muddled brain. Yet, her confusion had somehow added perception and clarity to her thinking. She saw how her grandfather's unreasonable terms and her own ambition had blinded her against Peyton's treachery.

Kate felt sick and ashamed, but she couldn't hold herself completely at fault for the cruel entanglement of fate. If Gabe had been honest with her from the start, she would never have turned to Lloyd Peyton for help. She drew little comfort from that fact as she glanced over the brochure announcing the afternoon's presentation.

"Designs for the Twentieth Century." She read

the words, running her fingers across the fine gold calligraphy. Peyton had printed and mailed a copy of the brochure to every prominent architect in New York City, including Gabe. The absence of Gabe's name anywhere on the program increased her dread.

She wanted to stop the presentation but knew she could no more accomplish that than she could halt the train now barreling through the tunnel. It arrived on schedule and with it her grandfather.

Kate braced herself, closing her eyes, feeling as though some invisible clock had struck, marking off an irrecoverable hour in her life. When she opened her eyes, all the jarring activity of the crowded terminal vanished as she focused on the face of her grandfather.

He stepped from the Pullman, wearing a dark business suit and carrying a black umbrella. His style and youthful stride made him look more like an English barrister than an aging upstate apple grower. Kate fought to hide her fatigue behind a painted smile, keeping her gaze fixed on his face.

Hard determination set his jaw and the deep lines etched around his light eyes and mouth were fixed in the same unyielding expression she'd squared off against so many times. Today, she had no stomach for confrontation. Her midnight soul-searching had left her listless and sapped of energy.

''Kathryn,'' he said as he drew near.

In his fleeting smile she caught a glimpse of the kinder man he must have been before life had hardened his heart.

She straightened her back and leaned up to kiss his cheek. "I'm glad you've come."

"I wouldn't have missed it," he replied. "It's exciting to have my granddaughter present a paper to such a prestigious group of architects. I'm proud of the progress you've made."

Her heart sank. She had to tell him the truth and it was better done now while they were alone. "Actually, I won't be the one giving the presentation."

"You won't?" he asked.

His disappointment left her undaunted. Losing the praise she'd longed for all her life no longer mattered. Strange, only a few weeks ago she would have never admitted failure. Compared to what she'd faced and still had to endure knowing his prediction had come true seemed unimportant. She had moved beyond the bonds of her ambition and the foolish agreement she and her grandfather had made. Somehow knowing that made facing the truth less painful.

"They won't allow me to present the paper." She left it at that, ready to accept his response.

His expression softened. "Well," he said after a moment. "You're still invited, aren't you?"

She hadn't expected that. "Of course," she said. "And you're my guest."

"It sounds like you've impressed them. I believe you may yet succeed and prove me wrong."

At that moment she wanted nothing more than to confide in him. Her fear of Peyton kept her silent. "I suppose you're right," she said softly. "You always are."

He didn't dispute that, but offered her his arm. "Hadn't we better go?"

Kate managed a weak smile and linking arms, they climbed the stairs to the upper promenade. She couldn't hide her distraction. Her grandfather noticed. "You're very quiet. Is anything wrong?"

Kate shook her head and held more tightly to his arm. "Just a slight nervous headache. I'm sorry you were upset by that newspaper article," she added to change the subject.

He smiled thoughtfully and patted her hand. "I should have known better. No mere man will sway you from your course."

Kate swallowed a pang of shame and said, "We'd better go."

They left the terminal. Kate caught the wet gleam of dark carriages moving along the avenue like a funeral procession. Her grandfather hailed a coach and held the door as she climbed in. After what seemed like a long ride in tense silence they arrived at the theater.

She walked beside him into the plush auditorium, feeling as if she were watching the proceedings from a vantage point outside herself. A thick haze of cigar smoke filled the vestibule. Her grandfather looked around, taking in the crowd of prominent men who assembled to hear Peyton. Men like Stanford White and Charles McKim, whose vision shaped Columbia University and Madison Square Garden.

"Impressive," he said. "You should be proud to be included here."

Kate felt anything but proud. She prayed that

Gabe would come forward and speak out against Peyton before it was too late. She knew the circumstances of his past made his accusations useless. She alone could act. Yet fear paralyzed her.

"Shall we find our seats?" Her grandfather's voice drew her back.

She felt him watching her, assessing her behavior as they made their way to the front of the theater. The uncomfortable silence stretched into an uneasy void. She didn't know what to do. Her desire to ask for his help became an intense pressure pushing against her rib cage. She noticed Lloyd Peyton talking with Conrad Hartford and shuddered.

They stood at the front of the auditorium, the carbide footlamps illuminating their faces. She kept her eyes on Peyton, her stomach constricted into knots. His predatory posture and the possessive way he held Gabe's notebook made her blood surge with a sense of urgency. She had to stop him.

Her grandfather leaned toward her. "Which of them is your instructor? I'm eager to meet him."

His question renewed the sharp pain in her heart and she answered softly. "I'm afraid he can't be here today."

Just then Peyton glanced up and caught her gaze. He pressed the notebook to his chest as if he held the Holy Grail. Every fiber of her moral tissue demanded she stop him. But how?

She found herself poised at this crisis of her life, fighting for an answer unassisted. She closed her eyes and prayed for guidance. Nervously, she smoothed the lapel of her navy pin-striped suit. The absence of her good-luck charm heightened her feeling of abandonment.

She alone held the key and as she looked at Lloyd Peyton once more, she knew what she must do. She dredged up every ounce of her courage she could muster, hoping it would be enough. He would not get away with this. No matter what the outcome, she stood ready to take the risk. She turned to her grandfather before fear could change her mind and somehow managed a smile.

"Would you excuse me?"

He stood, allowing her to move from the row of velvet chairs. Kate walked toward Hartford and Peyton, feeling as if she walked to a gallows. They ended their conversation and looked at her as she approached. She smiled, remembering the older man from the New Year's ball.

"Mr. Hartford, Mr. Peyton," she said. "Could I have a moment?"

"Of course," Peyton replied. He made a brief introduction. "Conrad Hartford, Kate Delaney. Gabe Murray's apprentice," he was sure to add.

"Charmed." The older man looked her up and down, his lecherous assessment making her skin crawl.

Kate forced herself to go on, moisture trickling between her breasts. She struggled to keep her voice from sounding tight and high pitched with nerves. "My grandfather came all the way from Elmira to be here today." She paused motioning to where he sat.

Hartford turned a curious glance in the direction

she pointed. "Elmira?" he said, studying the older man. "Tell me, Miss Delaney, what does a man of his bearing do for entertainment in a place like Elmira?"

He cackled arrogantly. Peyton joined in. The amusement they took in belittling her home infuriated her and made what she was about to do easier.

She squared her shoulders and lifted her chin, informing them, "His vast acreage produces some of the finest apples in all New York State. And for added entertainment, he manages his warehouse property here on the waterfront."

She had Hartford's attention. "Really. That area is marked for some development in the near future."

Kate seized her opportunity. "Well, maybe he would be interested in discussing the sale of some of that land after the presentation," she said, smiling. "As I was saying, he came all the way from Elmira for this program and I was hoping you might reconsider and allow me to at least introduce Mr. Peyton."

Peyton's warning glare made her stomach tight. She turned her attention back to Hartford. "It would mean a lot to my grandfather."

Hartford glanced at her grandfather, obviously calculating what he stood to gain. "I think we could arrange that."

Kate smiled, realizing how easy it was to play their game. "I'm honored," she said, shifting her gaze back to Lloyd Peyton.

He didn't seem at all pleased with the idea. His disapproval heightened her anxiety.

"I'll go and tell my grandfather," she said and quickly moved away.

Panic tightened her chest and she felt the blood drain from her face as she returned to her seat. She realized she didn't know what she would do next.

Her grandfather squeezed her hand. "Kathryn, what is it?"

"They've agreed to let me introduce Mr. Peyton," she said.

She took in every nuance of his expression, as she spoke, setting in her mind the pride she saw in his eyes. She heard someone behind her and turned as Hartford extended his hand to her grandfather.

"I'm Conrad Hartford." He smiled. "You should be very proud of your granddaughter."

The older man completed the handshake. "Indeed, I am."

Kate forced herself to smile though Hartford's patronizing tone made her sick. He gave her another quick once-over then shifted his attention back to her grandfather.

"I look forward to talking with you this afternoon."

He motioned for Kate to follow and moved toward the stage. She remained standing beside her grandfather suddenly unable to move.

He prodded. "Hurry along. Don't keep him waiting."

She glanced at him then moved swiftly down the aisle, fighting the inertia of fear. Peyton stopped her, grabbing hold of her arm. "Quite a coup," he said in a hushed voice. "You realize this could mean a place in the firm for you. If you support me, there will be no stopping us.''

Kate met his eyes squarely. He offered her the world, but the price of admission was more than she was willing to pay. Her loathing fused her courage. ''Mr. Hartford is waiting,'' was all she said.

She willed her feet to move toward the stage, knowing every step brought her closer to an irreversible turning point in her life. She stood slightly behind Hartford, staring at Peyton, her mind racing with a thousand disjointed thoughts. Yet knowing what she risked, she remained resolute.

The room fell silent, the last buzz of conversation fading as Hartford took his place at the podium. He removed his spectacles from his vest pocket and placed them at the bridge of his bulbous nose.

''Gentlemen,'' he began, his voice booming and confident. ''My firm is delighted to sponsor this presentation today. And, to prove that we are modern-thinking men who will set the standard for architecture in the Twentieth Century, I'm pleased to invite a lovely lady to introduce our speaker.''

His unexpected remark ignited the hum of conversation. Kate looked over the audience, swallowing hard as he relinquished his place at center stage. Except for the racing of her heart, everything else fell into a slow motion.

''Thank you, Mr. Hartford.'' She pushed the words out, but her voice, weak and shaky, was swallowed by the drone of conversation. Hartford left her alone onstage and took the seat beside her grandfather.

Her mouth went dry as she looked out across the room and fumbled for something to say. She took a deep breath, finding herself temporarily at a loss for words. A ripple of laughter came from the back rows. For the first time in her life Kate didn't know how to proceed and the pride she saw in her grandfather's face made her task that much harder.

"Gentlemen," she began. Her voice broke, forcing her to start again.

A nervous flush rose to her cheeks. She fought to get their attention, nearly shouting. "Distinguished gentlemen."

Quiet came over the room at last. Kate paused until it seemed every one awaited her next words before she began. "I'm honored to be here and it gives me great pleasure to speak on behalf of one of the most forward-looking talents of our age. A genius whose work will, indeed, set the standard for architecture in the Twentieth Century."

Peyton sat tall in his chair like a puffed-up gamecock. His vile treachery nauseated her and she had to grip the edge of the podium to keep from shaking. Her fear and animosity deepened with every breath she drew. She stared at him until the space between them narrowed, until she felt as if they stood alone, face-to-face, locked in mortal enmity.

Her heart pounding like a sledgehammer, she went on to say, "It is his dedication to our work that makes him stand out among us. The beauty of his work and his love of the pure undecorated line is what brings us here today. Yet I doubt that most of you understand the full measure of the man we've

gathered to honor. For that reason I'm going to ask
Mr. Lloyd Peyton to join me on the stage now.''

He rose without a moment of hesitation, like an
actor eager to take the stage. He whispered to her,
''You've done splendidly.''

Kate used her outrage to overcome her dread. ''I
asked Mr. Peyton to join me here because he is the
man I am eager and proud to introduce this morning.
A man whose selfless nature brings him before us
to praise the work of his former partner, Gabriel
Murray.''

She stepped back and caught Hartford glaring as
a wave of shock spread through the room. Visibly
shaken, Peyton's face flushed red with anger. He
moved to the podium, jaw clenched, eyeing her with
evil malice. ''You'll regret this,'' he growled.

Kate trembled and took another step back,
amazed that her legs still supported her. She felt the
depth of his hate and knew she had made a lifelong
enemy.

Chapter Twenty-Seven

The rain left puddles and mist-laced patches along the waterfront where Gabe nervously awaited Eve. He extended his hands to warm them over a trash barrel fire. Unshaven and lacking sleep, he thought he must look like a sailor back from months at sea.

Rubbing his stubbled jaw, he glanced around, unable to shake the feeling he was being watched. He wondered if Eve would show up or if second thoughts had changed her mind when the clipped sound of urgent footsteps brought his head around. A figure emerged from the shadows, heavily cloaked and carrying a valise.

She cast a furtive glance his way, then hesitated, drawing back into the alley. Gabe realized she didn't recognize him and stepped toward the fire, waving her on, afraid to risk calling out her name.

She moved forward cautiously at first, her pace quickening when she saw his face. Gabe was struck by the circumstance that had brought them to this point. It seemed ironic that he should be assisting

Eve to gain an uncertain future in order to escape the life that had promised her so much. He took her hand and drew her aside, away from the firelight and the possible scrutiny from unseen eyes.

"Were you followed?"

Eve shook her head. "I don't think so," she replied, a little breathless.

He felt her trembling and squeezed her hand. Her apprehension and uncertainty momentarily took his mind off his own life that was crumbling around him. The distraction came as a blessing and he kept his thoughts on her, his eyes fixed on her face. She looked afraid and unsure.

"Eve, if you've changed your mind, I'll understand. You don't have to do this."

Her gaze shifted toward the *Longview* moored a few yards away, its tall mast silhouetted against the slate-gray sky. "I haven't changed my mind," she said.

Gabe admired her courage and wanted to make things as easy for her as he possibly could. With time short he had details to explain. "Listen carefully," he said. "From now on you're Clair McAvoy, the widow of a Pennsylvania coal miner. You'll be met in Dublin by your brother-in-law, Evan McAvoy. You have no family here so he and his wife, Eileen, are taking you in. You can use your imagination to fill in the rest of your past any way you like."

"Something to occupy my time on the voyage," she said with a trace of nervous laughter.

"Something like that." Gabe smiled. His heart went out to her. "Do you have the money?"

Eve nodded, looking surprised. "I didn't expect so much."

He gave her hand a reassuring squeeze. "I told you we could count on Finn."

She smiled then, a brief smile that came and went like a fleeting ray of sunlight. "I never doubted I could count on you, Gabe."

Her trust in him moved Gabe, putting a lump in his throat, making him wish he could place that kind of faith in another human being.

"I wish you well, Eve."

"In spite of everything?"

He nodded slowly, taken by the forgiving nature of love. "In spite of everything," he told her.

"Then I have one more favor to ask."

Reaching into her cloak, she removed an envelope, placed it into his hand. "Would you post this after I've sailed? It's a note letting my parents know I'm safe."

He slipped the envelope into his pocket, wondering what the contents would mean to Peyton.

She leaned toward him, kissed his cheek, then drew back taking one long last look at him as tears filled her eyes. Gabe wrapped her in an embrace, drawing her close. He thought how quietly the significant events of life unfolded.

He held her until the ship's bell followed the sound of sails unfurling in the wind, telling him it was time to leave.

"I'll miss you." He brushed her forehead with a goodbye kiss.

Eve pressed her lips together and struggled to hold back tears. "We'll meet again." She squeezed his hand tightly.

Gabe knew they might not. They were on separate paths, each facing uncertain days. Yet unsure as her future seemed, she at least had a plan. He envied her that.

Offering her his arm, he escorted her up the gangway. Eve paused when they reached the midpoint of the narrow ramp. She turned to him. "I'd like to go the rest of the way myself," she said.

Gabe stood back, watching her board the ship alone, glancing at him once to wave goodbye. "Bon voyage," he whispered, turning the final page on a part of his life.

She disappeared from his sight, leaving an odd, sick feeling in the pit of his stomach. Now that she was safe and on her way, he had nothing to fill the emptiness or distract him from Kate's duplicity. He lingered at the waterfront, wondering what turn his life would take now. At last he left, fearing he might be seen.

He wandered aimlessly down sidestreets, trying to find his center, some steadying sense of purpose to cling to and get him through the empty days and endless nights.

He found himself at the Harp, pushed open the door and walked past the few disinterested patrons seated at tables. Gabe pulled a stool up to the bar to sit opposite Finn, who poured him a much needed Scotch.

"Thanks," he said, swallowing a mouthful. The Scotch warmed his body, but his heart felt as empty as a newly dug grave.

Finn placed the bottle back on the bar. "Did everything go as planned?"

Gabe glanced at him. "She's on her way."

Finn poured himself a shot and raised the glass. "Luck to her."

They toasted Eve, Gabe adding, "I think she'll be all right."

"Then why so glum?"

He looked at Finn and tried to sort out his emotions. He felt good about helping Eve, but it wasn't enough. Days of simmering frustration and anger boiled over. Knocking back the rest of his drink, he pulled the crumpled brochure from his pocket and slapped it on the bar for Finn to read.

"What's this?" Finn took it into his hand.

Gabe didn't hold back his hostility. "It's an invitation, damn it. Kate gave Lloyd the notebook with all of my ideas. That bastard had the gall to invite me to be there while he claims them as his own."

Anger sparked Finn's eyes. He shoved the brochure back at Gabe. "Well I hope you're not blaming her. You didn't give the lass much choice."

Gabe felt his temper heat. "I might have known you'd defend her."

Finn snarled back, "Someone has to, you blind fool. You've all used her—you, Peyton, even her own grandfather. For Pete's sake, lad, can't you see? You've just helped one woman escape a loveless marriage and condemned another to the very same fate.''

Gabe's eyes snapped to Finn's. "What are you getting at?"

Finn leaned his weight against the bar, lowering his face to within inches of Gabe's. He spoke in a tight voice, thready with emotion. "She made a bargain with her grandfather. She had one chance to succeed as your apprentice or go home with him to marry whoever he selects."

Gabe couldn't believe it. "You're not serious. Why would she do that?"

Finn replied sharply. "You tell me. You're the gambler."

Gabe stared blankly ahead, realizing the part he'd played in causing the disastrous events that were now unfolding. Kate was as blameless as Eve. All of her actions had been brought on by the men in her life. He envisioned his own life without her and the emptiness was more than he could stand. Scowling, he felt his pulse elevate. Lloyd Peyton alone deserved his rancor and it was time the bastard paid for his sins.

"I have to stop him." Gabe shoved back the stool.

He stormed from the Harp, out onto the street, searching for a carriage. He looked like a vagrant and none would stop. Running alongside the curb, he waved his arms in a frantic attempt to halt an approaching coach. The driver took one look at him and cracked his irate whip, knocking Gabe aside. He hurled himself out of danger, dodged the crushing wheels by inches and landed in a puddle.

"Son of a bitch," Gabe cursed, scrambling to his feet.

He sprinted to the intersection in time to catch a trolley. Completely winded, he pulled himself up the few steps to the platform, then backed away from the flood of passengers pushing out of the crowded car.

His temples throbbed. Waiting to board, Gabe pressed the bridge of his nose to fight the suffocating panic and stabbing urgency. As the last person stepped from the car, he bounded up the steps, searching his pocket for the fare. He came up short. The driver eyed him suspiciously and pointed toward the exit.

"We only take paying passengers."

Gabe pounded his fist against the side panel, unable to curb his frustration. He turned to leave when someone tugged at the hem of his jacket. He twisted around to find an elderly woman offering him change. He hesitated to take the money.

"Go on," she insisted. "I know what it's like to be down on your luck."

"Thank you." Feeling like a fool, Gabe paid the fare. He stepped back into the crowded car, catching wary glances from other passengers who seemed reluctant to make eye contact.

Standing in the aisle he clutched the handhold, keeping his eyes on the street, tension rising to a pulverizing ache at the base of his skull. The trolley moved in fits and starts, stopping again and again to let off passengers then take on more. The frustrating snail's pace was infuriating. His heart pounded, ticking off precious minutes as they sat stalled in traffic. He felt trapped, having no control. Gabe knew he'd never make it.

"Excuse me." Raising his voice, he pushed his way through the crowd to the front of the car as the trolley rolled to yet another stop. Gabe bolted from the door, stumbling out onto the curb. He ran up the avenue sidestepping crowds, his heart hammering so he thought it would explode.

At last he reached the theater and bound up the steps. He burst headlong into the auditorium, adrenaline pumping vengeance through his bloodstream.

Every head turned and all eyes swung his direction. One man at the rear of the hall studied him with a puzzled look, then rose to his feet and began applauding. Another joined in. Then another until Gabe found himself confronted by a standing ovation. He stared back at them, numb with amazement, as the surge of well-wishers moved toward him, surrounding him, patting him on the back with congratulations.

Confused, he searched the room for Kate. He saw Peyton fling the notebook at her feet and storm from the stage to exit through the side door. Kate stooped to pick up the book before a flustered elderly man ushered her from the theater.

In a flash of understanding, Gabe realized she'd sacrificed herself for him. He tried to break free and reach her, but the crowd kept him prisoner. His pulse raced as he absently responded to congratulations, nodding back at men, knowing if he didn't get away soon he never would. He shook as many hands as he could, managing at last to free himself. Without making excuses he ran up the aisle, sprinted across the stage and out the side door. Gabe pushed his way through the narrow alley, past trash bins and overflowing crates in a desperate race to catch up with Kate before he lost her forever.

The sound of approaching footsteps behind him made him turn. Peyton walked toward him, his face contorted in a look of pure loathing. "You think you've won, don't you, Gabey? Well, think again. You'll never have Eve."

Gabe ignored him, resisting the pleasure of telling him that Eve was gone. He turned to walk away. Peyton raised his voice.

"Go on, run after her. Your little trollop left with the old man."

Gabe spun around, landing a blow that broke Peyton's nose and sent him staggering back, toppling crates as he hit the wet cobblestones.

"That's for Eve. And my father." Gabe cringed, rubbing his sore hand. The satisfaction of finally flattening the bastard made up for the pain.

He grabbed Peyton by the collar, ready to hit him a second time, then let him go. Eve's letter would finish him soon enough. Turning his back he ran from the alley and reached the street just as Kate and her grandfather climbed into the carriage and drove off.

Chapter Twenty-Eight

Kate hurried her grandfather toward the study, past the stunned-looking Goodhue sisters. She closed the door behind them. The deepening flush of his face told her he was about to explode.

"What's going on?" His voice rose to a rumbling pitch that she was certain had the curious sisters poised at the door. "Mr. Peyton was furious. What have you done?"

Kate kept quiet, letting him rant, giving him time to blow off the head of steam he'd built up on their ride back from the theater. She felt strangely calm, at ease with herself, as if by defeating Lloyd Peyton she had somehow moved to a place beyond punishment where nothing could hurt her. She realized that while her grandfather's opinion mattered, it wouldn't change her feelings or make her regret what she'd done. Her placidity contrasted sharply with his mounting agitation.

He turned to her, waiting for an answer, looking hot under his high starched collar. Kate drew a deep breath ready to explain. "Sit down, Grandfather. Please."

She proceeded to tell him everything that had happened, editing only the intimate details of her relationship with Gabe. She gave him a moment to absorb what she'd said. His expression moved by degrees from one of anger and confusion to shock and disbelief.

"So, now you know," she said, bracing herself for the worst. "Go on, Grandfather, say it. I've failed both professionally and personally. You'll feel much better."

He sat for a long time staring at some undefined point beyond her. Kate remained quiet, waiting for his reprisal. His prolonged silence concerned her and she worried he might be suffering some kind of seizure brought on by shock.

"Grandfather?" she asked, leaning close to make sure he was breathing.

The sound of her voice shook him from his stupor. He slowly raised his eyes to hers. "You haven't failed."

Kate straightened, eyeing him suspiciously, more certain than ever that what she'd done had caused something in his mind to snap. She was about to send for a doctor when he pushed himself out of the chair, stood before her and took her hands.

"I'm proud of you," he said to her amazement. "What you did took courage and strength of character. I believe you'll always make the right choice, Kathryn, no matter how difficult."

She blinked her eyes in stunned silence, not

knowing what to say. They'd spent so many years
arguing, his compliment caught her unprepared and
left her speechless. The moment would have been
perfect if he'd left it at that, but he didn't.

"You've convinced me that you're not at all like
your mother."

Kate would not accept praise if it meant denounc-
ing her mother. She pulled her hand away. "Yes, I
am," she retorted, her tone defensive. "And I'm not
ashamed of that. I'll never be ashamed of having a
heart that can love and ache to be loved in return."

His expression softened and his eyes took on a
look of remorse she couldn't recall having ever seen
in them before. "Don't," he said. "Don't ever be
ashamed of your humanity. I was wrong to let you
grow up believing I despised your mother. I loved
her. She was a beautiful, spirited person and I never
should have let them take her from us."

"Why did you?" Kate confronted him at last.

"I was angry, embarrassed." He shook his head,
dissatisfied with his own answer. "Kathryn, I let
other people convince me it was the right thing to
do. I turned my back on her and in the end, that
destroyed her. My stupidity came between us. I'm
sorry for that."

Choking tears tightened her throat as she wished
with all her heart that her mother had lived to hear
him speak those words. He looked so contrite, his
regret so deep, she couldn't stand it.

"I'm sorry, too," she said, wrapping her arms
around him.

He embraced her, drawing her home to his heart,

making her feel she belonged for the first time in her life. "Can you ever forgive me?" he said, his voice tight with emotion.

Kate nodded, her cheek brushing his chest, unable to speak above the lump in her throat. When he released her, a trace of tears lingered in his eyes. Embarrassed by his emotions, he cleared his throat and pulled a large white linen handkerchief from his breast pocket. He offered it to Kate.

"Thank you." She dabbed at her eyes.

He straightened his tie and fought for composure. "If we hurry we can still catch the afternoon train," he said, once more in control.

Kate felt panic rising within her, tying her stomach into knots. He couldn't have stunned her more if he'd slapped her face. "I can't believe that after what you've said you would hold me to that stupid agreement."

He stared back at her, confused, deep wrinkles creasing his brow. "I don't expect that," he said. "But what's here for you now? Surely what you did today has ruined your chances?"

"Not all," she said, her thoughts turning to Gabe. "There's one more risk I have to take."

His eyes moved to hers and in them she saw understanding. "You're speaking of the young man you're in love with?"

Kate nodded and said with a hint of skepticism, "I owe myself the chance to know if he shares my feelings."

"A chance your mother never had," he said thoughtful for a moment. He laid his hand on her shoulder. "Take your risk. I'd expect nothing less from my granddaughter."

"Thank you." Once more she threw her arms around him. He held her for a moment, then still clasping her hands drew back to look at her. "I guess I'm on my own." He smiled sadly.

"You're not alone," she reminded him, forging the beginnings of a bond of love between them. "We're a family."

Tilting her head she kissed his cheek. "I'll write often," she promised him.

He glanced at his watch, taking a moment to choke back tears. "I'd better go if I want to catch that train." They embraced once more before he left.

Kate watched from the window seat where she could see a small portion of the street and sidewalk. Her grandfather's carriage had no sooner moved from view when she saw Gabe darting up the front walk. His disheveled appearance and insistent pounding on the door brought her to her feet. She raced from the study as Hattie and Vera ushered him into the vestibule.

He flattened one hand against the wall for support, his chest rising and falling as he labored to catch his breath. Hattie stared at him wide-eyed and alarmed as Vera exclaimed, "Good heavens, Mr. Murray. What's happened?"

Kate assessed his rumpled appearance wondering the same thing. His clothes were wrinkled and wet, his trousers torn at one knee. With his hair falling across his forehead he looked like he'd been dragged beneath the crosstown trolley.

"Where's Kate?" he gasped, struggling to get the words out.

The urgency in his voice drew her toward him. "I'm here," she said, his eyes following her as she moved closer.

A look of relief replaced the tension in his face. As he brushed the hair from his forehead she noticed a handkerchief wrapped loosely around his right hand.

"Gabe, you're hurt." She pressed her hand to her heart.

"It's nothing," he said.

Without giving it a thought, he stuffed the bloodied handkerchief into his pocket, revealing bruised knuckles. His eyes told her he had something else on his mind.

"I saw the carriage and thought you'd left with your grandfather."

She looked at him puzzled. "How do you know about my grandfather?"

"Finn told me everything," he said, his eyes never leaving her face. "Kate, I—" Gabe began only to stop, becoming suddenly aware of Hattie and Vera.

"Would you excuse us?" he said, directing Kate into the study. He waited as she preceded him into the room, then closed the door.

She stood facing him, wondering what he'd been about to say, stymied by his tattered appearance.

"How did you hurt yourself?" she asked.

He glanced at his hand, then back at her. "Settling an old debt," he said, shrugging it off. "You might call it my contribution to what you did to-day.''

An uncomfortable silence followed as Kate real-ized she didn't need to explain her motives. Gabe considered her for a long minute before reaching into his pocket to remove her gold filigree shamrock.

''This belongs to you,'' he said, holding it out to her.

''Thank you,'' she replied. ''It was kind of you to return it.'' As she took the pin into her hand, their fingers touched, igniting ripples of desire.

The feeling was so strong, she took a step back and gripped the arm of the settee. Her pulse raced and his knowing smile made her heart do crazy things. She didn't know what to expect when he took a step toward her.

''Kate, I didn't come here just to return your pin. I need to know, are you going home with your grandfather?''

Her heart leaped to her throat, making it hard to speak. ''Why does it matter?''

''It matters a great deal to me,'' he said. ''I want you to be my partner.''

Passionate fires lit his dark eyes which contra-dicted his tone and added to her confusion. She took another step back, trying to keep some space be-tween them and her wits about her until she figured out exactly where this was leading.

''Why me?'' She searched his eyes. ''You have the city at your feet. You can have any partner you choose.''

"I want you." His quick response came as he drew near once more.

His face was only inches from hers, his lips inviting. The air between them throbbed with possibility, but were they possibilities seen by her heart alone? She couldn't tell any more than she could retreat any farther without pitching backward onto the soft cushioned settee. Her imagination already put her there, locked in his strong embrace, his warm hands caressing her. Her eyes slid shut and she fought to remain focused and keep from falling.

"Why do you want me?" Her voice trembled as she pressed him for the answer she longed to hear.

An answer he withheld. He took her hand, lacing his fingers through hers. "I never thought I'd be able to trust anyone again, but you've changed that. Kate, you've changed me. I want you to be my partner in every way."

She felt a fluttering in her heart but kept a tight rein on her emotions. "Every way?"

"Every way," he replied with unmistakable conviction. "For better or worse. For richer or poorer. In sickness and in health."

Kate released a pent-up breath. "This is a proposal."

He surprised her by saying simply, "Yes."

She gazed into his eyes, finding in their depths all the love and commitment she'd longed for. He looked at her gravely, awaiting an answer.

Kate brushed a stray wisp of hair from his forehead, delaying her response, cherishing the moment.

His somber expression made her smile. She couldn't resist playfully turning the tables.

"Do you really think you can tolerate my constant difference of opinion?"

He answered quickly, "Life would be dull without it." His eyes roved up to hers then back to her mouth. "We have the rest of our lives to work out the details, but if I don't kiss you soon—"

He took her into his arms at last, closing the distance between them, opening himself to all the love she was ready to give. His hands moved to hold her tightly against him as he kissed her hard and long, making her yearn for more.

She draped her arms across his shoulders, still clutching the filigree pin in her hand. Fitting her mouth to his, she deepened the kiss, losing herself. In the years ahead she knew she might face days when luck alone would see her through. But for now, at least, she had everything she wanted.

*   *   *   *   *

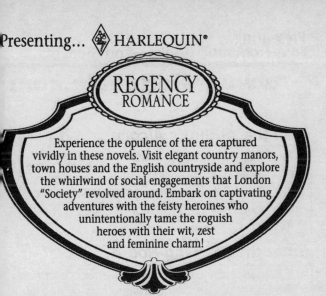
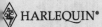

Presenting... 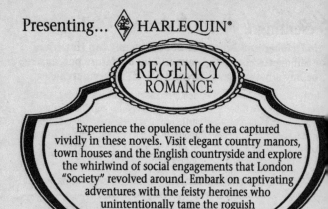 **HARLEQUIN®**

REGENCY ROMANCE

Experience the opulence of the era captured
vividly in these novels. Visit elegant country manors,
town houses and the English countryside and explore
the whirlwind of social engagements that London
"Society" revolved around. Embark on captivating
adventures with the feisty heroines who
unintentionally tame the roguish
heroes with their wit, zest
and feminine charm!

Available in October at your favorite retail outlet:

A MOST EXCEPTIONAL QUEST by Sarah Westleigh
DEAR LADY DISDAIN by Paula Marshall
SERENA by Sylvia Andrew
SCANDAL AND MISS SMITH by Julia Byrne

Look for more marriage & mayhem coming in March 2001.

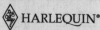

You're not going to believe this offer!

In October and November 2000, buy any two Harlequin or Silhouette books and save $10.00 off future purchases, or buy any three and save $20.00 off future purchases!

Just fill out this form and attach 2 proofs of purchase (cash register receipts) from October and November 2000 books and Harlequin will send you a coupon booklet worth a total savings of $10.00 off future purchases of Harlequin and Silhouette books in 2001. Send us 3 proofs of purchase and we will send you a coupon booklet worth a total savings of $20.00 off future purchases.

Saving money has never been this easy.

I accept your offer! Please send me a coupon booklet:

Name: _____

Address: _____ City: _____

State/Prov.: _____ Zip/Postal Code: _____

Optional Survey!

In a typical month, how many Harlequin or Silhouette books would you buy <u>new</u> at retail stores?

☐ Less than 1   ☐ 1   ☐ 2   ☐ 3 to 4   ☐ 5+

Which of the following statements best describes how you <u>buy</u> Harlequin or Silhouette books? Choose one answer only that <u>best</u> describes you.

☐ I am a regular buyer and reader
☐ I am a regular reader but buy only occasionally
☐ I only buy and read for specific times of the year, e.g. vacations
☐ I subscribe through Reader Service but also buy at retail stores
☐ I mainly borrow and buy only occasionally
☐ I am an occasional buyer and reader

Which of the following statements best describes how you <u>choose</u> the Harlequin and Silhouette series books you buy <u>new</u> at retail stores? By "series," we mean books within a particular line, such as *Harlequin PRESENTS* or *Silhouette SPECIAL EDITION*. Choose one answer only that <u>best</u> describes you.

☐ I only buy books from my favorite series
☐ I generally buy books from my favorite series but also buy
  books from other series on occasion
☐ I buy some books from my favorite series but also buy from
  many other series regularly
☐ I buy all types of books depending on my mood and what
  I find interesting and have no favorite series

Please send this form, along with your cash register receipts as proofs of purchase, to:
In the U.S.: Harlequin Books, P.O. Box 9057, Buffalo, NY 14269
In Canada: Harlequin Books, P.O. Box 622, Fort Erie, Ontario L2A 5X3
(Allow 4-6 weeks for delivery) Offer expires December 31, 2000.   PHQ4002

PAULA
HAMPTON

Paula Hampton attributes her romantic nature to her Irish-Italian heritage. She believes one gifted her with a love of language and the other with a sense of drama.

Having grown up in New York watching TV Westerns and news of space programs, it seems fitting that she settled in New Mexico. She lives with her husband in Albuquerque where she works for a research and development company.

In what passes for free time, Paula enjoys painting, traveling the western United States and gardening native desert plants. You can write to her at P.O. Box 51533, Albuquerque, New Mexico 87181-1533.

HH53